Worth It

Chloe B. Young

Riptide Publishing
PO Box 1537
Burnsville, NC 28714
www.riptidepublishing.com

Worth It

Cover art: L.C. Chase, lcchase.com
Editors: Veronica Vega, Carole-ann Galloway
Layout: L.C. Chase, lcchase.com

ISBN: 978-1-62649-916-4

First edition
October, 2020

Also available in ebook:
ISBN: 978-1-62649-915-7

Worth It

Chloe B. Young

To Leah, whose passion informed and encouraged me from day one.

Table of
Contents

Chapter  1

People cursed the unflattering light of department-store fitting rooms, but Elliott was positive the worst-lit, most terribly angled, and least confidence-inspiring place to try to put together an outfit was a coed bathroom of a bustling college dorm.

"Looking good, Meyer," Amanda from up the hall crowed on her way to the showers. Elliott cringed and tried to ignore her, along with anyone else who happened to come by.

Co. Freaking. Ed. Whose idea was that, even? Some sadist's, likely.

The girls weren't actually the worst part—that was the steady stream of guys who wanted to catch a quick shower before donning a thick layer of body spray and trying their luck at the local watering hole.

Elliott was focused on what he was doing, but the door squeaked, so any time someone came in, he knew it. He also had an eighty percent accuracy rate in guessing when it was a guy, because most of them would stop abruptly, their brain obviously catching up with their eyes and comprehending that there was a dude at the end of the row of sinks putting on eyeliner.

No one had given him a hard time, so far. It was unlikely anyone would, considering how liberal UCLA purported to be. They were young and Californian, living the dream with their progressive worldviews and leafy green vegetables. They were totally chill.

Yeah, sure. That was why eleven of the thirteen people who'd walked in on him had frozen in the doorway and clearly waged an internal battle. Did they want to proceed into unsafe territory or stage a retreat back into their comfortable world of polo shirts, classic rock, and chicken wings?

That wasn't fair of him. He really shouldn't stereotype, especially since—when he wasn't wearing skintight cotton-Lycra blend on top and equally figure-hugging black jeans on the bottom—he could appreciate a good polo. And he hated kale, so he didn't exactly fit the hippie-dippy archetype either.

Then again, he hadn't picked this school for its politics. Only for its great classes on ancient Greek politicians. And the inspiring faculty. And the PhD program a few years down the line . . .

The school had a lot to recommend it besides its atmosphere of acceptance.

Elliott finished connecting the soft-brown line that rimmed his eye, then uncapped his mascara. Before he'd bought it, he hadn't even known there was more than one color of mascara, but then he'd gotten one with a barely there green tint, because the salesperson had told him it might bring out the green in his hazel eyes. He wasn't so sure color theory worked that easily, but he figured as long as it stayed subtle, it couldn't hurt.

He wiped most of the gunk off of the wand onto a scraggly piece of two-ply, since he wasn't trying to kick up a slight breeze every time he blinked. All he wanted was to enhance what was already there, his best feature, according to one of his friend's ex-girlfriends. (*Unfair*, she'd pronounced his eyelashes, huffily, back in high school.)

Where he was going, a pair of eyes like his—big and bright and moist from the irritation of the chemicals—would be a hit among a particular demographic. It had been a while since he'd actually been as innocent as his eyes convinced men he was, but, oh, could he convince them. He could likely do it without the getup too, but he wasn't about to take that chance. He had bills to pay, and payment schedules would wait for no starving student.

When his lashes were as defined as they were going to get, he straightened and admired his handiwork. His clear skin was smooth, but not unnaturally so, and the eyes would be more of a draw than his pointed nose, or the hollows under his cheekbones that made him look gaunt at the wrong angle, no matter how many calories he pounded. He was too familiar with and critical of his face to be sure, but he thought he cleaned up well for someone who was objectively average.

The harsh light, unforgiving of his flaws, was actually the reason he was getting ready here, and not back in his room. Using a tiny hand mirror and the soft, fuzzy light of his desk lamp to judge the final product would be too big a risk. And if he could be halfway presentable in the godawful sickly glow of the fluorescent lights, he would look fucking fantastic under the flattering flashes of purple and green on the dance floor at Venom.

He smeared lipstick on his lips—barely darker than their natural pink color, but dark enough to give the illusion that they had already been put to good use that night. (They were his second-best feature, according to the same ex-girlfriend, though he disagreed. They were way too wide for his face.)

Wearing makeup was all a calculation. The eyes, to make him look innocent and awestruck. The lips, to make it obvious that, in spite of that, he wanted more than a free drink and a dance.

With every millimeter the pigment covered, more of the boring, nerdy Elliott went away. In his place? An Elliott who knew what he wanted and how to get it.

Thursday at a club like Venom was a completely unique experience. It lacked the crazed relief and barely disguised working man's misery of Friday and the manic desperation of a busy Saturday. Venom was the classiest, cleanest place in the area; the music didn't totally suck; and best of all, there was a roped-off VIP area with a regular bouncer who seemed to like Elliott in spite of himself.

"Well, what do you know?" Terry drawled, crossing his arms over his broad chest. His face was as stern and bored as always, but the tiny, almost imperceptible upward tic of his lips gave him away. "The cat came back."

Elliott rolled his eyes and leaned a hip against the heavy pole that the velvet barrier ropes were clipped onto. "Ugh. I hate cats. I'm more of a loyal lapdog, I think," he said, just loud enough to be heard above the thumping music. Then he held his hands under his chin like paws and gave his most charming puppy-dog eyes.

Terry snorted, unaffected. "It's been a while, Elliott. Did Innes finally get bored of that new place in Century Park?"

Ah, yes. There was the awkward moment Elliott had been expecting. He shrugged. "You'd know better than me. You seen him around?" If he was, then Elliott would have to cancel his plans for another week.

Terry's eyebrows rose fractionally, but he showed no other emotion. "You're not . . ." Elliott let him struggle for a few seconds, just for the fun of it.

"Together anymore?" Elliott finally prompted. "No. We broke it off a while back."

"And now you're here."

"Now I'm here."

Terry nodded and unclipped the rope barring the entrance to the upper level. He waved Elliott through without another word, or even a look that would betray what he was thinking. Terry's discretion was one of the reasons why Elliott liked him so much, despite the fact that none of their conversations had lasted longer than the one they'd just had. It made a refreshing change that he never seemed to have an opinion about what Elliott was doing. Or *had* been doing and was attempting to do again.

Elliott approached the VIP bar, which was smaller but still way less crowded than the one on the main level. So far, it was managing not to reek of spilled liquor and frantic borderline alcoholism, so it got a gold star, along with Elliott's patronage. There wasn't anyone sitting on the gleaming chrome stools, either. The customers in this section preferred the secluded and dimly lit booths.

Venom wasn't a gay bar, necessarily, and there was no advertisement about its free-for-all status, but the owners were equal opportunity moneymakers and kicked out anyone who had a problem with being hit on by the "wrong gender."

The only other person waiting to be served got his drink and walked off to join everyone else in the shadows, so Elliott took a seat and ordered a 7 Up in a small glass, pointedly ignoring the bartender's raised eyebrow. He didn't even like 7 Up that much, but it was what he always ordered when he didn't want his head muddled with alcohol, and he didn't want to be the only person obviously not drinking. A clear, fizzy drink could pass for a gin and tonic without him having to drink the gin. Or the tonic, because that stuff was like salty ass in liquid form.

When the glass was set in front of him, he dropped a five-dollar bill on the bar and perched on one of the stools, sipping from the little straw, running his fingers through the condensation seeping across the countertop, and projecting hopefulness. After all the time he'd spent here with Innes, the place felt almost as familiar as his living room back home. However, the kind of person he wanted to attract would be more interested in young, easily impressed guys who didn't know this club like the back of their hand.

He looked around the bar as he settled into his posture. Did he even like it here? Any feelings he had were amplified by nostalgia. He'd been here so many times with Innes. He'd met Innes here.

Those emotions were hard to forget: insecurity, baffled excitement . . . relief. A sexy, suave, rich lawyer had wanted to give him all the money he needed for whatever he cared to spend it on and all Elliott had had to do was have sex with the—hands-down—hottest guy who'd ever spoken to him and go to a few parties. Easy. No strings attached.

Elliott licked the sour taste of the 7 Up off his teeth with a small, bitter smile. Oh, yeah. So easy.

The worst part was that Innes hadn't lied to him. Elliott couldn't even curse Innes's name for manipulating an impressionable nineteen-year-old into a life of prostitution he didn't want and didn't have the fortitude for. Innes hadn't done anything except give Elliott the opportunity.

That was okay, though. There were plenty of other things Elliott had to curse Innes for.

"You look lonely."

Right on schedule. Elliott fought down his satisfied smile before he faced the guy who thought he could use some company. The guy was a bit of a cliché, really. Nice suit, clean-shaven, white smile. *Wide* smile, like a predator.

"Oh, yeah? Why do you say that?" Elliott asked, then he flicked his tongue out to catch a stray drop of 7 Up on his bottom lip. He'd never admit it out loud, but the move wasn't something that had come naturally to him. He'd practiced the tongue thing in the mirror until he was confident he could straddle the line between nervous and sexed-up.

"Well, you're all alone, aren't you?"

"There's a difference between being alone and being lonely." For introverted Elliott, at least. This guy seemed the type to go to five different bars in one weekend to avoid being subjected to his own company for longer than a few hours.

"And which are you?" The guy oozed into the bar, propping his leg on the rung of a stool, Captain Morgan style. Elliott barely restrained an eye roll at the display of Aggressive Body Language 101.

"You already guessed," Elliott said, despite his disinterest.

The guy's smile quirked with undeserved triumph. "Well, why don't you let me fix that? I've got a whole table of people who'd love to get to know you."

Ew.

Elliott was of the opinion that some guys needed to try their lines in the mirror and see if they could keep a straight face while they imagined saying them to their sister or mother. Elliott would probably have taken a pass after that poor display if he hadn't seen the table *Dustin*—Elliott was informed—was talking about.

The guy had friends. Wealthy ones, if the open bottles of champagne on the table were any indication.

Dustin settled a hand on Elliott's lower back as he introduced him to the group. Elliott only bothered remembering about half the names. The men who raked their eyes up and down his body in its tight, flattering clothes were the type he'd come searching for. The rest of them were probably part of the small demographic of people who came to Venom for the signature cocktails and the company, rather than the *welcoming* atmosphere.

There was an empty seat next to a man whose watch cost the yearly economy of a small country. Dustin pulled Elliott down next to him, instead.

"Sit with me, darling," he purred, but it sounded more like a pissed-off Persian grumble. "That's Kent's seat, right, Tom?"

"Kent?" Elliott's spine snapped straight from its shy, retiring curve, and his heartbeat picked up as he spotted a drink at the seat in question: an inch of amber liquid in a squat glass. It *could* have been Scotch straight up with a tiny spritz of lemon, just how Innes liked it, but there was no way to tell. The drink could belong to some other Kent. Kent was a first name too, right?

"Yeah, he'll be back soon," said Tom, the man across the table with the poorly hemmed cuffs. (And wasn't it sick that even though Elliott was entering panic mode, he could still strike off one potential customer from the list because he noticed when someone was hanging with a crowd he couldn't afford to be friendly with?)

"Who's Kent?" Elliott asked, as casually as he could, trying for vague curiosity, but overshooting it to mild interest, if the tightening of Dustin's lips was anything to go by.

"Lawyer. Expensive one."

"Good, though," one of the men across the table said, raising his glass in a salute. "You best not forget. His firm got my big brother out of a medium-sized problem just last month."

"Sure," Dustin said, with eyes only for Elliott. "Kent's great, but I want to hear about you."

Shit, shit, fuck. If "Kent" was Innes, then Elliott's innocent act was up. Innes had a well-earned reputation for letting no new thing go unspoiled, and there was every chance that he'd ruin Elliott's cultivated image with a sly remark.

Elliott needed to get out. He could try again another night with Dustin (or, more accurately, Dustin's friends), but only if they didn't know he'd been a fixture here until fairly recently.

"Uh, about me?" Elliott stammered, only half faking this time. "Not much to tell. Actually, I'm pretty boring, and it's kind of past my bedtime, so I think I'm gonna, um, go?"

"What?" Dustin caught Elliott's wrist as he stood to leave. "No, don't do that, we'd miss you. Wouldn't we, boys?" There was a chorus of noncommittal hums.

"Nah, really. I have to go. But it was nice meeting you." The first attempt Elliott made to tug his arm from Dustin's grasp was ineffectual, and that sent a frisson of fear down Elliott's spine, but the second yank earned him his limb back, and he turned away from the table—

Only to walk into a warm, but unyielding wall. He stumbled back a step, but the wall—person—steadied him with hands on his shoulders.

"Sorry," Elliott mumbled, and tried to step around them.

"Elliott?"

Elliott stopped and actually looked. The light was dim in the club, but it was bright enough for him to recognize the criminally square jawline, the strong eyebrows, and the frown.

"Kent," Elliott blurted. "*You're* Kent."

"Aiden," Innes's nephew replied, his face scrunching up in a universal expression of *duh*.

Elliott winced. Fifteen seconds into their first conversation post-Innes, and Aiden thought Elliott had forgotten his name. "Yeah. I mean, of course. How are you?"

"What are you doing here?" Aiden demanded.

"Same as you, I guess. Drinking. Socializing." Elliott jerked his head toward the table behind them, where Aiden's drink had almost certainly gone room temperature.

Aiden's lip curled as he glanced at the table, then it flattened into a neutral line. "With these assholes?"

"Yeah. Those ones. Who you were happily sitting with."

Aiden's eyes skittered down and away, and his jaw tightened. Interesting. "Or not so happily?"

"Come on." Aiden spread his hand across the thin material over Elliott's back and propelled him across the VIP section and down the stairs. Dazed, Elliott let himself be led, stumbling over his feet as they pushed through the throng of dancing clubbers, but steadied by Aiden's sweltering palm on his sweat-damp skin.

They'd made it to the exit and out into the cool air before Elliott realized that he could have jumped ship at any time. He'd been steered, not pulled, to Aiden's destination of choice, and the difference between that and Dustin's too-tight grip on his wrist was enough to make him decide to stick around.

"Can I help you?" Elliott asked, crossing his arms over his chest to seem unaffected, and to ward off the chill of the rapid temperature change between the stifling club air and the cool breeze. California was a sunny state, but January was still cold.

Aiden was taller than him, but not by much. With Aiden's lean muscle mass, combined with a thunderous frown and dark, villainous stubble, Elliott might have been uncomfortable if he hadn't learned from Innes that Aiden braked for butterflies that landed on the road.

"Why did you come here?" Aiden asked.

"The same reason most people come here. To hook up with someone." That was, perhaps, a bit of a stretch. The kind of hookup he wanted was a little more expensive than usual.

"Really? A one-night stand is all you want?" Aiden's face pulled into one of its default expressions: profound skepticism.

"And if it isn't? What could that possibly have to do with you? Come on. Give me one good—I mean *good*—reason why you hauled me out here to give me the third degree. I'm not with Innes anymore. Remember?"

There was no chance Aiden wouldn't remember. Aiden and Elliott hadn't been exactly friendly when Elliott and Innes had been a thing, but they'd made small talk at countless parties and dinners and fundraisers that Innes had dragged him to.

Aiden had been working his way up from his position as a highly capable associate to having his name included under one of the Kents in Kent, Kent & Morris Law Office, but he hadn't managed it before the end of Innes and Elliott's arrangement, which, awkwardly, Aiden had known all about.

Innes hadn't been exactly subtle.

Aiden didn't seem homophobic, but he did seem to be a bit of a prude. Not to mention, he always looked incredibly busy and moderately exhausted. They'd mostly ignored each other, which had been easy to do, despite the fact that Aiden and Innes worked at the same company, one floor apart.

(Elliott had gotten off at the wrong floor the first time he'd come to the firm for a quickie in Innes's office. He'd told the receptionist he was there to have lunch with Mr. Kent, and she'd assumed he'd been talking about Aiden, the younger of the two Kents. It had made for an uncomfortable conversation when Aiden had had to point him to the correct floor and watch Elliott do the walk of shame.)

"Of course I remember," Aiden snapped, then he visibly gathered himself, and his lips firmed into a line. It wasn't a smile, but it was closer to one than the glower from before. "Hard not to. It's been boring without you, honestly."

That surprised a laugh out of Elliott. "Innes hasn't found someone new to scandalize people with?"

"Not yet. I think he's finding you a tough act to follow. You were the most interesting person he'd seen in a while. Maybe ever. Definitely the smartest."

This time, Elliott's chuckle was bitter. "The smartest of all of Innes's playthings. What a compliment."

Aiden was too self-contained to shuffle his feet, but he looked like he wanted to. He stared at the brick wall behind Elliott's head instead. "I didn't mean it like that."

"How did you mean it? I never really knew how you felt about me. I don't know if you think I'm . . ." *Disgusting. Dirty. Stupid and shameless.* Elliott could take his pick of the usual assumptions people made. It didn't make a difference that none of them were true. People had a right to their opinions, just as Elliott had a right to ignore them.

"No. I don't," Aiden said. "Whatever it is you're thinking, I don't think that."

"Then what are you doing here, Aiden? Why did you drag me out? It wasn't for old time's sake, that's for sure."

Aiden's muscles worked under the taut skin of his jaw as he obviously tried to come up with an answer. The guy must have killer TMJ.

"Those guys are bad news," Aiden blurted eventually.

Elliott rolled his eyes. "Good god, you sound like a cop in a movie set in the fifties. 'I don't trust 'em, Sly. He's a rebel without a cause, ya see—'"

"I'm serious, Elliott. They aren't . . . good people."

Elliott threw up his hands. "You think I don't know that? You think I'm gonna go out looking for a saint? Why, sure, Elliott, of course I'll pay your tuition if you let me fuck you on the regular. But first, I have to feed the starving orphans. Oh, wait! You're half an orphan, let me write you a check, keep the no-strings-attached sex, I can do without—"

"Stop."

Elliott's mouth clicked shut, because Aiden no longer resembled a harried dad giving a last-minute lecture to a teenager. He seemed serious and genuinely concerned.

"Sorry," Elliott mumbled, unclear as to exactly what he was apologizing for. He didn't owe Aiden any explanations for what he did with his life.

"Please don't go back in there and sit with them." Aiden's eyes shone in the light of the club's neon sign, piercing and somber with streaks of acidic pink breaking up the dark brown. "I'm only here to keep a client coming back when his brother messes up again. If I had to worry about you as well as about keeping a straight face, I'd get another ulcer."

Elliott winced. "Ouch."

"Yeah. Innes would never let me hear the end of it. He already gives me a new bottle of Pepto-Bismol every week."

Elliott snorted. "I bet he owns stock in it."

He'd never laughed so much in Aiden's presence before. He'd never had much reason to, despite Innes often sinking his teeth into his own nephew with his casual, cruel humor.

When it was some poor schmuck Innes was pleasantly ripping to pieces, it'd been easy for Elliott to get caught up in it, but he'd never been able to snicker along when it was Aiden, an almost acquaintance. Thankfully, Aiden had usually ignored Innes's bait.

"I was glad to hear you weren't seeing him anymore." When Elliott frowned, Aiden rushed to explain. "I just mean that he isn't good for you. Or anyone, really. Innes is family, and I know he has some good qualities if you look hard enough, but his bad ones far outweigh them. You're better off without him, and I was happy when it seemed like you were done with this sort of thing." Aiden jerked a thumb at the doors of Venom, where just as many people were leaving as arriving.

Elliott shifted his weight, flexing his toes in his dress shoes. They were tighter than he remembered. "Yeah, I probably am better off. But a guy's gotta eat, you know?" And study at a school that was way out of his budget, and pour money into a debt incurred before the training wheels were off his bike. "So I continue to do 'this sort of thing.' Sorry to disappoint."

"I'm not disappointed, that isn't—" Aiden broke off and growled under his breath, glaring at the dirty sidewalk. The burn of bitterness and annoyance in Elliott's throat calmed.

"For a big-shot lawyer, you're putting your foot in your mouth a lot," Elliott said with a rueful grin.

Some of the tension leaked out of Aiden's shoulders. "'Big shot?' You must have me confused with someone else."

"Oh, really? Someone specific? What is he, about yea high—" Elliott drew a line across Aiden's shoulder. "—with obsessively groomed hair and a superiority complex like whoa?"

Aiden's lips trembled with suppressed laughter, like he thought Innes would jump out from behind a nearby dumpster if he badmouthed him too loud. "He's the one. I'm no big shot. I only keep crooked CEOs out of prison."

Elliott nodded sagely. "Noble."

Aiden grimaced. "It pays the bills."

"Lucky you." It came out harsher than Elliott had intended, and tense silence followed. "Well, this has been bizarre, but I should probably get back to . . ." He gestured vaguely to the club door. "I'll take your advice on Dustin and his friends. If you happen to know anyone in the market for someone to spoil in exchange for sexual favors, you know where to find me."

He resisted the urge to bring out the double finger guns and turned away from Aiden, heading for the front door.

"I do know someone, actually."

Elliott stopped and looked back over his shoulder, but he didn't turn around. "You don't say. And who would that be?"

Aiden's blush was ruddy and dark, visible even under the pink lights of the sign. He stared at the ground and got redder and redder until he jerked a vague hand toward his own chest. It took Elliott a good few seconds to figure out what he meant.

"You're joking," Elliott said.

Aiden clenched his fists, then dug them into his pockets, shaking his head in a quick snapping motion. "Never mind. It was stupid anyway."

He stepped past, but Elliott caught his arm before he could escape back into the club, digging sweaty fingers into the tailored suit jacket.

"No, it's not stupid. I was just . . ." *Surprised* felt like a weak word for what he was. *Absolutely floored* would be closer. "You never seemed the type."

Aiden froze, his eyes locked on Elliott's grip on his arm. "What type do I seem like, then?"

"I don't know, man, I haven't really thought about it," Elliott said, jabbing his fingers through his stiff, product-ridden hair. It was too easy to take a guess, though. Aiden seemed the type for an old-fashioned courtship. A standing appointment for movie night with popcorn and pj's. A tense and perfect meet-the-parents dinner. A long engagement, because they were going to be together forever, so why hurry?

None of that aligned with what was being proposed, so he couldn't be blamed for the spark of suspicion that flared neon bright.

"Are you doing this because you feel bad for me?" Elliott demanded, yanking his hand from Aiden's arm. "Innes was a dick sometimes, but I dished it right back. If this is some sort of sick apology for whatever you think he did, you can—"

"Do you honestly think I like Innes enough to spend my own money apologizing on his behalf?"

That bit of bracing logic cut through the haze of misplaced annoyance and embarrassment, and the fight went out of Elliott. The breeze picked up and he shivered. He wanted to go home and scrape off the thin layer of makeup that was making his eyes twitch, then shed his tight clothes and feel sweet air on his legs again.

"No. I guess you wouldn't. I just . . . It's been a confusing night, so I'm really not up for whatever game you're playing."

"It isn't a game." Aiden's stare was always intense, but tonight, his eyes seemed to glow. "I'm not Innes. I'm good at what I do, but I can't play people like he can, and I don't want to learn."

He reached into his pocket and fished out a business card from his wallet. He offered it to Elliott. "Call me if you want. We can work something out. If not, then good luck, I guess."

Elliott watched Aiden's back as he retreated into the building, then glanced down at the card pinched in his white-knuckled fingers.

The stock was thick, the typeface angular and unadorned. The lettering was black, not flashy gold or silver. Simple and straightforward. Like Aiden. Maybe.

Elliott tucked the card into the tiny, cramped front pocket of his jeans and kept his hand around it as he started his walk home under the bright street lights.

Maybe he could use a bit of simple.

As Elliott got to his door, some girls from down the hall went by, giggling and talking, their excitement peaked for a night only beginning while Elliott was turning in, like an old man waiting for the sun to go down so he could shut off the light.

Be safe, he wanted to shout after them, but he wasn't their grandad, even if they did seem painfully young. Their youthful exuberance would probably wake him up on their journey home, and in the morning, he'd be grateful for his room on campus when he wouldn't have to waste precious sleeping time on a long commute.

The pros and cons of dorm life were a constant struggle, but until 9 a.m. classes were banned, he'd pick proximity over peace and quiet.

In the privacy of his single room, he wiggled out of his pants and kicked them savagely into a corner, but they weren't his biggest hurdle.

Waterproof mascara was even harder to get off than it was to put on. When he'd bought the stuff, he'd thought, *Well, why wouldn't I want it to be waterproof?*

Because the way it clung was magic of the darkest variety.

After pitching his third makeup wipe, he gave up on getting the last traces of color. He might look haggard the next day, but he'd get extra participation marks for being more interested in the material than in sleep.

In his T-shirt and boxers, he climbed under the soft covers, fully expecting to drop off immediately.

No such luck.

All his tiredness vanished as soon as his head hit the pillow. He tossed around, trying to tap into the mental exhaustion he'd felt as he'd walked home, but eventually gave in to the inevitability of getting up again.

At his desk, he pulled out his textbook for his Rediscovering Rome class, clicking on his lamp to start burning the midnight oil.

Next to him, the heating vent puffed out tepid air uselessly, and Elliott's warm bed called him back.

He could give sleep another try. Or he could lie under his blankets and stare at his phone for a few hours, wasting time until the sun came up . . .

Not if you want to make the ancient history faculty list before age thirty, a voice that sounded suspiciously like his mom's piped up. If he wanted to stay in school until they had to give him three degrees to get rid of him, and make a living by publishing essays in esoteric journals for people like him to read, he couldn't waste unexpected opportunities for productivity like this one.

He traced the cover of his book: a stock photo of a bust of Julius Caesar. He smiled as he remembered the one exactly like it that his mother had owned. They used to say good night to it along with his teddy bears on the way to bed.

It'd fallen off the shelf a couple of years after she'd died. It'd cracked down the middle, and he hadn't wanted his dad to replace it, not when they hadn't been sure where they'd get the money to replace his cheap, crumbling running shoes.

He opened the heavy book up to his bookmark, shaking off his midnight melancholy. At least now he was pulling his own weight, financially.

As soon as Elliott had graduated high school, he'd been working at a factory and pouring most of his paychecks into their debts. Ignoring his dad's guilt and his own disappointment hadn't been easy, but his mom's medical bills hadn't cared that they'd both wanted Elliott to go to college.

If their bills hadn't been so high, Dad would never have let him put it off. He'd seen how much Elliott wanted to go, to fulfill both his own desires, and those of his parents, but Dad had needed the help, so UCLA had had to wait.

But he'd made it there eventually, and was working toward his dream. The payments were still high, but Dad never missed one, not with Elliott's help.

See, Dad, he wanted to say, by phone, in person, email, anything. *I'm doing exactly what you told me to do.*

Well, not exactly. He'd never told Elliott to go out and find someone to pay him for a few hours of sex every week, but he'd done it anyway, and he didn't regret it, not when it gave him the freedom to come back to this, his passion, while still having money to send, chipping away at the burden on his dad's back.

His dad had never told Elliott that borrowing money would ruin him either. He hadn't had to.

A burst of wild laughter from outside Elliott's door made him jump and drop his book to the desk. Instead of picking it up again, Elliott texted his dad about his new classes, and the professor he swore looked like an older, cooler version of himself. Wishful thinking, probably.

Despite the late hour, he'd barely put his phone down before he got a response.

Dad: *Your mom always thought you'd make a great teacher. Keep working hard, and you'll get there. Don't stay up too late!*

"Oh, Dad," he whispered to his empty room. "You're worried about the wrong things."

Putting his phone away, he turned his attention back to his book. He managed to get almost to the end of the assigned readings before his eyes started to droop and the tiny font started blurring. After closing the cover and giving good old Jules a tap on his Roman nose, he climbed into bed. But still, sleep didn't come.

He only had one person to blame.

Aiden Kent. The go-to guy for the less glamorous cases that needed competence, not flash—at least, according to Innes, who couldn't be called a trustworthy source. Everything else Elliott knew had been gathered through the colored lens of being Innes's pay-per-view boyfriend.

He'd never thought of Aiden in the way Aiden seemed to want him to. He had eyes, of course. There were some fabulous genes in the family.

But the bottom line was that he could do worse. Way worse.

He might have gone home with Dustin. The guy had been genuinely repellent, but if next semester's tuition bill had loomed a little more menacingly in the back of Elliott's mind, he might have sucked it up.

He would have felt like shit afterward, but his textbooks would've been paid off for the entire semester with the "gift" Dustin would've felt "generous" enough to give him. And if he was honest with himself, the shitty feeling probably wouldn't have lasted long, because he knew that putting in some time between the sheets didn't make him a bad person.

(He'd figured that out without a single therapy session. Not that he wouldn't have appreciated a chaise lounge and a PhD, but he'd never wanted to ask Innes, *Hey, could you pay for a shrink to screw my head on straight about me screwing you for tuition?*)

Elliott groaned and flopped over onto his stomach, shutting out the ivory light that filtered through his window in irregular bars across the bottom half of the bed. He couldn't do a damn thing without thinking of Innes in some way, which was highly annoying as well as illogical.

They'd never dated. They slept together, sat next to each other in clubs, and sometimes Elliott had let Innes dress him up and take him to thousand-dollar-a-plate fundraising dinners, but neither of them had ever forgotten that at the end of the night or in the morning, Elliott would go home to the dorm room that Innes's money paid for, and study from the books that Innes's money bought. That had been what they both wanted, until suddenly it hadn't been. So it didn't make sense that he felt like he was in a post-relationship slump.

Relationships involved trust. Elliott had seen that in his parents' marriage until the day his mother had died. Trust was not something Elliott had ever had in Innes.

Aiden, though . . . he screamed *trustworthy* in every tense line of his well-built body. Being with Aiden would be a completely different experience.

Probably.

His phone lit up in the darkness with a reminder about emailing Professor Martingale for book recommendations—the textbook for Poetry and Prose was fine, but uninspiring. Instead, he opened up his banking app.

His balance was the same. Enough to get him through a few weeks, if he managed not to run out of toothpaste, but not enough to start saving for next semester. Nowhere near enough to send to Dad.

A couple of excited whoops came from the hallway. Sighing, he reached for the earplugs on his nightstand. If he was going to call the number on Aiden's business card in the morning, he wanted to be at the top of his game.

Chapter  2

On Saturday, Elliott raised his hand to knock, lowered it, then raised it again.

He hated these fancy apartment buildings, mostly because he never knew whether he was supposed to knock. Aiden had buzzed him in downstairs, so was he going to open the door after a suitable waiting period? Was Elliott supposed to announce his presence, or would that be horribly gauche?

The door didn't even have a peephole so Aiden could see it was him instead of a stranger who'd shanked Elliott in the elevator and was about to rob the apartment blind. That wasn't likely to happen, but Elliott's dad had taught him well. He had all kinds of hang-ups from being a cop's kid.

He ended up knocking once, softly. Then he worried whether it was loud enough to be heard. Should he knock again? What if Aiden *had* heard? That would make him seem impatient.

Aiden opened the door.

"Hi," Aiden said with a small, neutral smile that thankfully didn't scream, *Come in, sit down, we'll have tea and discuss how much I'm willing to pay you to have access to your glorious booty 24/7.*

Elliott swallowed and stepped past the threshold, then hopped on one foot to remove one of his sneakers. Apparently Aiden's was a shoes-off household, a concept that shattered Elliott's unrealistic assumption that Aiden spent all day fully buttoned and laced.

He fell over into the wall trying to tug off his second shoe without untying it all the way, then blushed and grimaced when Aiden's expressive eyebrows rose to mock him wordlessly.

When Elliott was finally shoeless, Aiden led the way into the airy apartment. It was cozier than he'd have expected such an expensive piece of real estate to be. It had the kind of polished, ultra-coordinated, yet Cheerio-bland vibe of professional decorating, but there were a few more personal touches.

A couple of luridly covered crime novels had been shoved onto a windowsill next to a thriving potted plant. A pair of socks languished under the coffee table. Pictures lined the walls, blown up large so smiling faces took up most of the space.

Several looked familiar, though Elliott didn't think he'd met any of them. (He could have, given the circles he used to frequent, and might frequent again soon.) The recognizable features meant that some were probably Innes's nieces and nephews, who he talked about more than he thought he did. The rest would be Innes's siblings, who he never talked about, even though he worked with some of them.

"I thought we could sit in here," Aiden said, gesturing to the cluster of couches.

Elliott mentally shook himself back into his professional headspace. He'd learned with Innes that when he was working, he needed to be a different version of himself.

Here, he needed to be a confident, collected man about town, with enough knowledge on obscure topics to make conversation over dinner with anyone, and the experience in bed to please the pickiest partner. The experience part hadn't been a lie after about a month with Innes. The man had been a good teacher, and Elliott was nothing if not a quick study. What worked with the uncle should work just fine for the nephew.

That thought made Elliott feel gross, and he couldn't suppress a shudder as he sank onto the plush brown leather couch across from Aiden.

"Are you cold?" Aiden asked.

"What?" There was a special kind of intimidation that wealthy men wielded without thinking, and Elliott was out of practice with it. "No. I'm fine."

"Would you like a drink?" Aiden put his hands on his knees and froze, like he was fighting every instinct not to go and pour something, anything, in a glass, because that's what was expected of him.

Elliott shook his head anyway. I don't drink on the job."

"No, not— I meant water. Or I have tea. Green or chamomile. I'm out of peppermint."

Elliott really needed to quit being surprised by Aiden. "Thanks, but no. I'd like to get down to business, if you don't mind."

"Oh. Of course."

Aiden brushed his palms on his pants, then folded them in the air between his knees, then put them back on his thighs again. Watching those nervous hands, Elliott could finally take a full, deep breath.

"Are you still serious about what you said the other day?" Elliott leaned back against the couch. He let his legs relax so they were slightly open. The effect wasn't quite as good as that scene in *Basic Instinct*, but he liked to think he was channeling a bit of early-nineties Sharon Stone. "I figured when you didn't ignore my text that you were. But do you really want an arrangement like what I had with Innes?"

Aiden winced. "I'm not like Innes."

"I know. If you were, I probably wouldn't be here."

Aiden looked up at him, his eyebrows climbing.

"I was the one who broke it off, remember?"

Aiden's lips twitched in a smile. "I remember. He sulked for weeks."

"Did he?" Elliott slapped the leather couch cushion beside his knee and forgot about being seductive, bringing up his socked feet and crossing them underneath him, leaning forward like a kid at story time. "That faker, he acted like he was all relieved that I beat him to it."

"No, he was definitely put out. He had to go alone to the lymphoma research gala, and he was so pissy the whole night that he made a waiter cry."

Elliott laughed, though he felt bad for the poor waiter. "He would. He likes to deny it, but he actually loves those things. It's an excuse to get dressed up and pretend he's better than everyone else."

"That's Innes's favorite thing to do, aside from terrorizing his aides when he's in a bad mood." Aiden grimaced. "You might want to avoid them for a while. Last I heard, they were joking about getting your head on a pike for not giving them any warning before you left him in the bad mood to end all bad moods."

Elliott snorted. "He was probably mad that he had to go out and find somebody new to have sex with on the regular. The man is such a hedonist, he can't go a week without getting some before he gets whiny."

The amused half smile at Innes's expense disappeared abruptly, and Aiden coughed, looking down at the floor. Elliott's face heated up, and he swallowed a stammering apology that would only make things more awkward.

Blowing out a long breath, he forced himself not to play with the top button of his stiffly ironed collar. There was a reason why he'd bothered with business casual: he'd hoped it would remind him that they were making a new agreement, not reminiscing on old times.

They were never going to get anywhere if neither of them volunteered to start the necessary conversation. All he could do was hope that honesty was the best policy in this case.

"This is weird, isn't it?"

Aiden huffed a laugh, but his posture eased somewhat. "Yeah, a little."

"Listen." Elliott leaned forward again, trying to exude a self-assuredness he didn't feel. "I thought about coming in here and pretending I didn't even know your uncle. I could've put on an act like I hadn't done this sort of thing before. But somehow, I didn't think that would be your style. I thought you'd be the kind of person who wouldn't want the romantic bullshit when we both know I'm a done deal. Was I right?"

Aiden hesitated, and Elliott's heart rate rocketed, but he pressed harder.

"Tell me honestly. Would I blow this by treating it as the business arrangement it is?"

Aiden shook his head, but his shoulders were still up around his ears, so Elliott couldn't be entirely relieved.

"No, you wouldn't blow it," Aiden admitted. "I do appreciate you being honest with me."

He couldn't quite meet Elliott's eyes, though, so Elliott pressed, "But?"

The cracking of Aiden's knuckles was loud in the quiet room. In any other situation, with anyone else, it might've been a cheesy-mob-flick move, but Elliott could tell it was a stress relief thing. It must have worked, because Aiden let out a long breath and said, more confidently, "I don't think what I want from this is what Innes wanted."

"How so?" Elliott watched as Aiden struggled again, opening his mouth a couple of times, but failing to articulate anything. Elliott helped him out. "Innes wanted a trophy. An attractive statue he could parade around to make the execs uncomfortable at dinner parties. He also wanted sex that fit into his schedule without him having to put in the effort to go out and find someone to take back to his place who wasn't a thief, a psycho, or a legitimately good person who didn't deserve to get thrown out on their ass at dawn."

The description was frank. It was awkward too, and not just for Aiden. But Aiden needed to know how far Elliott was willing to go, and being honest was the only way to do that.

Aiden nodded, ruddy-cheeked. "That's what I thought." He looked slightly ill. Elliott didn't really have any family other than his dad, but he could imagine how much he wouldn't want to picture his uncle having sex with someone fifteen years his junior.

"That's not what you want, though?"

"No."

"So tell me." He sat through another taut hesitation, deliberately not thinking about the kinky desires that might be keeping Aiden tongue-tied, then bluffed through his unease. "Come on, lay it on me. I promise not to laugh. It wouldn't be good for business."

Aiden's eyebrows knitted up in a glare directed at the floor, but he also relaxed noticeably. It still took him a few long moments, but eventually, he met Elliott's eyes.

"I want— God, this is so embarrassing. It's such a rom-com cliché. Innes wanted sex." He pulled a face. "And I'm not going to lie and say I'm not interested in that, but the fact is, I don't want to kick you out."

Elliott was a bit perplexed. Maybe Aiden was working up to the request that needed safewords and negotiations. "What would we do instead?"

A small, soft smile flirted with Aiden's lips, and he stopped gripping his hands together so tightly and turned his palms toward himself, staring down at them like they'd give him the answers to the universe.

"Cuddle," he said, at length. "Stay warm under the covers. Get up when we feel like it."

Elliott sat back on Aiden's plush leather couch in his swanky high-rise apartment. "You want a relationship," he said slowly, feeling out the words.

Aiden sighed. "Not really. That's my problem. I don't want the stress that comes along with that. Sometimes—most of the time—I will want you to leave, but I don't want to be worried I'm going to mess things up by asking to be alone. I don't want to have to worry that I'm not texting you enough, or that my place isn't clean. I don't want to have to make conversation if I'm too tired."

Elliott nodded, a clearer picture starting to form. "So, basically, you want to skip past the dating stage to the meat and potatoes, but not have to give a shit about my feelings getting hurt when you forget to take out the trash."

Aiden stilled, barely breathing, then tension bled out of his body. "Exactly."

"Huh," Elliott said. "You're right. That is a cliché."

Aiden huffed a laugh. "God, I know. Busy lawyer doesn't have the time or the energy to date, pays someone to cuddle with him instead. It's almost as bad as *Pretty Woman*."

Elliott sat up ramrod straight, slapping his hands down on the gleaming black coffee table. "Okay, rule number one: *never* mention that movie again."

Aiden's eyes widened. "Sorry, I didn't mean to offend you—"

"Something about Richard Gere's stupid smug face makes me irrationally angry. I can't stand it. *Runaway Bride* is just as bad."

The switch in Aiden's expression from panicked to annoyed was so fast, Elliott got whiplash, but it was worth it. Aiden shook his head and gave his tiny almost-smile again. Elliott grinned and settled back into the couch, enjoying the buttery leather and plush cushions while he could. He didn't know if he'd get another chance.

But despite the surprises, he was starting to get hopeful.

He could work with this. It was different from what he was used to, but that wasn't saying much, since he only had Innes to compare to when it came to being compensated monetarily for sexual favors.

In his limited experience, when people shelled out the kind of money Elliott would ask for, they wanted intimacy far beyond cuddling on the couch. Aiden might want other things too, but if he spent even a quarter of his time with Elliott in a date-like scenario, with snuggling and foot massages, then it'd already be way more than Innes.

"Okay," Elliott said.

"Okay?" Aiden's face twitched into a confused frown.

"Yeah, let's do it. We need to discuss specifics first, some limits, what sort of schedule your bank account will let us set up, all that stuff."

"Just like that?"

Elliott blinked at Aiden's incredulous tone. "Yes? I mean, I'm not selling you my soul or running away to Mexico as soon as you give me a lump sum for the whole year. Neither of us are that stupid. What I'm saying is that I'm willing to try it out if you are. If either of us isn't feeling it by the end of a suitable amount of time—let's say a month—we can revisit it. But yeah, just like that."

Aiden nodded, relaxing by another couple of degrees. "Okay."

"All right. If you've finished freaking out, we can talk about what we're doing here." Elliott reached into his pocket and pulled out—with some difficulty, since he was sitting—a piece of paper that had been folded into the smallest rectangle he could manage. He spread it out on the coffee table, then turned it so that Aiden could read it. "This is what I'm comfortable doing in bed."

The list wasn't long, but neither was it extremely short. He was open-minded, and he wouldn't be okay with an arrangement like this one if he didn't like sex, but he was closer to vanilla than to dark chocolate.

"Other stuff is negotiable," he continued, since Aiden didn't seem to want to jump in. "But I choose when and how about anything that's not on that list. Anything that *is* on there, you can pretty much request anytime."

Aiden ran his finger down the bullet points, pausing only when he reached the bottom. "*Any*time?"

"Within reason. I have classes to attend and study for; I have assignments I have to do. I can't be swinging from the chandelier until three o'clock every morning. But then, you've got a day job, so neither of us are going to go crazy. A few nights a week, you can count on me to be ready and willing to do anything on that list."

"And if I want something that's not on the list?"

"Just ask. I'll think about it, but I reserve the right to say no. I have before, and I will again if I'm not okay with what you're asking for." He wasn't going to judge anyone on what they liked, but Innes's request for a cop/criminal roleplay had been a complete no-go. Elliott had hung out at the station with his dad as a kid way too often to get off on that scenario.

"Sounds reasonable."

Elliott reached forward, placing his hand on top of the list and pinning Aiden with the cold, hard stare he'd learned from his father. "And that doesn't just go for special requests. If I say no, for any reason, I mean it. You push, I walk away, no matter how much money you give me. Got it?"

"Got it." Aiden stared back, with a stony face he probably used when he told a jury, *No, my sleazebag client isn't a tax evader, he simply likes Swiss banks better than American ones.*

"Great," Elliott said, folding up the paper so the explicit words printed on it weren't visible, but leaving it on the table. "So what does your schedule look like? Is it consistent enough that we could have a few standing appointments every week? I don't have class Wednesday evenings, if that helps—"

"We're actually going to make appointments?" Aiden asked, his incredulity plain.

"Yes, we are," Elliott said, firmly. "I have a lot of shit I have to get done when I'm not here, so I need to know what my schedule is going to be week to week. Think of it as date night, if you're having trouble wrapping your brain around it."

"I guess."

Aiden was obviously having a hard time grasping how spontaneous Elliott wasn't. Maybe, in Aiden's mind, Elliott didn't have anything better to do than come when he was booty-called, but at the end of the day, this was a part-time job, not a full-time lifestyle, and the ability to control his schedule was reason *numero uno* for Elliott's trip down the road less traveled.

What other job—safe and legal one, at least—offered the same kind of money per hours worked? He could flip burgers for hours and never make the amount of cash he did now, and his grades would suffer as a result.

He couldn't allow that. He needed this to work out if he wanted a home to go back to, and his father to be happy.

"Have you ever had sex with a complete stranger?" Elliott asked. "Or someone you only sort of know?"

"Yes," Aiden replied immediately.

Elliott blinked, feeling the stirrings of attraction gone dormant with the winter. Since when had he been hot for Aiden's brand of straitlaced sexual confidence?

"Okay." Breathing in through his nose, Elliott filled his lungs with bravado and let it speak for him. "Well, you and me, for a while at least, are going to be like that. Don't make it into a bigger deal than it has to be. You're not going to be picking me up off a street corner. I'll come over, like I did today, we'll make small talk, we might have sex, or we might not. Whatever."

Aiden nodded. "Fine. It just seems a little . . . businesslike."

"Well, now we're back to playing pretend. If you want, I could let you sweet-talk me. I could be coaxed a little more, as long as I get a few promises by the end of today."

"I can make you promises." Aiden lifted a hand, loosely curled as if around a thick, heavy pen he was used to holding. "I could draft up—"

Elliott cut him off with a firm shake of his head. "No contract. Not in writing, at least. I don't want anyone looking my way when your practice gets audited."

"Okay." Despite his complaint about how businesslike everything was, Aiden's eyes had narrowed.

"I'm not a prostitute," Elliott said. Aiden frowned, then smoothed out his face as he seemed to realize how offensive his disbelief might've been. Elliott continued, "Or, more accurately, no court would bother to prove me one, because it'd take way too much effort. It's basically unprovable unless you confessed to paying me for sex, which you probably won't do. If your bank records are ever depositioned, all they'll show is that you're an extremely generous person who helps his completely legitimate, definitely not contracted lover through school by paying for his tuition and living expenses. That's why we're not going to bother with a written agreement."

He'd never had one with Innes, and he wasn't going to start now. Research was something he was good at, and he'd applied everything he'd learned about absorbing information and forming his own thesis to create the safest action plan he could.

"That's smart." Aiden's expressive brows had risen over bright, sharp eyes.

"I know. I have to be, doing this on my own."

"On your own?"

Leather creaked under Elliott's legs as he wondered how the hell they'd gotten here. "There are services that arrange this kind of thing," he said, carefully. "Matchmaking, with heavily suggestive wording about what happens after dinner and drinks."

"Ah." Aiden winced, and any fear Elliott had about Aiden turning to something like that vanished. "Not your style?"

"Not my budget. They take a cut, and I can't afford that. Speaking of."

It was the best segue he was likely to get.

There was a stack of note paper on the coffee table next to a decorative art bowl with nothing in it, and Elliott helped himself to a sheet. With the pen he fished out of his pocket, he wrote a number and *monthly* on the piece of paper, then slid it, facedown, across the table.

Aiden picked it up, looked at the number with all its zeros, and nodded. "That's fine."

Elliott took a quick breath in, his heartbeat speeding up. He'd expected a bit of tactful haggling, which he'd planned to counter with his meticulously crafted budget. He was only asking for what he needed so his dad could make debt payments and he could save for tuition, but he'd thought he'd at least get a pained hiss or a low whistle. *"That's fine"*? Not something he'd prepared for.

Aiden must have seen this on his face. "I don't make the salary Innes does," he said, wryly. "But I still have plenty. I also don't spend as much of my money on mani-pedis."

Elliott laughed. It seemed like Aiden was already unbending a little bit and getting more used to the idea of dating his uncle's former . . . whatever.

"Great," Elliott said. "I'll email you my banking details. You can get your secretary to deal with it, or do it yourself, I don't care much. I prefer payment on the first of the month for the previous month, but I can work around it if that doesn't—"

"How do you know I'll keep my end of the deal?"

"I don't," was Elliott's immediate reply. "That's why I use bargain-brand shampoo and mooch off my friend's Netflix. If you change your mind, I need savings to fall back on, since it's not like I'm going to get two weeks' notice."

And he'd never take a lump sum in advance, although he'd keep the reason to himself. He didn't think Aiden would like hearing how much he hated the idea of being obligated to stick around longer than he wanted so that Aiden could get his money's worth.

From the deep V of Aiden's eyebrows, Elliott gathered he was about to argue, to prod further about security Elliott didn't have. "Not that it's happening today," he said quickly, leaving money talk in his dust, "but do you pitch or catch?"

"Doesn't matter."

"Cool," Elliott said after a brief hesitation. "I prefer receiver to quarterback, so I'll assume you're okay with that until you say otherwise."

"All right." Aiden tapped his finger absently on the piece of paper with Elliott's salary on it. "Can I ask you one more thing?"

"Shoot."

"Why do you do this?"

Elliott jerked, faltering now that this was going in a direction he hadn't steered it to. "You know why. I'm in college, and it's expensive. Most people end up drowning in debt. I don't want that noose around my neck when I graduate."

"Is that it, though?"

"What, that's not a good enough reason?" His grip on the sofa cushion tightened, squeezing the leather and stuffing flat. "I have to be noble, selling myself for an orphaned younger sibling, or you'll keep asking?"

Aiden looked like he was struggling with himself. His jaw worked and his eyes fixed on Elliott's collar until some kind of decision was made and he doubled down on his line of questioning. "No, it's not that. Lots of people go to college without a scholarship, but not all of them do what you're doing."

"Don't you think our economy would be better if they did?"

"I want to make sure I'm not pressuring you. If you're doing this for school, that's fine. But is it just for that?"

Treacherous waters lay ahead. Aiden wasn't buying unrestricted access to Elliott's personal life, so this wasn't something to be encouraged, but neither was it smart to be so close-mouthed right away. He didn't want to scare off his best shot.

"Not that it's any of your business," he started, because surrendering didn't mean he had to like it, "but my dad needs help. He's got a mortgage, and since Mom died, he's been struggling. I'm trying to make his life easier."

Aiden's lips tipped up the tiniest bit, giving him the look of a panther who'd gotten a meager cup of cream. Placated, but not satisfied. "Thank you. If you weren't helping him, would you still be here?"

"If it was only tuition, you mean?"

Elliott had wondered before. His job solved both his problems, or at least came close. If he only had to deal with one of those things, then would he have gone to measures like this?

He'd never come up with a straight answer, but he knew which one Aiden wanted.

"Yes," he said, lifting his chin and meeting Aiden's eyes, trying not to blink. "I've got plans for my life that don't involve being weighed down by money problems. I'd be here if a PhD was my only motivator."

Regardless of whether it was true, Aiden seemed to accept it. He nodded, and another layer of tension seeped out of his shoulders.

Jesus, Elliott thought, eyeing those hard-looking muscles. *How stressed is this guy?*

The leather couch squeaked as Aiden's weight shifted. "So. What now?"

"That's up to you."

Elliott got up, walked around the rectangular coffee table, then forced himself between the edge of it and Aiden's knees. He sat down on it, confident that Aiden would be the type to buy sturdy furniture, and arranged his legs so they were pressed against Aiden's, knee to shin. It wasn't sexual contact, necessarily. Shins weren't inherently sexy. But he'd invaded Aiden's space, and let his own space become invaded, and that was enough to send a message that what was coming next wasn't going to involve paper, pens, or numbers.

"I could leave now," he offered. "Let you digest what we talked about today and get back to me in the next few days. But I don't really want to. You seem like a guy who sticks to a decision once you've made it, and you'd already made your decision before I knocked on the door. Hadn't you?"

Aiden nodded.

"Okay. So, yeah, I could leave. Or . . ." Elliott slid forward, claiming real estate for himself until he was on his knees between Aiden's, running his hands up strong, muscled thighs, tauntingly close to the fly of Aiden's jeans.

Aiden swallowed and licked his lips as he looked down at Elliott, then he croaked, "Or?"

"I could stay."

Elliott ran his thumb over the thick line of the right inside seam of the jeans. The material was rough against the pads of his fingers, and Elliott wanted to be even more rough with them. It'd been a long time for him, and he'd always loved oral just as much as the tragically closeted jocks in high school had told him he would, with that annoying mouth of his. Joke was on them, though. He was the one having fun, while they were enjoying their lackluster heterosexual college flings and probably flunking Psych 101 for nonattendance.

He dove for Aiden's fly. Aiden twitched as the button was opened and his hands leaped from the indents they'd made in the leather couch, but he didn't stop Elliott. He only stared down with his mouth parted, so Elliott quirked an eyebrow to ask: *Is this okay?*

"Yes. Stay," Aiden stuttered, his hands fluttering up again, and settling at his sides.

Elliott grinned and slid the zipper down with an aggressive tug, revealing black underwear from a brand even Elliott recognized. After an encouraging push, Aiden reclined to make room.

It was some view. Shoving up Aiden's shirt revealed an expanse of toned abs—probably part of the reason why Aiden didn't have the time to waste impressing dates with his hard work—and pulling down the band of his boxers revealed . . .

"Wow." Elliott leaned back to take it in. He opened his mouth to say something complimentary, but everything he could think of involved a comparison to previous partners, and that was just too strange, considering the last person he had to compare to.

He didn't have to come up with anything, however, because Aiden stiffened and started to sit up, his jaw set in an uncomfortable line. "Elliott, do you think . . . What I mean is, should we . . . without—"

"Got it covered." Elliott pulled a condom from his pocket. He wasn't offended in the slightest by Aiden's visible relief. They definitely didn't know each other well enough to put that amount of confidence in their respective sexual histories.

He made quick work of the condom, wrapping his hand around Aiden's dick and getting him fully hard—"Jesus," he breathed, while Aiden turned red—then rolling it down to the base. It wasn't his favorite way to do this, but he was used to the taste of latex. Innes had used to spend a night with a boy toy occasionally, and every time, Elliott had made him get tested before they could do it without the condom again. He'd always had to spend a night on his knees to make up for it.

Before he started, Elliott quashed a bolt of nerves. He'd had plenty of practice, but his pool wasn't varied, and it had been weeks since the last time. Was he as good as he thought, or fooling himself? Only one way to find out.

It was like riding a bike, apparently.

He went slowly at first, learning the feeling of Aiden in his mouth, but he didn't speed up by much, like he would normally. Aiden was far from an open book when his pants were on, but with them undone like this, he relaxed enough for Elliott to read him. The times Aiden's legs tensed or his spine arched weren't when Elliott took in as much as he could. No, Aiden's reactions were the biggest when Elliott slowed down, dragging his tongue up Aiden's length, sucking gently on the head, using all the tricks he knew to draw it out longer.

It couldn't last forever, though. Elliott had started to wish he'd had the foresight to ask for a pillow for his knees when Aiden's groans began to sound less ecstatic and more pained. The perfect tipping point. Elliott doubled his pace, using both hands to work the slick surface of the condom and his mouth on the place that made Aiden shiver every time Elliott's tongue passed over it. It was all over pretty quickly.

Aiden wasn't capable of being very helpful after, but his stunned inertia was funny, so Elliott didn't mind finding the nearest trash can on his own. Aiden was back online by the time Elliott returned from throwing out the condom and wiping the plastic taste from his mouth. At least, he was awake enough to snag a belt loop as Elliott went past and pull him closer.

"What about you?" Aiden sounded like he was moving in slow motion. Elliott smiled at a job well done.

"I'm fine. You can get me back next time." Elliott leaned down and planted a kiss on Aiden's mouth, making sure to fix the angle, even though Aiden's head was lying on the couch at a slouching tilt. Upside-down or sideways kissing was always weird outside of movies.

His breathing was as quick as Aiden's when he finally pulled away, but he still didn't opt to stay. No, he hadn't gotten off, but he didn't really care much since there would be time for that later. Elliott was looking forward to it, and the waiting—that sweet anticipation—was one of the best parts of sex.

"I'll see you later, Aiden," Elliott said, and he headed for the door of the apartment.

Aiden mumbled something unintelligible in reply, which made Elliott snort with self-congratulatory laughter. The sound seemed to prod Aiden out of his postcoital stupor because he shook himself, fixed his pants with fumbling hands, and stood up. He hadn't made it to the door before Elliott was letting himself out, but Elliott caught a glimpse of him just as the elevator doors shut. He seemed a bit stupefied, but in a good way.

Elliott grinned to himself in the middle of a mirrored, gold-paneled box in an apartment building that was way fancier than he'd ever want to live in, and saluted his reflection.

He'd landed on his feet once again, it looked like. He was *so freaking lucky* to have landed right in the lap of someone who was not only physically attractive, but also not morally reprehensible. He'd gathered that was pretty much unheard of in his field, so he was going to take the gift he'd been given and appreciate it.

The elevator *ding*ed and he stepped out, then he waved to the stone-faced doorman behind the counter. Might as well start to butter up the staff now, since if he had his way, he'd be a regular fixture until he could introduce himself as Professor Elliott Meyer.

Chapter  3

"**F**ucking die, you elderberry-smelling motherfucker!"

"Dude, chill. You're letting the thirteen-year-old trolls get to you."

Elliott sighed and dropped his controller into the laundry basket next to him. He flopped back into his beanbag to the soundtrack of explosions and probably the cackling of evil pubescent demons who had way more time to practice their raiding skills than he did. (He had them muted, so he couldn't know for sure, but he could hear it in his mind.)

"I know," he grumbled to Kevin's sympathetic face in the corner of his laptop's screen. "It's just a stupid game, but we got murdered hard."

He made himself feel better by curling up fetal and pushing his face into the beanbag, then regretted it immediately because the smell of Cheeto dust and excess testosterone was overpowering. Its stink wasn't surprising, considering it didn't get aired out much. It spent most of its days in the bottom of Elliott's closet and only saw use when Kevin was up for gaming over Skype.

As chairs went, it wasn't very practical, but he kept it because it contributed to the general atmosphere of carefree nostalgia that manifested whenever he saw Kevin, even if it was only digitally. He always felt like the twenty-one-year-old he was supposed to be when Kevin spent time with him.

"It's okay, man, don't be so hard on yourself," Kevin consoled him, nodding wisely. "It's easy to get caught up in the competitive spirit."

"Damn right."

"You're a lot more busy than you were in high school." Kevin's voice changed from teasing to disarmingly neutral. "Not as much time to practice, with your classes and, uh, stuff."

Somehow, Elliott managed not to laugh at the unsubtle transition. "Yeah. That's true."

"So, how's it going with your . . ." Kevin's face creased like a particularly underweight shar-pei as he hesitated. *Boyfriend* was apparently too sacred a title for Innes.

As far as Kevin knew, Innes had been Elliott's long-term fuck buddy, and Elliott was racking up as much debt as Kevin had, but without the guaranteed middling-salaried job at a local veterinary practice right after graduation.

"His name was Innes," Elliott said, amused. "And we're not together anymore. I broke it off before Christmas."

"Oh. Why didn't you tell me when you were home?"

Kevin's voice had the same tightness of pushed-down hurt as it had when he'd told Elliott he didn't care that he'd never met Innes and knew next to nothing about him.

(That was a can of worms Elliott was not willing to open, since he never could come up with a reason why he'd date Innes that wasn't *He's extremely wealthy, as well as controlling enough to get off on employing someone for regular sex.*)

"It was really recent. I was still working through everything and remembering why it was a good thing we weren't together anymore."

It was as close to a lie as he'd ever let himself tell his best friend. It would work because it fit right in with Kevin's adorable world view: casual sex was a myth, all fuck buddies were always secretly in love, and everyone needed someone or they'd be tragically lonely, no matter how many scented candles were lit or body parts self-explored.

"I'm sorry you had a hard time, but this is for sure a good thing. He didn't sound like a good guy—" He gamely ignored Elliott's snort. "—and you deserve better."

"If you say so."

Kevin gave him a thoroughly unimpressed glance, so Elliott raised his hands in surrender. Far be it from him to disagree with the captain of his personal cheering squad.

Elliott! Elliott! He's so cool! He is not a total tool!

"Well, you've still got some time before Valentine's Day," Kevin said, his sudden smile wide in his small space on Elliott's screen.

"Time for what? Ordering a massive chocolate cake to eat in one sitting?"

"No. Time to get over him. To move on."

"Oh, I'm over it, don't you worry," Elliott said, pulling a face.

"You are single, now, right?"

"Um."

"No way, Elliott. You're not dating again so soon." The look was back, and this time, Kevin managed the disappointed-dad face better than Elliott's actual father.

"What? I thought that's what you wanted me to do!" Elliott squirmed in his squishy, Cheeto-y seat. "And I wouldn't call an entire month *soon*."

Kevin's face blurred on the screen as he shook his head. "I didn't think you'd actually do it. You need time to get over this. You have to pack up the house you built with your relationship and unpack it in—"

Elliott gagged and flopped off his beanbag. "Stop! Stop, I can't take it!"

"You're so immature," Kevin's tinny voice came through the speakers.

"Augh, it burns! The maturity, it burns me! The power of Cosmo compels me!"

"Knock it off, you child."

Elliott could hear the smile in Kevin's voice, which had been the goal, so he crawled back onto the bag, collapsing stomach first.

"Don't worry, Kev," he said, seriously. "I'm over Innes because I was never under him."

"What?"

"Never mind, that doesn't make sense." It was also completely untrue, if he included the biblical definition. "What I mean is that I didn't have feelings for the guy beyond attraction and award-worthy tolerance of his awful personality. So don't start thinking that I'm pining for anyone."

Kevin hummed skeptically. "And this new person?"

Elliott scratched at a tiny burnt patch on the carpet. "What about him?"

"Do you have feelings for him?"

He honked a laugh. "God, no. Well, one, actually. Amazement, at the size of his c—"

"Ew, stop. I don't want to know."

Elliott opened his mouth and raised a finger, but Kevin didn't stop.

"And don't start with me about it being homophobic not to want to hear about your boyfriend's dick. I have never described any of my girlfriends' parts in that much detail."

Elliott deflated and slumped back into the bag. "Fair."

"You can tell me other things about him, though. Is he nice?"

Was Aiden nice? He made his living getting shady rich people out of legal issues, and he was morally flexible enough not to mind that paying Elliott for sex was technically illegal. He was also related to Innes, which didn't recommend him. But the proudly displayed pictures in Aiden's apartment of his sisters in graduation caps told a different story of his character.

"Yeah, I think he is," Elliott said, with more hope than hard evidence. "It's too soon to tell. And don't start getting ideas about meeting him or adding him on Facebook or something. We're not serious. He doesn't want lovey-dovey shit any more than the last one. Or me, for that matter."

Kevin nodded sadly, and Elliott had to look away from his computer screen. It said something about Elliott's dating history that Kevin didn't even try to argue anymore. He'd finally learned, after Innes and the short string of pointless hookups before him, that it was useless to try to convince Elliott that he totally would like his alone time filled up, his independence stolen, and his heart broken. Elliott was surprised to find that he missed having the debate.

And there sure wasn't anyone else around he could have it with.

"Does this guy know you just got out of a relationship?" Kevin asked.

Elliott snorted. "Oh, yeah. Definitely."

Kevin narrowed his eyes. "Do I want to know?"

"Nope." Elliott flipped around, wiggling until he found a position that didn't make his back hurt. Stupid impractical beanbags. "You really don't, and I wouldn't tell you if you did, because it would probably change your mind about me deserving better."

"No, it wouldn't." Kevin ignored Elliott's disbelieving huff. "Everyone deserves to be loved."

"Ack, the pain! Wisdom is my only weakness!"

"Shut up and play, you goof. You're starting to sound like the thirteen-year-olds who thrashed your ass."

"Oh, you bastard. That's it, you're going down."

Playing with Kevin like this was totally worth putting off a few piles of reading he had to do. It was a melancholy kind of happiness, a carefree moment that contrasted sharply with the specter of his rigid ten-year plan and measures he'd taken to make it happen. The innocence of it all made his life seem a lot more sordid.

He didn't hate himself for what he did. Far from it. He had a pretty healthy relationship with the profession he'd fallen into, mostly because he'd chosen the job himself. He knew how privileged that made him, and he didn't take it for granted. That life wasn't for everyone, for good reason, but he was doing okay because he was realistic enough to be able to make off-color jokes about *Pretty Woman*.

"I saw your dad yesterday," Kevin said, yanking Elliott's thoughts from one extreme to the other.

Elliott mashed his keyboard buttons without pausing. "Oh?"

"At the grocery store. He told me about your basement." The game lay forgotten, the music still playing. "That's tough, man."

"Yeah. Did he mention whether the insurance company has called him back?"

"Nah. Last I heard, he was still bailing out the water and waiting for the phone to ring."

Elliott perched higher on his beanbag, but it immediately sank down under him. "I keep meaning to call him myself. I still can't believe what a mess it is. I've only seen pictures, but it's bad."

"Yeah. Not that surprising, though." A hollow, plasticky noise clicked across the computer connection as Kevin fidgeted with his mouse. "From what your dad was saying, all of those pipes are as old as the house. One of them was bound to blow sooner or later."

"I guess. Bad timing, is all. The roof will probably have to be fixed soon if the window in my room keeps leaking."

"Your dad's pullout couch is calling your name," Kevin teased—as if Elliott didn't know full well that he'd be staying in Kevin's spare room next time he came to town. "Home, sweet home."

"Yeah." Elliott smiled for the low-res camera so Kevin wouldn't see how hard he was trying not to think about the crumbling Corinthian porch columns his mom had been so proud of.

"You should visit him again soon."

"I know." Christmas was starting to feel like it'd been months ago, rather than weeks. "I'll try, but with midterms, I'll be—"

"I get it. We just miss you when your head is buried in exams. Don't drop off the face of the earth this time, okay? Or I'll start mailing you condoms and Valentine's cards until you pay attention to me."

"You fiend! One more round, I swear this time I'll finish you."

Elliott's mood was boosted high until Kevin signed off. It was hard to feel isolated when the presence of his best friend still filled his small room, but after the screen went black, he spiraled like he usually did when Dad or Kevin called and asked how he was doing.

It wasn't just the empty room that pulled him back to earth. It was the overthinking too. Their possible reactions to his present choices played over again in his mind: explosive and angry, or chilly and disgusted by turns. Today it was worse, with Kevin's disappointed face fresh in his memory.

What made this one of his top ten waking nightmares was that those negative reactions were the most likely to happen. At the very least, Dad and Kevin would be upset—he knew they hoped for better for him. There wouldn't be much he could do to change their mind, to tell them that it was the best thing he could possibly do to make sure he and Dad didn't have a cent to worry about paying back when he finally started taking money from an accredited college instead of paying it.

Instead of stewing about it, he distracted himself by reading, and he got a bit of research done for his next paper. He had weeks before he'd planned to start it, but the topic—the actual war *300* was based on—was to die for. (It was hard not to feel bad for anyone who thought the movie was more fascinating than what actually happened.) He was interrupted by the rumbling of his stomach and the buzzing of his phone with an incoming text.

He dealt with the hunger first, grabbing an age-speckled banana from his "adult food" stash to counteract the junk fest of his afternoon. His finger dragged a smear of sticky banana mush across the screen of his phone as he opened the new text.

You said you were free Wednesdays.

It wasn't exactly a question, but he answered Aiden anyway. *Yeah. You want to meet?*

He bit his lip. After the success of yesterday's meeting, he was actually excited at the prospect of his first "date" with Aiden. They were about to enter into Elliott's favorite stage of any relationship, however casual. The first sexual encounter was over with, and any last-minute insecurities had been shoved to the back burner and replaced by the sweet, sweet anticipation of getting into the groove of each other's rhythm. And Aiden seemed the type to cha-cha real smooth.

His phone beeped again.

Aiden: *Only if you're free.*

Elliott rolled his eyes. *I said I was. Your place, 7 too early?*

Aiden: *No, 7 is fine. See you then.*

Just like that, it was in his calendar, and he was bumping up the laundry that he'd planned to do on Wednesday to earlier in the week, so he could do a different kind of bumping. Elliott looked down at the barely touched banana in his hand and smirked at its frowny, bruised, judgmental face.

"Knock it off," he told it. "You wish you were getting the action I'm about to."

Then he threw it away and finished the bag of Doritos instead. He could go back to being an adult tomorrow.

Aiden answered the door on Wednesday wearing tight-fitting black boxer briefs and a soft-looking white T-shirt that was so thin Elliott could see the dark shadow of his belly button through the worn fabric.

"Wow," Elliott said, rocking back on his heels to take in the view. "You weren't kidding about letting it all hang out."

Aiden gestured him in and closed the door behind them. "No, I was not. I can't tell you how much of a relief it is not to have to put on pants."

"I get it. Lazy pj days are the best days."

Innes's pajamas, the couple of times Elliott had seen them, had been made of actual silk. *Of course* they had been. But Innes was more likely to stay in his fancy tailored suit until the moment he got into bed and not bother to put a layer in between him and his Egyptian cotton sheets.

Elliott grimaced at Aiden's back as he was led to the living room. He really needed to stop comparing Aiden to Innes. They were related, had the same profession, worked at the same office, and wore the same label of fancy tailored suits, but Elliott was coming to see the little differences. Like lazy pj days. And the bottle of water that was sweating a ring directly onto the coffee table in the living room.

Elliott ignored his urge to find a napkin to wipe up the mess. (Intellectually, he didn't give a shit if there were rings on the table, but his great-aunt Harriet had done her job of teaching him how to take care of furniture well. Too well.)

Aiden didn't waste any time getting—even more—comfortable on the fluffy leather couch in front of the expensive TV mounted on the wall. Elliott found himself hovering a few feet away, shocked silent. He checked his phone—the international symbol for *I'm uncomfortable and looking for a distraction*. It was 7:02. He'd officially been fully clothed and upright for a minute longer than he'd expected.

"I gotta say, I feel a little overdressed," he said, on a laugh that he hoped didn't sound forced.

Aiden's response was to reach for the remote, then he settled deeper into the couch. "Don't worry about it," he said brightly, with a small smile that changed his face. "I'm not going to."

"Cool," Elliott said slowly. "So, is this a good time? Or should I come back—"

"Oh, yeah, sorry. That's not what I meant." Aiden sat up and shifted his lower half a couple of inches closer to the arm of the couch.

"Would you sit with me? I've been meaning to watch this movie for forever."

Elliott sat down immediately, relieved to have a place to be. He didn't leave any room between himself and Aiden, who seemed to like that just fine, since he wrapped an arm around Elliott's shoulders and left it there.

Aiden clicked through his Netflix queue with the remote, found the one he'd been dying to see, and pressed Play. The first five minutes of the movie were promising. Elliott had heard of it when it came out and been intrigued, so he was entertained. But he found it a little difficult to stay focused when Aiden's mostly naked thigh was pressing against Elliott's clothed one, and . . . not doing anything else.

Aiden was absorbed in the action, apparently, and seemed to have forgotten Elliott was even there, going by the blank, relaxed look on his face. Elliott subtly watched him for a few more minutes, waiting for some indication that he was supposed to be doing something other than sitting like a lump. It was easy work, and he didn't mind doing it, but the work ethic his dad had taught him through strict chore schedules, report card appraisals, and after-school volunteering prevented him from simply relaxing and enjoying the easiest shift ever.

He couldn't stop calculating how much he was earning, breaking the monthly number down in his head, by day, then by hour, then by minute, watching the cents Aiden was paying him slip away.

"Seriously?" Elliott finally burst out, during an excruciatingly quiet point of the movie. "You're actually going to give me money to Netflix and chill with you?"

Aiden reached for the remote, paused the movie, and calmly looked down at him. "Yes. Problem?"

Aiden had told him he wanted all the perks of a boyfriend but without the inconvenience or emotional entanglement. So, why was he thrown off by Aiden keeping to his word? He supposed he'd been prepared for Aiden's version of a boyfriend to be a person he fucked more than a single time. Which made no sense, because he remembered teasing Aiden about the cute, couple-y things he wanted to do with a guy who was paid to do it.

"Nope," he blurted. "No problem at all."

He settled back in and tried his best to let his anxiety go, to enjoy the proximity of a warm, attractive body like most people would, but he couldn't, and apparently didn't do a great job of hiding it, because they only got through a couple of scenes in the movie before Aiden paused it again.

"Okay, this isn't working," Aiden said.

Elliott's panic flared, and he immediately started calculating whether he could afford to spend another few weeks searching for the least-creepy guy on the short list of people who'd be willing to pay for his ass. It didn't look likely.

He rushed to fix his mistake. "I'm sorry I'm being weird, ignore—"

"It's fine. I think you need to understand how much I'm enjoying this."

Elliott blinked at Aiden's emphatic tone.

"Here's the thing," Aiden explained. "Watching TV used to be a family event for me. We'd get everyone together, take turns picking what to watch, share a big bowl of popcorn. It was fun. College was like that too, only . . . different."

A hint of a blush rose on Aiden's artfully scruffy face, clearing up what kind of *different* it was. With Aiden's good looks, he must have had his pick of people who'd "watch a movie" with him.

"I have a lot of memories that start with turning on the TV and getting comfortable," Aiden continued, "and that's probably why I never feel more lonely than when I'm watching TV by myself. I'm too wiped after long days to do emotionally complicated, so I don't want to go out. But if I got a friend or someone to come over, I wouldn't be able to use my free time to relax the same way as when I'm alone. So, this works, and I don't mind that I'm paying for the privilege of not feeling like a complete loser for watching *Die Hard* for the fifteenth time alone in my underwear."

Elliott could picture Aiden when he was younger, hanging out with his siblings, then later, at his fancy school for prelaw, stealing an hour to be a young, hot guy with game to spare. And he got why Aiden didn't want to do it by himself. Elliott didn't play video games without Kevin for the same reason.

"Okay," Elliott said.

Aiden smiled slightly. "Not to mention, this outfit might be comfortable, but it's not exactly sweltering."

Elliott laughed, picturing Aiden hugging a hot water bottle in the middle of summer with the cool air on full blast. "Well, then. It's my solemn duty to cuddle you for warmth."

He started to shift over, but at the last second, he paused and made a decision. He stood and undid his jeans, pushing them down and tossing them over the other end of the couch. His boxers were a lot looser than Aiden's, but they were still fairly new and presentable since he hadn't expected to be wearing much more than them for so long.

He plastered himself to Aiden's side this time, snuggling in and making sure there was as much of them touching as possible. The movie started again, and then Aiden reached down and scared the shit out of Elliott by popping out the footrest.

"Look at you, big spender," Elliott said, smirking. "The height of luxury."

"You should see the cupholders."

Elliott laughed, then something exploded on the screen, and they were both distracted. Paying attention to the movie was easier now that he didn't have to worry about what was expected of him. He had to crane his neck a little bit to see the screen since he was so attached to Aiden, but it was worth it to feel Aiden's chest as he let out a monster sigh of relief and comfort. Within a few minutes, Elliott had arranged them so their legs were tangled together and they'd reached optimal levels of skin-to-skin contact.

Elliott was good at cuddling. He knew it, Kevin knew it, and a few random people in attendance at Elliott's after-prom party knew it as well. He knew just how often he had to move so that they didn't get sweaty or have their extremities fall asleep. He had long, thin limbs that looked like they should have been too pointy, but they made up for that slight disadvantage by being able to wrap around someone like a warm, easygoing octopus.

The rest of the movie was good, too. Not the best he'd ever seen, but entertaining. They weren't completely silent throughout—Elliott never could keep his commentary to himself, which was why he preferred watching movies at home—but the longer the movie was on, the less Elliott felt like he had to speak. Aiden was as laid-back as Elliott had ever seen him, which made Elliott relax even more.

This could work, he thought, and finally convinced his brain to stop drawing up Plan B through J in case Aiden cut him loose and he was back to square one.

When the movie was over, he untangled himself and got up, since no amount of adjusting could keep him from getting antsy for that long.

"There's water and other stuff in the fridge if you'd like some," Aiden offered, stretching his own legs, and drawing Elliott's eyes to his powerful quads.

Jeez Louise. Elliott made it to the gym a couple of times a week himself, but he'd always tended toward leanness, rather than muscle-y and broad like Aiden. He was fine with their differences, especially since he was the one who got to see instead of being seen, but he felt almost bad about how hard he was objectifying Aiden. Almost.

The kitchen was easy to find, and like the rest of the apartment Elliott had seen, it was clean, simply outfitted, and shiny with chrome. He opened the monster-sized fridge right as he heard Aiden get up from the couch in the other room.

It was as spotless inside as it was outside, but that wasn't what drew Elliott's attention. He was mostly interested in how little there was in it. Water bottles lined the bottom shelf, and the door was stuffed full of condiments, but two-thirds of the remaining space was empty. The last third, the shelf at eye level, was taken up by neatly stacked plastic containers full of food. They were a little like homemade Hungry Man dinners, meticulously packed and ready to go, with labels showing the contents and a best-before date. It was pretty impressive, actually.

Aiden came up behind him. "The water is— Oh, you found it."

"Um, yeah." Elliott shook himself out of his envious daze and helped himself to a bottle, then pointed to the open door and fumbled, "What is—"

"Oh, yeah. That." Aiden reached over him and pushed the fridge closed firmly, then coughed. "I didn't make those. I don't like cooking because it takes too long."

"So, you have a personal chef?" Who was a master at meal-planning, apparently.

"Not exactly. A friend of mine is a stay-at-home dad who cooks for his family every day. I pay Vernon generously to make twice as much as he needs, and a couple times a week he brings over the leftovers he froze. It's a win-win situation." Aiden sounded like he was having an argument he'd had a hundred times before. "He makes money for doing something he was going to do anyway, and I don't have to live on takeout. It's hard enough to keep in shape with the hours I work."

"Cool."

"Cool?"

Elliott nodded. "Yeah. It's a good idea. Convenience is most of the reason why I still live in the dorms. Like, I could cook for myself, but why bother when I'm happy eating the dining-hall food?"

Aiden smiled, his shoulders untensing. "Exactly. I'm fully capable of not starving. This is just easier."

"I totally get that."

Aiden helped himself to his own bottle of water, and they sipped in silence for a few minutes. Elliott was starting to wonder if he should make some kind of move when Aiden twisted the cap onto his drink and suggested they watch something else.

They ended up in the same position as before, but this time, Aiden chose a movie Elliott had seen. His attention drifted away from the movie periodically, which was probably why he noticed the difference in Aiden. Before, he'd been completely relaxed, almost melting into the buttery leather couch. He'd allowed Elliott to place him where he wanted him, clearly basking in the presence of another living human.

This time, there was an unmistakable tautness in Aiden's body. He'd directed Elliott's arm higher a couple of times, and was twisting his body away from Elliott's hip in a way that must have been uncomfortable—

Elliott was such a dumb ass.

He reached over Aiden for the remote on the end table, unconcerned that his torso was covering the screen. Aiden didn't protest, just looked at him questioningly. He paused the movie, and his face must have given him away because by the time he'd twisted in Aiden's loose hold and faced him, straddling his legs, Aiden didn't seem confused at all.

Aiden's hands automatically came to his waist to steady him, even though he hadn't lost his balance. Elliott smirked. If Innes hadn't already told him, he would still have bet money he didn't have that Aiden was bi. The *hands circling a tiny waist* thing was something Elliott used to do, back when he'd had lackluster makeouts with girls in closets in high school. Now that he was a solid Kinsey five, he didn't go in for things like sensual hair stroking or delicate touches. There were probably men in the world who liked those things, but they weren't the men who Elliott was having sex with.

Elliott dipped his head and kissed Aiden properly and forgot everything he was thinking. It was nice. Better than nice, and it got better the longer Aiden let him have control. They made out, slow and lazy as though they were a couple of teenagers who had the hotel room until 11 a.m.

Aiden was an exceptional kisser, Elliott found out, once he'd been given the time to gain confidence. His hands, when they left Elliott's waist, were sure and warm, and they took their time sliding up and down Elliott's back. It said something about how touch-starved Elliott had gotten that the press of fingers through the cotton of his T-shirt could get him revved up.

When his lips were tingling and hot from kisses and the scrape of Aiden's facial hair, he pushed himself up and stumbled onto his feet. Aiden watched him as he peeled off his shirt and tossed it to the end of the couch with his jeans. He stared intensely as Elliott fingered the band of his boxers, drawing out the reveal.

He didn't have anything special to gawk at. If anyone asked him to describe himself, he'd say he was pretty average, looks-wise. But he'd learned firsthand how large a role confidence and bluffing played in attractiveness. In that moment, he believed wholeheartedly in his own appeal, so Aiden must have too, or he wouldn't have looked like a thirsty canine when Elliott's boxers finally hit the floor.

With Elliott's help, Aiden's joined them, along with his shirt, but it wasn't a quick process. While the reclining sofa was comfortable, it would've been a lot easier if Aiden had stood up. Elliott loved a challenge, though, and the bonus was that when Aiden had finally lost his clothes, Elliott was in the perfect position to kiss his way up Aiden's hard stomach. It was extremely difficult for him to stay north of Aiden's navel, but he didn't want to fall into a routine. Besides, he could still remember how Aiden's dick had felt in his mouth, and he had a few other places he wanted to feel it in before he started repeating himself.

Aiden, the good man, followed Elliott's lead, staying still while Elliott settled. Elliott was starting to see a pattern there. Aiden let himself be led up until a certain time, at which point he'd start taking a bit of control. It was a fantastic push and pull, and Elliott wanted more of it. He wanted to see how much he had to push before Aiden would stop pulling.

When his legs were on either side of Aiden's, Elliott kissed him again, then grabbed Aiden's hand and guided it to his ass, right to his rim, where—

Aiden's fingers spasmed and withdrew. "When did you—" Aiden sputtered.

"Before I left home. It's been a while, though, so go slow."

Aiden's tongue peeked out to wet his lips, and his cheeks reddened. "You didn't have to do that yourself," he said, his voice lower and rougher than it had been earlier.

"You're paying for convenience, right?" Elliott quipped, then he tried to move Aiden's hand to where it had been, but Aiden had gone stiff. His face shut down a bit, not frowning, but carefully blank. Elliott's stomach clenched. He was going to get abs like Aiden's if he kept making Aiden so uncomfortable.

"Would you mind not bringing it up like that?" Aiden asked, not meeting his eyes.

"Uh, sure." Elliott couldn't even pretend he wasn't weirded out. "But are you sure, though? Like, this is what it is, and not mentioning it isn't going to make it—"

"No, no, I know that," Aiden assured him, and he sounded panicked enough that Elliott was inclined to believe it. "I'm not romanticizing you or anything. I don't know if anyone could."

"Hey, watch it." Elliott smirked, relieved, and gave Aiden's jaw a tap.

Aiden grinned and batted his hand away, then his face got serious again. "So, yeah, I'm good. But it just kind of—" He stopped, shook his head. "I don't know, it's stupid, forget I said anything."

He leaned in for a kiss and stroked his hands down Elliott's sides. Elliott shivered, but turned his head away. He was way too jittery right then to enjoy it.

"No, I get it," he said. "It ruins the mood. I totally ruined the mood."

"No, it's fine. We can get there again."

Elliott let Aiden kiss him this time, and as if Aiden had read his mind, he took charge right from the beginning. His hand came up to hold Elliott's jaw, tilting his head and devouring Elliott's mouth until he forgot to be worried. Until he had no reason to be worried because the mood he was afraid they'd lost bounced back, like the trooper it was.

They only stopped making out when Elliott couldn't stop gasping at Aiden's searching fingers. He buried his face in the crook of Aiden's neck as Aiden finished working him open, made easier by the slow half hour Elliott had taken before he'd left the house, weak-kneed and ready for anything. He moaned as the fingers probed deeper, but it was too awkward an angle to be truly satisfying, so Elliott pushed Aiden's arms off of him with one last, breathless kiss and reached for his jeans on the other end of the couch. The condom was right where he'd left it, in his pocket with some extra lube that they'd definitely need.

He peered at Aiden, intending to make a joke about what size of rubber he wanted out of Elliott's extensive (imaginary) collection, but two things stopped him. First, he remembered that Aiden didn't want to be reminded at each turn that Elliott was used to casual sex in every regard. Second, Aiden's expression took the words out of his mouth.

Aiden's eyes were heavy-lidded, roaming ceaselessly over the expanse of Elliott's twisted body. His mouth hung open, closing only briefly so that he could swallow deeply, then falling open again.

Elliott almost hated to move and spoil the view, though he wasn't sure what was so enticing about his bony rib cage and pink-flushed neck. But Aiden didn't lose the look even while Elliott knee-walked over his lap, stilted, but eager. That probably had something to do with the fact that he was doing it to reach Aiden's cock, and started stroking him lazily, using the pre-come that had gathered at the tip to swirl his thumb around the head with no resistance.

When Aiden's hips began to buck slightly with every pull, Elliott rolled on the condom with practiced ease, then drizzled lube over top. Messy, but effective. Aiden watched him do it all, not offering to help but clenching and unclenching his hands at his sides like he wanted to. He did steady Elliott when he struggled into place, which was appreciated. It took Elliott a minute to predict where he needed to be to get the right angle, but until he was sure, Aiden was patient.

"Go slow," he said again as he sank down on Aiden's cock, even though he was going to be the one doing the lion's share of the moving.

Or so he thought. Aiden stayed still for a while, silent except for a rough exhale of breath every time Elliott jerked out of rhythm and moaned from a brush near his prostate. Then, without any warning, Aiden slid down lower in his seat and gripped Elliott's straining thighs, his fingers denting the skin as they held him in place.

A whine was punched out of his throat when Aiden's hips slammed up into him, using the leverage he got from the footrest. Elliott's head fell back as Aiden kept up his momentum, taking over and giving Elliott a break. Sort of. He'd been a bit fuzzy from the burning in his thighs, but with Aiden taking a turn, he was very fuzzy from the pleasure, first from Aiden's cock hitting all the right places, then from his own hand on his dick.

The time for slow was over.

"Faster," Elliott panted. "Come on— *Yes.*"

Aiden sped up, and his breath started to come out in near subvocal growls that sent electric sparks up Elliott's spine. Aiden finished first, his hips crashing up suddenly and stilling, a groan tearing from his throat, the loudest sound he'd made the whole night.

Elliott kept up a steady, lazy motion of his hips until Aiden had melted into the couch. He hesitated for one uneasy beat. Should he finish himself off, or wait for Aiden to recover and return the favor? Did Aiden care whether or not he came? The point of Elliott being here was so that he didn't have to worry about the tit-for-tat grunt work of a real relationship, so did that extend to mutual orgasms?

Elliott didn't have to worry for long, because Aiden came back to himself a bit, sorting out his limbs, then fisting Elliott's dick where it had been resting, leaking a tiny patch of pre-come on Aiden's stomach.

Aiden didn't waste time teasing. He set a rapid, jerky pace that had Elliott's tired thighs bunching with pleasure as he surged to a height that forced Aiden's softening cock to slip out of him. It was a weird, half-remembered feeling, but it was what made him tip over the edge; the familiar sweet soreness and slide of lube that hadn't evaporated.

He spilled on Aiden's abs, adding to the mess already there. *At least we only have one place to clean*, he thought, a bit hysterically, high from endorphins and the loosening of taut muscles.

Aiden didn't seem to be in any more of a hurry than Elliott was. Only when sweat began to chill and itch did Elliott untangle himself, flopping next to Aiden on the couch and grabbing his T-shirt to use as a towel for his face and neck. Tomorrow, he'd be groaning every time he had to bend over or climb a set of stairs, but it was worth it.

Screw deadlifting. Good sex was easily the best way to get in leg day.

Out of nowhere, Aiden released a huge, happy sigh and said, plainly, "Fuck."

Elliott couldn't help but laugh in a loud burst. "Yeah, same," he said, when he was done.

Aiden got up and left the room, and Elliott heard a toilet flush a minute later. When Aiden came back, Elliott took his turn, then returned to the couch to find that Aiden had resumed optimal Netflixing position.

"Do you want to go right away?" Aiden asked, giving himself away by fingering the remote control.

"Not unless you want me to." Elliott couldn't get into the habit of staying late on weeknights, but for their first real date? He could make an exception. Besides, they hadn't finished the movie they'd been watching before they'd gotten distracted.

"I'm okay with you staying, if you don't mind."

"I really don't." He climbed onto the couch, reattaching himself to Aiden's side in a way that was starting to feel routine. "Play away. I've got all night."

The movie was okay. The company was better. The afterglow lasted until the end, at least for Elliott, and he was willing to bet for Aiden too.

"This was nice," Aiden told him, out of the blue about fifteen minutes before the end of the second movie.

"I'm glad."

The rest of the evening was just as nice. They watched thirty minutes of some period drama before they both confessed that it was boring as shit and decided to mute it and make up more interesting dialogue for the characters. It was late by the time they were finished and highly amused with themselves, so Elliott elected to stay over.

The only snag came when they realized how painful it was going to be to get unstuck from the leather of the couch. But that was solved with the incentive of another piece of furniture Elliott had yet to try out: Aiden's bed.

(Its score: A-plus, 10 out of 10, would give a blowjob and get spooned in it again.)

Chapter 4

Elliott sat down at the end of an empty table in the dining hall with a tray of eggs and toast, still damp from Aiden's shower, his laptop bag at his feet. He chewed mechanically, eternally thankful he didn't have to wait in line at the coffee shop near his first class or, worse, cook for himself. It made everything else that came with living in the dorms—the sleepless nights and the cramped illusion of privacy—worth it.

He'd been too busy catering to Innes's whims to make friends to move in with after his freshman year. He also didn't want to share rent with strangers for the same reason he shelled out a bit more extra money for a single room. Yes, he could've saved a few hundred bucks, but the odds he'd be questioned about his movements would be astronomically higher.

So, instead of constantly making excuses for his absence, he'd hide away in his little corner, alone.

A shout that was way too loud for pre-lunchtime pulled his attention across the hall. One of the tables was full of students who'd dragged themselves out of bed, probably with the promise of waffles.

Their smiles were wide, their eyes squinted against the sun that poured in through the tall windows. Elliott's eyes smarted too, the students' incandescent happiness almost painful to look at, but lovely all the same.

Egg fell off his fork with a *splat*. He shook his head to clear it, then picked up his book on the Minoans of Crete—the only one of his class texts that could fit in his back pocket. Matriarchal religion would be a better use of his focus than the people he lived with, not to mention was more interesting.

But he was scanning the lines without seeing them, blinking past the gunk in his eyes. The trip from Aiden's place hadn't been long, but he'd still had to wake up earlier than normal to make sure he was back on campus in time.

He gave up reading and headed to his class a little early.

The lecture hall wasn't open yet, but a few other keeners milled around, like the girl who always nabbed the best seat, no matter how early he showed up.

In retaliation, he now claimed the only bench within view of the door, and just barely resisted putting his feet up on the other seat.

"Is class canceled?"

He looked to his left at the speaker and got an eyeful of bedraggled hair and candy cane-colored eyeballs.

It was Matt, one of the few people on his floor whom he shared a couple classes with. At least, it was most of Matt. The rest of him might have been left in a toilet bowl back in their dorm.

"No, the professor's not here yet," Elliott answered, keeping his voice library-low for Matt's sake.

Matt's face creased—emphasizing the red indents on his cheeks from pillows well-used—and his backpack thumped to the floor. "I thought class started at nine?"

"Nope. Nine thirty."

After a few seconds of blank staring in the direction of the locked door, Matt claimed the empty spot on the bench, sending out a puff of deodorant that wasn't quite hiding everything else. "Damn. I could've slept longer."

"Bummer."

Neither of them spoke for a few seconds, long enough for Elliott to wonder if he could pull out his book again and get to the end of the chapter before class started, but Matt spoke up, with a clearer, less alcohol-soaked tone.

"Hey, man, did you do the readings for today?"

Man? He hadn't thought they were at that level of acquaintance, but maybe Matt just used it like punctuation. Or he couldn't remember Elliott's name.

"Yeah," Elliott answered. There was another uneasy beat of uneasy silence during which Matt nodded and bit his lip, so Elliott took a shot in the dark. "Do you . . . want me to summarize them?"

"Oh my god, would you? I meant to do it, but then stuff happened, you know? And the professor goes so fast, I can't keep the Apostolic and the Ante-whatever straight."

"Ante-Nicene. Yeah, he's a bit nuts. He also gets spitty when he's passionate, which is always. The splash zone is why I don't sit in the front row."

Matt's laugh was choked, like he was afraid their teacher was around to hear them. They weren't in a movie from the nineties, but Elliott snuck a glance behind him anyway. Nothing.

Relieved, he kept going. "But he's a rock star when it comes to the Achaemenid Empire, so you win some, you lose some."

"Sure," Matt agreed, his glazed eyes giving away his eagerness to move on.

Elliott cleared his throat and reached into his bag for his laptop, booting it up to retrieve the notes he'd already made on the chapters. "Yeah, so today, we're talking second and third centuries."

The recap didn't take long, since Elliott had simplified the text to the level of someone who was probably only taking the class as a required elective.

"Thank you so much," Matt said, picking up his backpack so none of the rapidly arriving students would trip.

"It's nothing. Christianity really starts getting interesting around this time."

"I bet. You really get this stuff and, you know, enjoy it. As soon as I saw you, I was like, 'Elliott will have done the reading!'"

So Matt did know his name. He must have had a good memory, since Elliott didn't have his name written on his door anywhere, and he tended to stay quiet during floor meetings.

A selectively good memory, maybe. Early Christian History not selected. His loss.

"Man, is the prof ever going to get here?" Matt mused out loud, peering at the door down the hall. "I'm not usually so early, I guess."

"He'll fly in at the last minute with his briefcase half open. I think he lays on the absentminded-professor aesthetic pretty thick, honestly."

Matt laughed again, crinkling the fading acne scars on his cheeks. "Dude. He totally does. That hair makes him look like a cartoon character."

Out of nowhere, Elliott's palms started to sweat, as though a timer had gone off. He'd been doing so well. Meaningless, easy conversation. It was his turn to keep their rhythm going, but his tongue was heavy with nerves. With every word he might say, he worried he'd accidentally spill something incriminating about his bank account or his odd "friendships."

Irrational? Yes. Unshakeable? Also yes.

"Totally," he said, then clamped his lips together.

The gods—the whole pantheon, except for Zeus, maybe—must have been looking down and taking pity, because their professor raced in just then. With five minutes to spare even, according to the clock, but speed-walking like a white rabbit.

Matt lifted his backpack and slung a strap over one shoulder, then with the casual nonchalance of someone posing a question to which they already knew the answer, asked, "See you tonight, then?"

Elliott blinked, flipping through his mental calendar and coming up empty. "Why? Is there a meeting?"

Matt's eyes widened and he tripped over his words. "There's, uh, a party. On the fourth floor."

"Oh."

A big one, then, if the engineering cabal from one floor above him was involved. Something everybody would have heard about already. Except him.

He'd be hearing it, though, while he tried to read or sleep off the weight of his decisions.

It was probably a good thing his invitation had gotten lost in the mail. Relaxation was the aim of parties like that, but as long as Elliott's job was not-so-technically illegal, he couldn't fully join in. He couldn't have one too many drinks and blurt out his secrets to the wrong person.

"You should come," Matt said, needlessly bright. "It's Mariah's birthday."

Elliott forced a smile. "Thanks, but I've got studying to do."

Matt's relief was palpable. "Man, it's the worst, right? But it'll all be worth it when we graduate."

"Sure." No grad school plans for this one, apparently. Would he even make it to spring break if his enthusiasm for learning was already waning?

Matt's red eyes sharpened, and his fingers toyed with the zipper pull on his bag. "Actually, it's good I caught you. A couple of people from this class have been studying with me." Ducking his head, he assumed a deservedly sheepish expression. "I've missed a couple of sessions. But you could join us if you want. You're so good at all this."

Oh, no. Elliott had been down that road before. Groups like this started with good intentions, left him alone in the library most sessions, then frantically searched him out for his immaculate study guides a couple of days before the exam.

"That's—"

"You could tutor us," Matt went on. "I think we could scrape together some money for your time."

Of course. What other reason could Elliott have expected? Disappointment still made his stomach sink to his knees.

But even if he'd wanted to help Matt's group, he couldn't. He'd thought about tutoring, in the beginning. As far as Dad and Kevin were concerned, his tutoring side hustle was thriving. But when he'd run the numbers, he'd worked out how many clients he'd have to have and how many hours he'd have to spend to make enough money to send to his dad, and it hadn't worked.

That, and all the reasons why he had to keep to himself, made it an impossibility.

"Sorry, I'm pretty busy already." Elliott scratched the side of his face, then craned his neck to look at the opening doors of the lecture hall. "I could suggest a few names, if you like?" He had a list of people he didn't avoid, since they might one day be his colleagues.

"That's okay." Matt stood and shuffled closer to the line of students entering the unlocked hall. "See you in there. And thanks again."

"Yeah, for sure."

They were both swept up in the crowding at the entrance. Matt headed up the stairs to the back, while Elliott took his usual seat in the second row, sharing a nod and a smile with Professor Handwavey McSprayerson.

He was a good guy, really. His actual name was D. Salter, and he didn't seem to mind pestering questions or a good debate when Elliott couldn't hold himself back.

What did it say about him, that he talked to his professor more than he did his classmates? He didn't care to answer himself, distracted enough by the stream of people coming in the door, chatting and settling themselves.

Elliott could hear them all as they talked about everything and nothing. This class, other classes, dates, jobs. The frightening potential of the world outside the cozy bubble of college life.

Elliott had already had a taste of it, and had decided he'd stay in academia as long as possible, burying his head in ancient stories and the smell of new textbooks. All he had to do was keep giving them tuition money without letting them know the source.

A pang of phantom panic squeezed his ribs as he imagined the fallout if the college ever did find out.

Weighing the risks and rewards of hooking was the first thing he'd done when Innes had made his offer. Despite the fear, it was worth it, so far.

A career that could potentially be ruined by his other work was better than no career at all, or one that came at the expense of thousands of dollars of crippling debt.

Right?

The beginning of the lecture helped him shake off his anxiety, and he shoved it to the back of his mind like he usually did until he could almost forget about it. The material was familiar, so he had lots to say when Salter opened up the floor for discussion.

But toward the end of the precious time with Salter's expertise, while pointless questions were asked about chapters they were supposed to have read weeks ago, Elliott's attention span wavered.

Did kids these days even look at the syllabus? (*Yes*, he thought, bitterly. *Once at the end of the semester, to find the professor's email so they could ask them if the Peloponnesian War would be on the exam*. Duh.)

His phone buzzed on the top of the desk, and he swiped it into his lap before its bleating could reach anyone else's ears.

1 New Text from Aiden (Kent)

The other Aiden in his phone had to go. There could be only One True Aiden, and the old classmate who'd switched majors after their disastrous group project because *"Greeks are boring, dude"* certainly wouldn't win that battle.

Thanks for staying, the text said, and as Elliott was reading it, another one came through. *And thanks for leaving too. I would've been useless as a host anyway.*

Elliott smirked, imagining Aiden pressing the Snooze button until the last possible minute. He typed out and sent: *Not a morning person?*

Not really. So thanks again.

You don't have to thank me, he sent back. That was what Aiden was paying for, after all. Cuddling with benefits, without the side of inconvenient obligation.

Aiden was quick to respond. *I want to. And I'd like to thank you again, in person.* Then, before Elliott could laugh at Aiden's lack of subtlety: *I spoke to my secretary today. She's going to set up an automatic transfer of funds. 1st of every month.*

Elliott breathed out a sigh and put his phone down for a minute to simply stare at the ceiling. That was great news.

He'd been taking his chances on Aiden by letting him take his time with the payment, but it was a bet he'd been sure of winning. Still, getting confirmation of a scheduled payment was a relief.

That's awesome, Elliott texted back. *When do you want to meet?*

Is 3X/week too many?

Elliott raised his eyebrows. He'd been expecting to make another one-off appointment to let Aiden get used to the idea of having him there regularly.

Elliott: *Not at all. I can even stay over one of those nights, every couple of weeks. Not every week, tho.*

Getting too busy with his side hustle to focus on school would kind of defeat the purpose.

Aiden: *Understood. W/F/Su work for you?*

Elliott: *Totally.*

Aiden: *Great. I work late most days, but I'm almost always able to get home by 7. We can plan on that.*

It worked fantastically. He could stay over on the occasional Friday, have most Saturdays to himself, then round out the weekend with one last visit on Sunday evening. It would be nice to have a little time to himself on the weekend, instead of spending all of it with Aiden and getting sick of the sight of him by Sunday night. He'd had enough of that with a different Kent.

In his lap, his phone buzzed again, and he snuck a look at the professor to make sure he was still being sent on tangents by the non-history majors.

Aiden: *We might have to skip a few Sundays. Not too often though.*

Why? Elliott asked, brave and curious.

Aiden: *I play football once a month with some friends. We're usually done by dinnertime, but sometimes we go out for drinks if we get trounced too badly.*

Elliott was treated to another mental picture of Aiden, this time in a thin, loose jersey without all the padding underneath, and those tight pants football players wore, whatever they were called . . .

Elliott's fingers fidgeted even as he typed, *Ooh should I get a cheerleader outfit and tag along?*

Aiden: *You could, but I don't think the organizers would appreciate your charms.*

Elliott slumped a bit in the uncomfortable lecture hall seat. Three dots wiggled on his phone to say that Aiden wasn't done yet, but Elliott was still oddly disappointed.

Another buzz.

We play for charity, Aiden's text said. *We fundraise at the game, donate the profits, usually to a kid's cancer ward.*

Innes had told him once that the only thing Aiden did was work and give his time to worthy causes. The way he'd said it, with a roll of his eyes, had implied that this was somehow a bad thing. Elliott had already known Innes was an asshole before that, but if he hadn't, that would've been a big clue.

That's really cool, he replied, hoping his embarrassment wasn't readable over text. *Let me know when they're happening.*

Aiden: *Maybe you could run a kissing booth? I wouldn't mind.*
Elliott: *Har har.*

Maybe embarrassment didn't translate, but somehow Aiden's humor did. Maybe a few months ago, Elliott wouldn't have been sure Aiden was joking, but now? He had to bite the inside of his cheek to keep from snickering.

Elliott let the phone screen go black and refocused on what was being said. Despite his good intentions, he was distracted again when his phone lit up.

Can I ask a question? Aiden said.

Elliott: *Yeah?*

Aiden: *On your "will do" list, you said you're okay with barebacking. Is that still true?*

Elliott was liking this bluntness Aiden was striving for, but it made him aware of every minute he spent composing his answer in a diplomatic way.

Yes, but only if we're exclusive, he decided on. Then, *Are we exclusive?*

Immediately: *Yes. On my side, at least. I don't need to go out and find anyone else.*

It'd taken six months for Elliott to even suggest a similar arrangement with Innes. They were both too cynical by nature to put their health in each other's hands until there'd been a wealth of evidence that they were each too lazy to fake the official papers or deal with the inconvenience of chlamydia. (Or the life-altering shittiness of something permanent.)

Okay, Elliott texted, shielding the screen of his phone more than was probably necessary, given that the closest person was two desks away. *Do you trust me enough to get you accurate test results and keep it in my pants so we don't have to worry about protection?*

Yes, if you trust me.

The funny thing was, he did. Aiden had proven to be trustworthy in every aspect so far. A true gentleman, if such people existed. It was out of character for Elliott to be putting that kind of faith in Aiden so quickly, but if he was honest with himself (and he usually was), constant vigilance was exhausting.

Elliott: *K. I'll show you mine, you show me yours. Let me know when you've made an appointment. I'll reward you ;)*

There was a long silence, long enough that Elliott tuned back into his class again. Finally, Aiden responded, *There's no need,* and Elliott amused himself by imagining Aiden in his fancy office at the firm, fretting over what to say.

There's EVERY need, he typed. He also sent a couple of eggplant emojis and some ambiguous droplets. That'd put a fire under Aiden's ass.

As he'd expected, Aiden didn't text back, and Elliott went back to struggling to pay attention. It didn't help that they were covering the historical Jesus Christ . . . again. The story itself was rad, but he was a little too aware that he hadn't made it home last night to get sucked into a topic he'd covered on his own in high school.

It was a purely psychological concern, that was for sure. He'd showered and changed at Aiden's place, so he was certain he looked presentable, but he didn't feel like his normal self. That always happened when he didn't use his own bathroom and his own shampoo, soap, and hot water. It didn't matter how clean he was, he always felt like he was only half-washed until he got back home.

"Elliott, could I speak to you before you go?"

Class had ended, and Elliott had been too out of it to notice, and now Professor Salter was staring right at him.

"Yeah, sure," he said, needlessly bright and perky. While the room emptied out, he went up to the podium, his shoes squeaking on the floor.

"Your essay from last semester," Professor Salter said, his laptop shutting down. "'Human After All,' right? It was good."

"Thanks." Elliott's chest warmed with pride. Out of respect, he'd refrained from calling his thesis about the graffiti of Pompeii explosive, but he'd definitely knocked that essay out of the park.

"I want to submit it to our undergraduate conference in September," Professor Salter said. "With your permission, of course, and your name on it. That sound like it's up your alley?"

Fighting down his happy dance was truly a Herculean task. "Sure," he said, keeping his voice artificially low to compensate. Talking about the long-dead people who wrote so-and-so was here on ancient walls in front of people who'd find it as cool as he did? Where did he sign?

"Fantastic, excellent, brilliant." Professor Salter closed the laptop with a snap and started packing it up, along with the power cord. "I'll send you an email with all the details. I also haven't forgotten about that reference you asked me for."

Tension crept into Elliott's shoulders and the flutters of ego evaporated under the embarrassing reminder. It was bad enough he'd had to ask for help in the first place.

"Great," he squeaked. "The scholarship committee won't start evaluating them until next month, so no rush."

"Don't worry, I'll get a move on." Professor Salter hefted his bag over his shoulder and they both headed for the lecture hall door.

"Thank you," Elliott said, before he lost the opportunity. "I really appreciate it. I don't want to take up too much of your time."

"It's nothing," Professor Salter called out, heading down the hall to his office. "See you next week!"

It probably would be nothing, in the end, Elliott reminded himself as he walked out into the late-morning air. Or close to it. He applied every semester for scholarships, and sometimes he was even awarded a small grant, but there was only so much to go around, and however much he appreciated it, it didn't come close to covering all his costs.

His walk home was short, and made quicker by planning what he was going to get done that day. The list was long, so as soon as he got home and high-fived the life-size poster of Alexander the Great on his door, he jumped onto his bed to shut his eyes for a few minutes.

Naturally, that was when his phone rang.

"Hey," he answered, throwing his free arm across his eyes. "I keep meaning to call you."

"Great minds think alike, kiddo."

His dad's rasping voice warmed the sterile insides of Elliott's dorm room more than any of the pictures and posters he'd put up. "Yeah, yeah. You should be here instead."

"Nah, I could never get into those Romans as much as you. I did see something in the paper the other day, about those statues that get you so riled up?"

"Ugh, the Elgin marbles! It's just more bullshit from the British Museum about why ancient Greek statues should be in England instead of, you know, Greece."

It'd been Elliott's mom who really cared about that sort of thing, but his dad let him go on about it, making all the right noises as Elliott relieved tension by going over arguments he'd already made or read about in books.

"You're getting a good start to the year, then?" Elliott's dad asked, after his ire had petered out.

"Definitely. One of my favorite TAs is running my Poetry and Prose seminar. I'm going to be watching her every move so I can figure out how to be her in a couple years."

"Fantastic."

"Oh, and my tutoring is picking up again for the semester. I should have enough clients to send you some money next month."

He'd meant to sneak it in as an aside, but his news dropped like a stone in the conversation.

Dad sighed. "Elliott—"

"Can we not do this? I'm kinda tired."

"I'm not your responsibility. I don't like borrowing money from anyone, least of all you. It gets people into worse trouble."

"I know, but you're not borrowing it, and I'm not some stranger."

"I just think you should be worrying about yourself."

He blinked up at the ceiling, seeing his dad's frowning face there. "But then who would worry about you?"

"You shouldn't be racking up debt when you could be paying it off as you go, instead of taking care of me. I'm fine."

Elliott's stomach tightened, but he wouldn't be put off. "What about the roof, Dad?" As expected, his dad didn't have an answer, not even when he pressed, "Will you be fine when it caves in?"

Elliott wasn't there at the house, in his mother's small, beloved kitchen with its outdated cabinets, but he could still tell that they were thinking of the same things. The dollar signs that would start to build up when they tried to get a new roof. The years and years it would take to free themselves of the debt, only to probably need to make another big purchase.

"Sometimes I think this place is more trouble than it's worth," Dad said, quiet enough that Elliott could hear the old fridge spitting in the background.

Elliott swallowed. "I'll send you something next month. Don't argue."

"Okay. But just from tutoring, right? No funny business."

"None," he promised, lying for the hundredth time, but not about what his dad thought.

It'd been a year since they'd argued about how Elliott could afford to send the money he did, and Elliott had "confessed" to selling essays to other students. He'd never actually done it, but the concept was unsavory enough for his dad to disapprove, but forgive. Now, he had to stick to the tutoring story.

"Tell me about your other classes," Dad said, blustering to move them along from hard topics.

"Sure. I had Early Christian History today."

"Ooh, sounds riveting."

"It is, surprisingly."

When they finally hung up, Elliott's phone was warm from the heat of his cheek, but he stayed on it long enough to check his bank balance one more time before he put it from his mind, diving deep into the past instead.

Chapter  5

E lliott slammed the door behind him and yanked off his shoes right away.

"God, I'm so sorry," he shouted, assuming Aiden would be in the living room or kitchen, as he usually was on Wednesdays. "My bus was at a dead stop for ten minutes. There was an accident or something, we were completely trapped—"

"It's okay," Aiden said, poking his head around the corner from the living room and raising an expressive dark eyebrow at Elliott's frazzled state. He was holding a fork and one of his dinner containers, so he'd evidently been running late as well.

Elliott stumbled into the living room and collapsed face-first onto the couch, then he grabbed a pillow from the end closest to his head and groaned into it.

"Bad day?"

Elliott flipped around, slinging an arm over his eyes. "Just busy. And long. It should really be against college policy to make students take three quizzes in one day."

Aiden moved Elliott's feet, lifting them up and setting them down in his lap as he sat down. "And knowing you, you were up studying for all three until late last night, even though you learned the material a month ago."

"Naturally. I aced them, though, so it was worth it."

"I'm sure."

Elliott wiggled down the couch on his back so he was close enough to pet Aiden's arm underneath its soft shirt. "In other news, whatever we do today, let's strike handjobs from the schedule. One of those quizzes was an in-class essay, and I am not ambidextrous enough to use the hand that isn't still cramping like crazy."

"Noted."

"So what *are* we doing today? Do you want to finish season three of *Game of Thrones*? Or just read?"

Aiden gave Elliott's feet a shove so he was forced to sit up or fall off the couch.

"Actually," Aiden said, "I was thinking we might do something different today."

"Yeah?" It'd taken Elliott until that moment to realize that Aiden was wearing jeans instead of sweats. They were nice jeans, probably more expensive than the ones from Walmart that filled Elliott's closet. It was odd to see them, though, and Elliott was curious what had convinced Aiden to wear real-person clothes outside of work.

"Well, not really that different," Aiden explained, "but a change of location. How would you feel about going out to see a movie?"

"Oh. Sure."

"Great. There's a small theater I want to go to, not too far from your school."

Elliott would have been happy to go even if Aiden's eyes hadn't been sparkling with contained glee. Something about seeing Aiden's normally rigid calm unbend a fraction was more gratifying than seeing a normal person let it all hang out.

That was Elliott's idea of job satisfaction.

Aiden had friends. Elliott had heard a little bit about each of them, but he'd also heard that Aiden's schedule and theirs prevented them from doing much socializing. Vernon, the guy Aiden paid to cook for him, was busy with his kids most of the time. And Aiden's football team practiced without him whenever work demanded he give up his Saturdays.

So Aiden hadn't seen a movie in a theater in years. He'd stoically borne Elliott's teasing after letting slip that he always felt skeezy if he came by himself.

The movie Aiden picked had come out months before, so they saw it at a dingy three-screen cinema. It smelled a little suspicious, and everywhere they walked, the floors were slightly sticky, but it had a certain charm.

"Wow. Happening joint," Elliott said as they entered the auditorium. It was empty, and showtime was only a few minutes away. "Maybe we'll get the place all to ourselves."

They did, and it was a lot of fun: they heckled the actors and commented on the plot as loudly as they wanted, though Aiden kept Elliott from throwing popcorn at the screen.

Elliott had seen the movie with Kevin over the holiday break, and he had to admit, it was better on the big screen. He got as swept up in it as Aiden did, until they reached a low point, a side-plot for a handsomely paid guest star.

Elliott looked down at the carpet. He couldn't see anything much in the darkness, and he didn't want to. The less he thought about it, the better. He grabbed the thick stack of paper napkins he'd taken from the concession stand and spread them out on the floor in front of Aiden.

"What are you doing?" Aiden asked, but he didn't have to be told to make room when Elliott went to his knees in front of Aiden's legs. (Who said he never made sacrifices? He was making one now, committing to washing his jeans that night.)

"What do you think?"

He started working on Aiden's fly. He could barely see his fingers in the dim light, but he'd done it enough times that it wasn't that difficult.

"The movie—" Aiden started, but his protest was feeble right off the bat.

"It's okay. We have at least ten minutes before it starts getting interesting again."

There was no one to be quiet for, but Aiden didn't make a sound the whole time Elliott was blowing him. When the action changed to an outdoor scene, Elliott took the opportunity of the brighter, blue-tinged light to pull off, drinking in the sight of Aiden dazed and panting, his eyes glassy.

The smooth line of Aiden's forehead and his soft, open mouth as he looked down made the unfortunate sacrifice of Elliott's pants worth it.

Aiden finished in Elliott's mouth at the same time as a few gunshots went off in the movie, which made Elliott cackle, muffled in Aiden's thigh. After a few minutes filled with explosive sound effects that Elliott imagined were coming from Aiden's brain, Aiden pulled Elliott over to sit in his lap, fiddling with the buttons on his jeans in an obvious invitation. Elliott declined, pushing his hands away. He wanted Aiden to see the movie more than he wanted to get off.

(His teenaged self would have been floored. According to Desperately Hormonal Past Elliott, turning down an orgasm at the hands of another person was a sure sign of insanity.)

"I've never done anything like that before," Aiden said as they left the lobby. The way his eyes sparkled and his gait rolled loose over the sidewalk made him seem younger than he was.

"Shocker," Elliott said, ignoring Aiden's soft squawk of outrage. "Did you like it?"

Aiden rolled his eyes instead of answering, which Elliott took to mean *Of course*.

"I can be spontaneous," Aiden burst out, seconds later.

Elliott looked up from checking his phone, schooling his expression so he didn't show surprise. Aiden sounded like he was in the middle of a long-standing argument with someone Elliott couldn't see or hear.

"Sure you can," Elliott allowed. "In the correct place, at a convenient, prearranged time, right?"

Truthfully, Elliott wasn't that fond of going with the flow either. Scheduled sex wasn't any less fun.

"That's what you're here for, isn't it? Spontaneity might not come naturally, but I can get on board with it with someone like you."

Someone like him? Elliott wasn't sure what that was supposed to mean, but it was obviously complimentary, from the way Aiden's lips tightened against a grin.

"Thank god for me, then," he said, a breathy laugh shaking his voice. "Expect the unexpected!"

"I always do, with you." Aiden smiled, and his eyes sparkled in the street lights. "It's . . . gripping. Like the movie, but with no guns."

"Not yet," Elliott joked, already in the midst of checking his phone again. "Well, it's getting late, so I should probably head home from here."

It was only ten, so he wasn't in danger of turning into a pumpkin, but the theater was much closer to his dorm than it was to Aiden's apartment, and the quiet simplicity of his bedroom was sounding better by the minute.

"Yeah, that's a smart idea," Aiden agreed. "But could I walk you home?"

Elliott stared at him for a few seconds, waiting for the punch line. He wasn't sure what he expected—*Ha ha,* gotcha*!* Or *Should've seen your face!*—but he hadn't thought Aiden would simply continue to gaze earnestly back at him.

"You're not joking, are you?" Elliott barely resisted checking the street for cameras to see if he was being punked. "Do I look like a chick from the first fifteen minutes of a horror movie?"

Aiden rolled his eyes. "No."

"You do know that I make my way home later than this on a normal Wednesday, right?"

"Yes, but you take the bus. Walking is—"

"Dude. I'm a dude. You don't have to worry about me."

Aiden stood his ground. "So you can't get mugged unless you're a woman?"

"No, I only meant—"

"Would you just indulge me? I know I don't have to worry about you the same way I worry about my sisters, but it's still not safe."

"That's cute, but it really isn't necessary. I barely have anything to steal." Except for his phone, his wallet, and his peace of mind.

"I could pay for the Uber back—"

"Absolutely not. You already paid for the one to get here." Elliott didn't have the budget for it, and there was no way in hell he was letting Aiden pay for something that his legs could do for free. His dad had taught him better than that, and shared his dislike of owing people and working for free.

The casual affection Aiden wanted was already blurring the line between business and friendship.

"It's not a big deal," Aiden said, his hands shoved into his seemingly bottomless pockets. "I can afford it—"

"But I can't," Elliott said, sharp and serious after all their teasing. "And I'll be the one paying for it. Or not paying, in this case, because I don't need it."

Aiden's forehead creased with the force of his scowl. "Then let me walk you home. It's a nice night, I'm as able-bodied as you are, and you still have to summarize that part of the movie I missed while you were—"

"Yes, yes, I get it. I just . . ." Elliott ran out of new arguments. He could continue to resist, and he was confident that Aiden would back down without too much of a fuss, but the more he tried to find reasons why not, the more he talked himself into giving in. "Ugh, fine."

He didn't wait for Aiden's response, simply did a one-eighty and headed in the direction of home. Aiden caught up to him quickly, and when Elliott glanced at him, he had a self-satisfied half smile on his handsome face.

"Thank you," Aiden said neutrally, as if he didn't resemble a cat cleaning yellow feathers out of his claws.

"You did that like a lawyer," Elliott accused.

"Making convincing arguments is my job. Can you blame me?"

Elliott shrugged and stared forward again so he wouldn't trip on something. "Guess not."

Elliott's hoodie was too light for the weather, but the chill was a mild burn that reminded him of winters farther north, where he grew up. He liked the relative cold. It felt like excitement did, like when he was a kid, and every high didn't have a fiery crashing low.

The weather was easier to ignore, given the company. Aiden and Elliott both knew how to talk movies, getting into a rhythm right away, debating some things and agreeing about others.

"But the secret-sister plot twist made no sense," Aiden argued as they turned a corner.

"Well, no. But it was entertaining, right?"

"Undeniably. But in a thriller or a horror movie, not in what we were watching."

"That's entirely fair." Elliott looked up at the sky, at the permanent beige-ish light pollution of the city. "But, *undeniably*, you're boring for thinking that."

Aiden scoffed, not even close to being offended. "That's undeniable, is it?"

"Absolutely, you boring— Oh, wait." Elliott's pocket had started vibrating.

He took out his phone. *Kevin Chan calling*, the screen read, next to a picture of his smiling face with a slobbery English Bulldog.

"Uh, give me a second, I'll call him back later," Elliott said, stopping in the middle of the sidewalk and untangling his other hand from his pocket so he could decline the call.

"I don't mind," Aiden said, stopping as well. "Honestly, go ahead. I'm still holding back tears from being called boring. This'll give me a chance to put on a brave face."

Elliott forced a laugh, and his thumb hovered over the Answer button. It was nice of Aiden to be so cool about Elliott taking a personal call while he was still on the clock. Not surprising, though, because Elliott was already used to how Aiden didn't count the minutes and watch the dollar signs get bigger like Innes had and Elliott did. But Aiden being okay with it didn't necessarily mean that Elliott was.

If he pressed Accept on Kevin's call, who did he answer as? Would Kevin notice a difference in his voice if he kept playing this version of himself, the slightly elevated, confident pretense? And if he acted normal for Kevin, would Aiden suddenly realize he was fucking a college student who still ate dry cereal in his underwear on Sunday mornings?

And would that change anything, or did Aiden know exactly what he was paying for?

With milliseconds to spare, Elliott answered Kevin with yet another persona. Dedicated Mature-for-his-Age Student Elliott, a pleasant, yet professionally cold demeanor that had impressed many professors and might have been a little bit inspired by Innes, that bastard.

"Hello?"

"Elliott! I'm so glad you answered. Are you busy?"

"Hi, Kevin. Am I busy?" Elliott chanced a look over at Aiden, who shrugged and lifted his hands in a *don't mind me* gesture. "That sort of depends, I guess. What can I help you with?"

Kevin laughed. "What can you help me with? When did you start forwarding your calls to a customer service center? Can I skip by the representative and talk to Elliott, please?"

Elliott blew out a short, firm breath, making their connection pop and fizzle. "Yeah. Sorry, man. You just caught me at a weird time."

He felt Aiden still beside him more than he actually saw it, but Aiden didn't say anything, though he was clearly listening.

"Oh, well, that's fine," Kevin said. "I just wanted you to know I can't Skype tonight. Boss is keeping me late to watch a panicky golden retriever."

Unsurprisingly, Kevin didn't sound upset about it. He'd followed his passion as much as Elliott had, though his passion had only taken him a few miles away to a local college with a two-year vet tech program, then to an animal hospital fifteen minutes from their elementary school. It was only Elliott who'd run a hundred miles from a town filled with memories, good and bad, and who had no plans to go back to stay anytime soon.

"Okay," Elliott said slowly. "And is there any reason why you couldn't have told me this by text?"

"Ah, good point," Kevin admitted, and Elliott heard his sheepish grin in his tone. "The condition of me staying after closing was that I needed an extra five-minute break so that I could call and change my plans. I wasn't about to pass up additional break time."

"Uh-huh. So, this is you actually using your five-minute grace period to call and change your plans, when you could have just texted me with that same information and used your remaining four minutes and fifty seconds to do whatever you wanted."

"Exactly."

"Are you sure you weren't a Boy Scout, Kev?"

"Absolutely sure. You got us kicked out, remember?"

"Yeah, I do." He had fond memories of those three weeks, in which he'd convinced the rest of their troop to rise up against the adults' tyranny in a rebellion worthy of any history book. His mom had been proud, even if Officer Dad hadn't appreciated his criminal leanings.

"Well, there's your answer, then. Anyway, that's all I wanted to tell you. So, maybe we can catch up on Friday instead?"

"Uh, Friday?" Elliott said, stupidly. Their Skype hangouts were normally planned so carefully that he hadn't yet had to tell Kevin how often he saw the mystery Not-Boyfriend neither of them liked to talk about. "I can't. Got a thing."

He whacked himself on the forehead the moment it came out of his mouth, because Kevin wasn't some acquaintance he could wave off with a lame excuse. This was his best friend.

"A thing?" Kevin asked, predictably.

Elliott tried to play it off, dialing down the Young Professional and kicking up the Buddy Ol' Pal. "Yeah, dude, you know. College thing, studying."

He didn't do it on purpose, but his eyes flicked over to Aiden, who was staring straight-ahead, down the deserted street.

Kevin seemed mollified. "Oh, right on," he said. "I'll talk to you later, then. Maybe next week?"

"Sure, yeah. Of course," Elliott said, relieved that the conversation was wrapping up. He felt like a bug under glass, but he couldn't resist adding, "Don't miss me too much, okay?"

"Yeah, whatever, you know you're the one who pines for the fjords of home."

"Since when does home have fjords?"

"Since you started missing them, and me, you sap."

They said goodbye, and Elliott turned his phone off before he put it back in his pocket. It would be just his luck if his dad phoned and he had to take another personal call in front of Aiden.

"Sorry about that." They started walking again, more briskly than before, Elliott jittering along the sidewalk.

"No problem, really," Aiden said.

They lapsed into silence for a short while, punctuated by the sound of passing cars and some Wednesday night college student revelry a block over from them. They turned a corner, and Elliott could see the top of his building getting closer. He slowed down. Maybe he could convince Aiden that he was safe from here.

"Brother?"

"What?" Elliott said, thrown by the non sequitur. "Oh, Kevin. No, he's a friend. We've known each other forever, so we might as well be brothers."

Aiden nodded slowly, looking so politely apathetic that Elliott had no idea why he'd asked the question in the first place. "Ah. That's nice, that you have someone you're close to, outside of your family."

"Yeah, it is."

Aiden probably meant that it was nice to have a surplus of affection, a place to turn for help that wasn't a support network as large as Aiden's was, with his many family members. Elliott's situation was different. For him, it was nice to have someone he could count on who wasn't a family member.

Elliott's support network was less of a net to catch him and more of a single line that he could try to grab when he was plummeting to the ground.

"Do they know what you do?" The words erupted from Aiden's mouth with a clumsiness and lack of deliberateness that wasn't like Aiden. "Your family, I mean."

Elliott looked down at his feet as they walked. The sidewalk was old and well-traveled enough that it was a dalmatian-spotted sea of stains and smudges and black gum pieces tossed away and incorporated into the landscape.

He could blow off the question. Make a joke about it, or bluntly inform Aiden that it wasn't any of his business, which it absolutely wasn't. It was the first time he'd been asked, though.

"No, they don't. My life is a lot simpler that way." Aiden didn't comment, so Elliott kept going. It felt good to tell someone that he hadn't forgotten his family in his yearning for a debt-free college experience. His family was his whole reason for the work he did. "It's easy to keep my dad and Kevin in the dark, since they're so far away. I can tell them I'm tutoring on the side, and if they notice I'm doing better than I should when I'm five or ten years out of school, well, maybe I'll tell them then, when it's something I did, rather than something I'm doing. They'll be mad, maybe horrified, but it'll be over."

"And you couldn't just do that? Tutoring, I mean. If it would make you happier."

The question was so earnest, like Aiden really believed he wouldn't have thought of it already.

"Sure, it would. Teaching is the ultimate goal, so yeah, it'd be great. But you pay my salary. You think I could make money that good by teaching freshmen how to cite in Chicago style a couple times a week?" A stone caught under Elliott's shoe, making a record-scratching noise.

"It's worth it, though. I just have to believe that Kevin and my dad will be okay with it in the end."

"Do you worry that they'll think differently of you?" Aiden asked.

Elliott tripped over his feet, his stomach cramping up, then blurted, "What happened to not talking about it?"

Aiden winced. "I'm sorry, don't answer that. It was a stupid question and there's no reason—"

"It's okay," Elliott said, quieter. He should have apologized, but the question was too pressing for him to waste time. "I think my mom would have known. She saw right through any bullshit, even when I was young. Especially then. I don't think I would have been able to keep secrets from her in the same way I can from Dad. She was that kind of person. If I'd told her that I was seeing an older guy and that it wasn't romantic, she'd have wondered what was up. Then I'd have had to explain why I don't have a part-time job, and then the whole thing would have come out.

"But, the thing is . . ." He squeezed and released his thumb a couple of times, remembering how his dad had cried when he couldn't afford to send Elliott to piano lessons like she'd wanted. "I can't be sure of what she would have thought. I like to think that she'd be okay with it. But 'okay with it' might mean that she would have kissed my cheek and told me to do what I thought was right, or it might have been that she'd still have loved me, but would have wondered where she went wrong, and cried into her pillow at night. I just don't know. It's been over ten years since she died. I've lived more of my life without her than with her. We never got the chance for those serious discussions about her views on prostitution."

"Were you close?" Aiden asked, letting his hand brush against Elliott's.

Elliott squinted up at him. "She was my mother."

Aiden shrugged, seemingly unfazed by Elliott's disbelief. "There's a difference between having children and being a mom. She sounds like she was a good one."

"Yeah, she was." The warm tickle of Aiden's hand against his wrist pulled his focus, but memories still came flooding back. "She had this book of Greek myths, and she'd read them to me. I loved them. They were so brutal, so sad, but ridiculous at times. I don't know when she started reading me history books, but I was young enough that I didn't notice when it wasn't fiction anymore. By the time I was reading by myself, I just wanted more like that."

"You must have been an interesting kid."

"Oh, yeah." Elliott grinned at his own recollections. "When I was nine, my favorite superhero was Alexander the Great."

"Of course it was." Aiden shook his head, his eyes twinkling again.

"And who was yours? Atticus Finch? That book came out around when you were born, right?"

The look Aiden shot him could have petrified wood, but Elliott wasn't fazed by it, or the bump of Aiden's shoulder. "You're hilarious. I'm not that much older than you, smart ass."

"Only a handful of decades."

"Try *years*. At least I've been able to buy my own alcohol for long enough that my favorite wine doesn't come in a box."

"Sure, you spend your money on fancy glass bottles. Me and cardboard get along fine."

Aiden snorted, his lips still quirked, but there was a tension in his shoulders that wasn't there before. His proud bearing was hunched a little, the weight of Elliott's age pressing on his neck.

"You know I don't care, right? A couple years between our birth dates isn't a big deal."

Aiden didn't straighten, but he did flash a more genuine-looking smirk. "I'd be surprised if it did. Though seven years is a little more than a couple, but I'll take your word for it."

For all Elliott's teasing, the gap between them honestly didn't feel so wide, in terms of life experience. And besides that, Aiden carried his advanced age incredibly well.

He had a couple of years to go before he hit thirty, but Elliott could picture how he'd look when he was middle-aged, and it was a very attractive vision in his crystal ball. He'd already had a preview of what Kent genes looked like pushing forty in Innes. There wasn't a ton of resemblance between them, but the DNA that wrinkled eyes and preserved hairlines had probably been passed down.

"My favorite superhero was Peter Pan," Aiden said, from the corner of his mouth in the middle of an empty street. "Since you asked."

"Why?" Elliott had never read the book, but he knew enough to wonder what qualities Aiden could admire in a violent elf child.

"He was so strange, but he was never afraid, and when he spoke, people listened. I liked that."

Elliott let a breathy laugh escape him, then they walked in silence for a while, Elliott's mind filled with imaginary home videos of what Aiden must have looked like as a child.

All he could picture was the seriousness and dark eyebrows of the current Aiden, which summoned a terrifying image, like the Antichrist in OshKosh.

Up ahead, Elliott saw the entrance to his building, and he started calculating the risk versus reward of letting Aiden escort him to the door. At the start of their walk, he'd been determined to shake Aiden before there was any chance of someone in his building seeing him and asking him personal questions, but somehow, they'd gotten sidetracked by childhood fantasies.

There was no one around, since the weekday partiers had moved on to the frat houses in search of better prospects. The only person he could see for miles was the bored security guard manning the desk just inside the main building, and that was through a pane of glass and a sheen of complete disinterest in the activities of students who weren't breaking any rules.

So Elliott let it go. He let Aiden walk him all the way up the driveway and to the outer door, the one that didn't require a key card to get in. He took another glance around, but Security Guard Ajit (Elliott's favorite guard because he never seemed judgy when Elliott forgot his key card) looked about as close to asleep as he could get while still doing his job.

It'd been a night of firsts. First "date" with Aiden where they went somewhere that wasn't Aiden's couch or bed. (Or kitchen. That table was sturdy as hell.) First time giving a blowjob in the middle of a movie theater.

Elliott was still unsettled in the pit of his stomach from the phone call and the weirdly intimate conversation after it. He wanted to turn that anxiety into the good kind of unsettled. With one last glance at the doors behind him and the long driveway—both deserted—he grabbed Aiden's neck and pulled him down for a quick but hard and thorough kiss.

"This was fun," Elliott said when it was over. Their casual conversation had gotten a little probing for him, since it wasn't the fun probing, but he'd had a good time.

"It was. We should do it again." Aiden smiled ruefully. A tiny spot of moisture clung to his bottom lip, glinting in the light slipping from the lobby. "I need to leave my apartment more often."

Elliott nodded vigorously. "Oh, yeah. Otherwise you might get boring. Oh, wait. You already are."

With a cheeky grin, Elliott waved and darted for the door, expecting to hear Aiden's outraged denial at his parting shot, but Aiden did something unexpected. Before Elliott had even opened one of the double doors, Aiden grabbed his upper arm and pulled him back and to the side, pushing him with his body face-first against the glass of the other door.

He wasn't trapped. Aiden was too much of a gentleman for that. Elliott could have shrugged him off at any time and given him shit for being pushy, but he didn't. Instead, he froze with his forehead pressed to the cold glass, and trembled when his hoodie was yanked out of the way so that Aiden's mouth and stubbled chin could press against his neck. Not kissing him. Just gently rasping, sensitizing the skin until it was burning from the contact. Only then did Aiden attach his mouth to the place where Elliott's neck and shoulder met, and apply warm, wet suction.

That particular area had always been responsive for Elliott. The only time he'd ever hit Kevin with any real intention was when Kevin hadn't noticed that he'd been serious about not wanting to be tickled. But this was a different situation, and Kevin was pushed far from Elliott's mind.

He moaned when Aiden's teeth scraped across tender skin and then soothed the sting instantly with his tongue. A cloud of condensation grew next to Elliott's mouth on the glass door, reminding him that they were very visible.

Elliott was paralyzed. If Ajit the Security Guard turned his head, he would definitely be able to see them. That was only one possibility, and the others were even more embarrassing: another student could walk out of the inner door for a late-night smoke break, or come up the sidewalk behind them, quiet enough that Elliott wouldn't hear them.

Without stopping his assault on Elliott's neck, Aiden started creeping his hand down the center line of Elliott's stomach, slow enough that if Elliott hadn't been so very aware of its band of warmth across his middle in the first place, he might not have noticed it. His fingers spasmed on the glass with a soft squeak.

He should have put a stop to their display, laughed it off, and made a joke about an undiscovered exhibition kink. He *should have*, but god, he didn't want to. Aiden's body was a wall of warmth, and Elliott was still tightly wound from being on his knees earlier and choosing to leave himself wanting. They were in the doorway of a highly populated college dorm, an unsuspecting security guard less than thirty feet away, and Elliott was unbelievably close to getting off, just from hot, wet pressure on his neck, and Aiden's fingers pressing in just below his belt, under the button of his jeans—

Aiden stepped away, his hands withdrawing and leaving Elliott cold, aching, and twitchy with lust. He leaned in tantalizingly close one more time, but now, it was to open the door Elliott wasn't leaning on for support. With his other hand, Aiden peeled him off the glass and nudged him through the open door.

"I'm only boring when it suits me," Aiden said as Elliott stumbled by him, then he *slapped Elliott's ass* and closed the door on Elliott's surprised squawk.

Elliott would have attempted to come up with some parting remark, despite his brain being the consistency of porridge, but Ajit the Security Guy chose that moment to glance up from his Sudoku— the same book he'd been working on since the beginning of last semester—and give Elliott a friendly wave. Elliott jerked guiltily and returned it, then headed for the elevator right away, since he probably looked like he'd barely escaped a rabid dog with his neck intact.

He didn't turn back until the doors were closing. Aiden hadn't left yet. There was just enough light shining through the entrance that Elliott could see him wave and turn away to walk back down the sidewalk, but not before he raked his eyes down and up Elliott's disheveled clothing and smirked.

Elliott let out a shaky breath and as soon as he was truly alone, collapsed against the wall. Technically, Ajit could still see him on the security camera, but he'd told Elliott he'd learned his lesson. People could get a lot done in a thirty-second ride, and Ajit wasn't interested in seeing any of it.

Letting his head fall into his hands, he started laughing, the delicious tension that had kept him on edge all night finally unwinding.

Chapter 6

Elliott contemplated his options in the vending machine, wishing he hadn't eaten his Pop-Tarts so quickly. The machine was only stocked twice a month, and since it was already the middle of February, all that was left was the gross and the pseudo-healthy.

He needed something to keep him going, though. There was so much material to sift through for his essay on Julio-Claudian emperors, and if he wanted the TA to critique it before the deadline, he needed to finish it this week.

Elliott's forehead *thunk*ed to the plexiglass. Red Vines would taste like plastic, but at least keep him occupied for a while. Decision made, he fished his change from his pocket.

His phone rang just as he was about to put the first quarter into the machine. His fingers hovered over the right buttons, but he decided to answer the call before making his choice.

Elliott frowned at the phone before he hit Accept. Aiden only ever texted him, usually when he was schmoozing clients in bars after work, hating his life and lamenting the fact that he couldn't have been anything else but a lawyer.

"Hello?" Elliott said, suspicious already.

"Hi, Elliott." Aiden sounded relieved to hear him, and a little like he'd just woken up, strangely, since it was six in the evening and Aiden hated napping. "Sorry to disturb you, I know I'm not seeing you until tomorrow. I have a bit of an emergency, and I— Uh."

"You wanted to make sure I wouldn't ignore your texts."

Aiden gave a surprised laugh. "Yeah, maybe."

Elliott waited for Aiden to elaborate, but there was only silence, with a soft *clink*ing in the background. Maybe he was doing dishes?

The pause went on long enough to be awkward, so Elliott, impatient as ever, gave Aiden the prodding he needed. "So, is there something I can do for you?"

"Oh, yes, actually." Elliott could almost picture Aiden starting guiltily. "I need your help."

"My help?" Elliott's brain started automatically searching for something he had to offer Aiden that he wasn't already giving. He really didn't think he was about to be asked for pointers on blowjob technique and couldn't imagine Aiden needed a well-researched paper on the greatest hits of Julio-Claudian emperors.

"Yes. Now, you can feel free to say no—it wouldn't be a big deal. I'll work it out on my own if you can't, but if you would consider it, I would be extremely grateful."

"Aiden, you're worrying me a little. What the hell is it?"

Aiden sighed, and there was more *clink*ing and a small *thud*, like Aiden had put down a particularly heavy dish. (Except, when did Aiden ever wash dishes that weren't plastic?)

"I have to go to a gala next weekend," Aiden admitted, and from his anxious, sheepish tone, it was clear where he was heading. "It's a big charity thing, two grand per plate, live music, all that stuff."

"I know the kind." Events like that had been a big part of Elliott's first job. Innes's flagrant disregard for conventional—read: heterosexual—relationships was something the older partners had attempted to use against him.

As a partner of his grandfather's firm, Innes was untouchable, but that didn't keep the other partners from making assumptions that he was a spoiled brat. That being true didn't stop Innes from showing off a guy half his age as a giant fuck-you to people who didn't want the "icky gays" on top.

"I thought you might be familiar with them," Aiden said, then he let out a long, relieved breath. Maybe Aiden expected him to groan theatrically at the very mention of the word *gala*. "Innes usually goes to these things to represent the family and the firm, but he has to go out of town suddenly."

"Suddenly," Elliott confirmed, crisply.

These things were planned for a year in advance, sometimes more. They were on the same weekend every year to make sure the same people were able to show up. Elliott would be willing to bet that if he looked in his datebook for a year ago, he would've been ready for the exact same occasion.

"Yes." Aiden's voice was absolutely neutral, giving nothing away.

Prior experience with the scary time-management skills of Innes's PA made it difficult for Elliott to believe he could've been taken by surprise, so there was a good chance he was faking.

To punish Aiden? Maybe. But it would probably be unrelated to Elliott's lateral move. Innes wasn't the possessive type. Not about Elliott. His attempts to push expensive gifts on him had been more about the wealth the jewelry or watches represented.

Right?

"So, I have a problem," Aiden said, predictably. "Innes had already told them he was bringing a guest along with him. It's a sit-down dinner thing, and a plus-one is pretty much expected. His assistant told me that the number of people at each table in the seating plan is vitally important, for some reason, and the organizers would threaten her with bodily harm if she told them only I was coming."

"You want me to come with you, then?"

"Yes. If you don't mind."

If Aiden and Elliott had had a contract, this wouldn't have been on it. Aiden had made it clear from the beginning that he wasn't interested in parading Elliott around like Innes had.

"If Innes was planning on going, that means at least a few of his friends will be there," Elliott pointed out. "Are you prepared for people to recognize me? He never did tell me whether some of them knew what our deal was, or if they all just assumed I was a gold digger with daddy issues." One of those was half-true.

"Yes. We can keep it friendly and you'll be a familiar enough face that people might not even question it. They don't need to know we, uh—" Aiden cleared his throat, and it was a good thing Aiden wasn't in the room to see Elliott's majestic eye roll. "—have an arrangement. It's none of their business."

"Sounds reasonable."

Elliott could've said no. Aiden would probably have to increase his dosage of antacids again until he found someone else, but he wouldn't blame Elliott if he was too busy with school. With that in mind, Elliott still didn't seriously consider refusing. He'd get an extra day of work on his paycheck, and enjoy a fancy dinner as well.

"Okay, sign me up," he said. "What's the dress code?"

"Black tie, but—"

"Ooh, fancy."

"Are you sure you don't mind?" Aiden sounded hilariously incredulous, which said a lot about how different his opinion was from Elliott's when it came to charity galas. For Aiden, they must come with their own dramatic theme music. A benefit for underprivileged kids? Horror! Dancing starts at 8 p.m.? Dun dun *dunnn*!

"I don't mind at all. It's not like I haven't done this kind of thing before." So many times. Truly, he was a pro. "I'm curious, though. Why are you asking me? Couldn't Innes's assistant come with you? Or one of your sisters?"

"My sisters had already RSVP'd. And his assistant was the one who brought me the news that I'd have to go and followed it up with way too many details about the holiday to Majorca she's taking with her husband that week. I didn't even get the chance to ask before she was telling me that the answer was an unequivocal no."

Elliott's hand had frozen around his pocketful of change at the mention of Aiden's family. "Oh, your sisters will be there?"

"Yes." Aiden sounded so happy, and Elliott could almost feel the affection in his voice. "Jill's home from college for a visit that weekend and Shannon just moved back into the area. I guess you've never met them."

"Nope." Meeting Aiden had been unavoidable, since he and Innes had worked together and gone to so many of the same work functions, but Innes had been pretty adamant about not wanting to explain himself to anyone else who shared his last name. "You're the only other Kent I had the pleasure of meeting as Innes's—"

"A true honor," Aiden drawled.

Elliott smiled into his phone and graciously allowed him to change the subject. "You better believe it, peasant. I'm a delight."

Aiden snorted and Elliott grinned into the phone. "Yeah, sure. You should buy yourself a tux—"

"I can rent one, I know a guy."

"Seriously, get it tailored and keep it. You never know when you'll need one. Get them to send me the bill; I'll take care of it."

Elliott's stomach twisted, and the appeal of red candy vanished. "Ah, ah, hold your horses. Because this is outside of my normal area, and I'm your employee, I'll allow you to pay for the cheapest rental I can get my hands on, but anything more than that is unnecessary."

"I appreciate this, though. It's the least I could do to give you something that will last you for years—"

"No, the least you could do is pay me for my services. That's all I'll accept, because you're not my sugar daddy. This isn't personal, Aiden. It's overtime."

Aiden was quiet for a while, and Elliott started to panic. First, that Aiden might dig in his heels, and second, that he'd gone too far.

He'd just bitched at his boss.

"Fine," Aiden said. "If I can't change your mind, then I'll pay for the rental, and you can't convince me otherwise."

"Deal." That made sense, in the strange leger of debt and payment Elliott had built in his head. He wouldn't owe any gratitude, and he wouldn't expect too much in return. "I appreciate that."

"Sure. It's two Saturdays from now, by the way. In the evening."

Was that it? Was Aiden going to accept that Elliott had come close to yelling at him? Elliott wasn't going to push it, but Aiden seemed pretty chill for someone who'd been on the receiving end of Elliott's displeasure.

"Okay," Elliott said, his hand jingling his collection of quarters again. "Let me check my calendar before I let you go, just to make sure I don't have anything else I promised to do that day. Gimme a minute to get to my computer."

Giving up on the idea of the Red Vines, he walked briskly to his room, then warned Aiden that he was being put on hold before he placed his phone facedown on the desk. His laptop groaned to life, protesting at having to do anything quickly in its advanced age. When he was finished scrolling through dates filled with his carefully crafted study schedule, he lifted the phone to his ear.

"Yep, we're free and clear and—" Elliott's ears perked at a new sound in the background that stopped a second after he went quiet.

It was a familiar noise, but it took a few seconds for him to place it. It brought him back to his first semester and the few wild nights he'd allowed himself, but also to his dad's garage every time he was home from college and wanted to unwind. It was so incongruous that it took Elliott way too long to recognize what was unmistakably the wet, bubbling sound of a bong hit.

"What are you doing?" Elliott asked, even though he knew the answer.

"What? Nothing," Aiden said, immediately, guiltily, and that was all the proof Elliott needed.

"Oh ho, you are definitely doing something!" Elliott accused, gleefully. "You are partaking in a controlled hallucinogenic substance, Mr. Kent!"

"What? No, I'm—" Aiden started choking, a dry, hacking cough loud enough that Elliott had to take the phone away from his ear for a minute until Aiden got it under control.

"Elliott, I— It's—" Aiden croaked.

"You fucker. Stay there, put your lung back in your rib cage where it's supposed to be, and don't finish it without me."

"What?"

"Give me fifteen minutes and I'll be there."

Elliott hung up and snagged his jacket and key card, almost dancing out the door to catch the bus. Julio-Claudian emperors could wait. Elliott had invited himself to a far better use of his Tuesday night.

"And then, I kid you not, this guy said in his most stereotypical stoner mumble that he'd never seen the full moon when he wasn't high."

Aiden snorted, sinking further into the couch. "Bullshit."

"Yeah, that's what I said. Like, did he never go outside after dark as a kid? Apparently not, though. His mother was super strict or something."

Aiden raised a skeptical eyebrow. "Strict, huh?"

"Yeah." Elliott let his head loll to the side, pressing his warm face into the cool leather. "And all it got her was a neurotic college dropout with enough in his trust fund to surround himself with deadbeat college-dropout friends. And me, who isn't any of those things."

Aiden's face scrunched up adorably as he let out a little laugh.

"Oh my god. No way," Elliott cried, grinning from ear to ear. "Are you one of *them*?"

Aiden's snickers, which were way disproportionate to the joke Elliott had made, tumbled past his rigid lips. "One of what?"

"A *giggler*," Elliott accused, then he slapped a palm over his face. "I can't believe it. My image of you is completely ruined."

Aiden whacked his arm, but not hard enough to hurt. "Fuck off, that's the euphoria you should have learned about in high-school health class last week."

"Hey, fuck you right back, I'm twenty-one." Elliott yawned and stretched out, crossing his legs next to the sensible breath mint tin half-full of Aiden's supply. There wasn't much, since, according to Aiden, he only needed it once every week or two.

"So, what about you?" Elliott asked.

Aiden blinked slowly, staring straight-ahead. "Hmm?"

"Were your parents strict? I'm just a little shocked that this is something you do. High-flying-lawyer type that you are."

"Why? It's perfectly legal." Aiden's voice was lower than normal, with a sexy rasp that was doing unexpected things to Elliott. "I've got a medical card and everything. My job is high-stress, so I need a way to relax from time to time."

Elliott had one too, though he'd only used it once. Smoking helped him sleep, but he didn't like to rely on any one form of sleep aid for any length of time. He'd learned other ways to relieve stress.

A thought occurred to Elliott, and he found himself giggling like Aiden.

"What?"

"It's just—" He waved his hand lazily between them. "This, the whole you-and-me thing. That's stress relief too, technically, so I was imagining something. What if you could claim me on your taxes as a business expense?"

Aiden's jaw hung slack for a few seconds before he lost it and started laughing harder than before, dragging Elliott with him. They snickered like children until the joke died away and Elliott was pleasantly relaxed. He adjusted his position, swinging his legs off the table and into Aiden's lap, but Aiden didn't seem to mind. He started trailing his fingers up and down the fabric of Elliott's jeans, above his ankle. It was rhythmic and soothing, a hypnotic caress that could've put him to sleep.

"Do you like your job?" Elliott asked.

The rubbing stopped and he opened his eyes. When had they closed?

"What do you mean?" Aiden asked.

"I mean, do you like it? Are you excited to go to work every day?"

"Is anyone?"

Elliott lifted his head to see Aiden's face clearly, just in time to see him shrug, his face open and honest. "Sure," Elliott said. "Lots of people love their job, or at the very least, they don't mind it."

"What's your point?"

"It seems like you actively dislike what you do."

Aiden's hand started its rubbing again, slower this time, and purposeful. "I don't know if I dislike it. Parts of it are satisfying."

"But?"

"But sometimes I sit in my car in the mornings and I have to force myself to go in. Sometimes I make deals with myself, like, if I buck up and go in right now, I can take an extra five minutes for lunch. Or if I call this client I hate without procrastinating, I can eat a muffin."

A lazy laugh bubbled out from Elliott's chest. "Naughty."

"Is that what you mean?"

"Yeah. So, I guess the answer is no, you don't like it."

Aiden shrugged again, staring placidly down at the foot in his lap. "Not really."

"Why do it then?"

"I thought I wanted to." Aiden's voice was soft. Not sad, exactly, but resigned. "Law school was tough, but at least I was accomplishing something. I liked learning the theory and reading case studies. Sometimes my job feels almost the same, but usually, it's all the worst parts of college."

"Like with police officers and paperwork."

"What?"

"Dad says police work is eighty percent drudgery and twenty percent high-octane stress. If you don't like the boring stuff, the cool things won't make it worth it."

Dad also said that new officers wanted the heroism without putting in the work, but that wouldn't be helpful to point out, especially considering that Aiden did put in the work. He just hated it.

Aiden snorted. "Yeah, that's about right."

"So, why don't you quit? You've given it a good college try. Why not move on?"

"My family would . . . It's complicated." Aiden let out a long breath, his eyes flicking around the room for a few moments before he shook his head. "Speaking of your dad, what about you? Was he strict? I imagine, being a cop, he would be."

Elliott generously took the bait, sinking deeper into the couch that was starting to feel more like home than the chair in his dorm. "You'd be right—to a certain extent. He works a lot and I was responsible for myself a lot, so it wasn't like he could get on my case about curfews and things. But if he'd ever caught me doing this before it was entirely legal, I could've said goodbye to my freedom, so I never wanted to risk it."

"And after that? You didn't mind the risk?"

He shrugged. "Not really. It's a bit of a cliché, isn't it? A police officer's cherished only son, an upstanding, rule-abiding honor student, beloved by everyone he meets—" Aiden snorted with laughter so Elliott dug his toes into his thigh and ignored him. "—gets to college and goes wild."

"Oh, yeah, so wild. Studies constantly, gets good grades, has a ten-year plan, and *sometimes* smokes weed. You wild thing."

"I don't do it often," he told Aiden, truthfully. "I don't have the kind of disposable income for that, so I just mooch off other people when I can. Like you."

"I don't mind," Aiden said, a soft, dazed smile on his handsome face. "It isn't much fun on your own, anyway."

Elliott gasped, his hand going to his smoke-warmed chest in feigned outrage. "Aiden, you rebel. I thought you did it for the stress relief, not the *fun*. Shame on you—"

"Yeah, well, I do *you* for the fun too, and I don't hear you complaining." Aiden pushed Elliott's legs off his lap but didn't protest when Elliott dragged his bulky arm over his smaller shoulders instead, only laughing as Elliott burrowed in.

"No. No complaints here."

He melted into Aiden's side, breathing in the scent of Aiden's laundry detergent with the new and intoxicating sweet-sour tang of weed smoke. The couch was their territory, where they spent most of their time that wasn't in the bedroom. This tangled position was still a familiar one for them, comfortable and routine. As familiar to Elliott as being on his hands and knees for Innes.

He shook that thought off, chastising himself yet again for comparing the two Kent men. There was nothing to compare, really, only to contrast. Trying to stack them up next to each other was an insult to Aiden and far more complimentary than Innes deserved.

"God, can you imagine me doing this with Innes?" Elliott blurted, then immediately wished he could staple his mouth shut. Whatever strain Aiden had access to was loosening Elliott's tongue.

"Not at all. It isn't his thing."

"Yeah, no doubt. A glass of wine is the only—"

"I used to be jealous of him."

Elliott blinked, his reaction time slowed to a crawl. "Of Innes? Why?"

Aiden stared straight-ahead, his throat bobbing as he swallowed. "You."

Seconds ticked by as Elliott attempted to wrap his head around what Aiden was saying. Aiming for casual, he said, "Oh, yeah?"

He must have sounded as nonchalant as he'd intended, because underneath his legs, Aiden's body lost some of its insidious tension.

"I thought it would be nice to have someone," Aiden said, his head dropping back against the couch again. "He could just call, and an intelligent, nice, and . . . vibrant guy would come liven things up. Of course, he had to be all sleazy about it, but I could understand that a bit."

His head rolled toward Elliott, warmth glinting in his dark eyes as he let his hand rest on Elliott's knee.

"Flatterer," Elliott said, struggling for any other response. "Well, now you've got me."

"Yeah."

They enjoyed a few more minutes of vacancy, then the jitters Elliott sometimes got when he was high made his legs and fingers too twitchy to ignore. He needed a distraction. A good one immediately came to mind, which he initially dismissed, but then he couldn't stop thinking about it.

Halfway to Aiden's apartment, he'd remembered that he'd still have to come over for his regular Wednesday appointment. Since he wasn't on the clock, he wasn't required to do anything except steal some of Aiden's stash and leave. Aiden's fingers on a lighter, though . . . they made Elliott forget the days of the week.

Elliott relinquished Aiden's arm, then got up on his knees, straddling one of Aiden's legs.

If he was a bit prone to clinginess while sober, he was a limpet while drunk or stoned. Weed made any touch twice as intense, which wasn't always a good thing, but with a guy who knew how to go slow and steady like Aiden? It was a great thing. A very tempting thing.

He kissed Aiden in slow motion, giving him his tongue like Aiden had given him the smoke from his mouth earlier while they both laughed at the silliness of it. Elliott tried to ramp it up, but Aiden didn't take his lead.

"What's wrong?" Elliott asked when he pulled away.

Aiden looked directly into his—probably bloodshot—eyes. "Is this a good idea? Neither of us is sober. Are you going to regret this tomorrow?"

Elliott blinked. No one had ever asked him that before sex. Most likely because he'd always been at a comparable level of intoxication as his partner, but still.

"Dude," he said, laughing. "I'm California-born and raised. This is nothing."

"You don't get an automatic tolerance from being born in a California zip code. You just told me you didn't start from the cradle."

"Exactly. So, me taking to it like a fish to water in my first week of college proves that I was born to blaze. Occasionally. When the moment is right, and someone else is paying for it. Come on."

He got up off of Aiden's lap and tugged his hands until he was standing, then pulled him backward across the living room and down the hall. Aiden followed, stiff as a zombie all the way to the bedroom, but he didn't put up any resistance. Elliott let go of Aiden's hands when he crossed the threshold, and started taking off his clothes, while Aiden watched, leaning against the door. Elliott knew, when he was naked and lounging in the center of Aiden's ridiculous bed, that he'd won. Aiden hadn't stopped him, even as he'd cocked his knee and stretched his arm up over his head.

They were mildly relaxed, not wasted. He knew Aiden, trusted him. They were good, and they were going to do this, and enjoy every second of it.

Aiden made him wait for it. He made him arch his back and run his hands over his exposed skin, avoiding the place that wanted to be touched the most. He let Elliott tempt him into sin, rather than jumping into it feetfirst, like normal.

Elliott loved it more that he'd expected to. Under Aiden's assessing gaze, he felt as a subject in a great painting might, so different from timeless, placid Greek statues. Legs open, beckoning, lips bitten and wet, no blanket or sheet, nothing hidden from the white light of the ceiling fixture.

Elliott was *naked*, exposed and vulnerable to judgment, but powerful too. He could choose to offer sex or withhold it, and his body—his everything—had the ability to tempt Aiden off his teetering ledge of impractical morality.

It ended up not being a jump, but a slow tilting to resignation. Aiden shed his clothes leisurely, still making Elliott wait and wait. He prowled until he was hovering over Elliott's body in the center of the bed like a giant cat, pressing him down into the mattress at his own pace, ignoring clinging arms and legs trying their best to bring him closer right away, right *now*.

Both of them were too worked up and chemically slowed down to do more than rub off on each other, grinding and stroking against whatever they could reach without having to move too much.

Elliott felt seventeen years old again, fumbling on top of the covers, no idea what he was doing, but enjoying every second of it anyway. He loved kissing normally. When he was high, it was even better, though it balanced on the edge of too much for his textbook heightened sensory awareness.

He almost fell asleep before he came, too caught up in the hedonistic journey to care much about the destination, but Aiden clearly hadn't forgotten it. After a few minutes, he sat up, and Elliott was suddenly cold from the absence of his humid body heat, but he didn't have long to be distracted by the chill. Aiden quickly fisted their dicks and got them off in a fraction of the time it usually took them, like a train speeding to a fiery crash after hours of crawling along the track.

Elliott was too energized after that to fall asleep, so he enjoyed the afterglow to the fullest, grabbing Aiden's head and kissing him stupid, long after the tremors of orgasm had passed. As usual, Aiden was too out of it to participate much, but from the smile on his face when Elliott brought him a towel from the bathroom, he wasn't complaining.

After they were both clean, Elliott shuffled across the carpet. "See you tomorrow," he told Aiden as he flicked off the overhead light on his way out of the bedroom.

"Mrfm," Aiden said.

That razor-sharp lawyer intellect, Elliott thought, amused.

He got his jacket from the closet and toed on his shoes, all in the semidarkness of the hall that'd been lit by natural daylight when Elliott had arrived. It was early yet, though, enough that he could go back to the Julio-Claudian emperors if he wanted to. He was still a little buzzed. Maybe all he needed to get the words flowing was a change of perspective.

He wondered if ancient Romans had blazed and abruptly had to know with a burning passion.

Well. Guess I know what I'll be doing with my evening.

They hadn't, he discovered, a few hours and a few dozen Wikipedia articles later. They had seriously missed out.

Chapter 7

"**O**kay," said Elliott. "But putting aside whether or not they're 'cool,' I think we can both agree that bow ties are objectively goofy."

Elliott adjusted the one he was wearing—stupid dress code—then gave up on trying to make it sit nicely and flopped onto the end of Aiden's bed on his back. "It might be a tiny bit more comfortable—and that's entirely debatable—but I can't think of a single person who doesn't look three times more stupid with a damn bow tie. The Cat in the Hat wears one, for god's sake. How is something supposed to be fancy on a human being when a giant cartoon cat wears it?"

"You're asking the wrong person, Elliott," Aiden's voice floated out from the attached bathroom. "I don't disagree with you."

"I know, you're the worst." Elliott slapped both his hands down on the covers and wiggled miserably, wrinkling his dress shirt. "I'm bored and I want a debate, but you're Switzerland on everything I can think of today."

"How tragic for you. That's probably because all the things you keep having opinions on are about fashion." Aiden said it like anyone else would say *sewage*. "You know I don't give a rat's ass about that stuff."

"Yeah, talk about tragic. Monday to Friday, you look like you walked off the pages of *GQ*, but if your assistant didn't pick your outfits for you, you'd be like a human resources nightmare in a blazer with a turtleneck underneath."

There was a long pause, in which Elliott was treated to a vivid picture of the monstrous image he'd just created.

"I don't think I even own a turtleneck." Aiden's confused frown read from across the room where Elliott couldn't see him.

"Praise Jesus."

"Well, I don't care as much as you seem to about bow ties, so how about you tie mine for me?"

Elliott groaned but sat up on the bed, then nearly swallowed his own tongue when Aiden strolled out of the bathroom dressed in black tuxedo pants, a white shirt undone at the neck, the bow tie loose and hanging at his collarbones, and a pair of thin black suspenders instead of a belt.

"Holy god, you look like a stripper," Elliott blurted.

Aiden stopped and glanced down at himself, then raised an eyebrow at him.

"No, I just mean, you . . ." Elliott faltered, then shook his head. "No, you actually look like you're about to ask which one of us is the birthday girl and start taking those things off."

Suspenders. Elliott had forgotten Aiden might be wearing them. He was suddenly short of breath, all because of a couple of stretchy black strips that did amazing things for Aiden's pecs, framing everything just right—

"Carol dropped the suit off this morning," Aiden said, stiltedly, interrupting Elliott's daydreaming. "I could wear something else? If you think I should, I mean. I probably have—"

Elliott choked again. "No! God, no. It's great."

"Okay?"

Elliott ran his hands down his thighs, then stood. Aiden dutifully held still while Elliott took the ends of the bow tie in his fingers, but Elliott didn't fold it up. He rubbed the fine material between his fingertips, then stared up at Aiden, trying to telegraph all the things he'd like to do to him that would feel even better than the expensive silk against skin.

Aiden got the message. "Elliott," he said, frowning a warning.

"Hmm?"

"No."

"But why?" Elliott whined. He ran his finger down the center of Aiden's chest, next to the line of black studs that kept the shirt closed. When he reached the bottom, he hooked his thumbs under those suspenders and followed them all the way back up, loving the burn of the rough elastic. Aiden covered his hands before Elliott could push the straps right off his shoulders, though.

"Elliott, we can't. Our chariot awaits."

He hummed, moving his fingers under Aiden's, testing the give. "Did you know that expression is Welsh? Not Roman or anything. And most chariot racers were teenagers. They had to be small to—"

"Interesting, but you're stalling. The Uber is going to be here in twenty minutes."

"Thirty."

Aiden checked his watch. "I ordered it for 6:15."

"I know, I saw." Elliott crowded in, breathing in the spicy scent of Aiden's aftershave. "But it's Glenn, and I've driven with him before. The man knows his way around the neighborhood, but he's always ten minutes late."

Aiden opened his mouth, but Elliott cut off his response by planting a kiss on his lips, taking it long and slow before pulling away. His puppy-dog eyes tended to make him look like he was guilty of mischief rather than innocent and deserving a reward, but today, they did the trick. Aiden sighed, but Elliott had already seen the smile tugging at his lips, and he wasn't imagining the way Aiden's eyes dipped to Elliott's lips.

"Fine," Aiden said. "We'd better make those ten minutes count."

Elliott whooped, then used Aiden's shoulders and a flying leap to launch himself into his arms, wrapping his legs around Aiden's hips. Aiden caught him, of course, then laughed as he carried him over to the bed, wrinkling their clothes even more.

They were out on the curb with five minutes to spare, their tuxedos straightened as much as they could manage. Elliott was smug. Aiden was dazed and delicious with his bow tie tight at his neck.

The event was one of the better ones Elliott had been to. The hall was full, but not overheated, so he wasn't sweating in his rented tux. And the cause of the day was underprivileged children, which Elliott could definitely get behind.

Not as many people recognized him as he'd feared. As arm candy for Innes, he'd been essentially invisible, not important enough for rich, busy people to remember after the first introduction. Or third, or fifth.

One lady who he remembered as an entertaining old bat made eye contact with him and raised a thinly penciled brow at Aiden. Elliott smirked back. *I've upgraded*, he thought, and he was pretty sure she approved. She used to call Innes *Ian* all the time, pretending she was too senile to remember his real name, which had been incredibly aggravating for Innes and immensely amusing for Elliott.

Another few people might have remembered him, but saying anything would involve acknowledging his presence, so that would never happen. That meant Elliott was pretty much left to his own devices, at least until dinner started. The cocktail bar was wasted on him while he was working, so he stuck close to Aiden rather than mingling on his own, since there wasn't anyone else he'd rather talk to.

Not to mention, it felt as if a step out of Aiden's reach would bring a wall of disapproval and dirty looks.

Aiden was different here. Elliott had almost forgotten about the unapproachable facade Aiden assumed when he was working—the cool demeanor that had convinced Elliott that he was a stuck-up, humorless prude, when he was really anything but. Elliott, too, was different here, which surprised him.

He was finding it difficult to slip into the Vapid Arm Candy role that he'd always played so well, because he hadn't been playing it with Aiden. When a colleague of Aiden's jeered something casually misogynistic, he almost jumped down the asshole's throat. The only thing that stopped him was the way Aiden's jaw visibly worked, clearly holding back a scathing comeback. If Aiden could keep his mouth shut, Elliott could too, even if it nearly killed him.

In the brief moments that they were alone, between the lackluster greetings and obvious attempts at networking, they didn't mesh as well as they usually did. There was a distance, physical and otherwise, that insinuated itself between them.

"I'll be back," he murmured to Aiden when boredom and jitters teamed up to make it impossible for him to stand still.

He didn't wait for a response, weaving through the glittering throng to the nearest restroom, and not because he'd had more than a couple of sips of liquid all night. It was some place to exist, to do something in silence without having to come up with a reply that was the right mix of uncomprehending interest.

After checking every social media he had, as well as his banking app—twice—he stared in the mirror as the water splashed on his wrists until a few people had come and gone and he wondered if Aiden might be missing him.

Back through the crowd he went, and as he got to where he'd started, he noticed that the group they'd been talking to had moved on. Aiden was now stuck talking to someone who looked far more like Innes Jr. than Aiden ever would.

"I just wouldn't have thought it of you," the man said, loud enough to be heard from almost ten feet away.

"Thought what?" Aiden's voice was tight, and his hand was white on his glass.

"That you'd bring along a boy toy. Seems a little graceless. Is he even legal?"

From this angle, Elliott saw how red the back of Aiden's neck was getting, but no retort came to defend himself or Elliott.

"I am, actually," Elliott said, stepping up behind Aiden's shoulder. This close, he could feel Aiden's tension, and could find the words to defend them both while Aiden couldn't. "Graduated from the kiddie table a few years ago."

"Well, good for you." The man's tone was sickly sweet and his smile playing at friendly charm as he slapped Aiden's arm. "And does Kent make you sit on his lap?"

"Nope. But I sit on his dick all by myself."

Next to him, Aiden choked into his flute of champagne.

"Jesus," their new friend said, his face contorted in disbelief.

"Oh, sorry. Was that a little too much info? I've been told I'm lacking grace."

The guy shook his head as he left, shooting a look at Aiden that was probably aiming for incredulous sympathy, but passed the mark right into pity. Elliott watched him go, making the defiant eye contact that Aiden seemed unable to do.

They hadn't won anything with that short battle. He might even have shot himself in the foot if Aiden had been holding back for some other reason than his obvious discomfort over Elliott's age, and other people's reactions to it.

But at least that asshole had been scared away.

"Sorry," he said. "I couldn't help it."

Aiden drained his drink, then shook his head. "No worries, honestly. I hate that guy, and I should have—" He broke off, fidgeting with the stem of his glass. "Do you want to get out of here for a minute?"

"God, yes. Any suggestions?"

"I know a place. Come on."

The raised terrace was like something out of a cheesy romance novel where the billionaire sweeps the office worker off their feet in an emotionally abusive whirlwind. It was beautiful, all marble and weathered iron and a tropically inspired garden.

"Are you angry with me?" Elliott asked as soon as they left the doors behind, then wished he could take it back. Hadn't Aiden already said it was fine? Wasn't Elliott perfectly within his rights to defend himself against some stranger who had a problem with him?

"No," Aiden said. A hollow *click* announced the champagne flute's abandonment. "Seriously. I'm only sorry I froze. It made him feel like he was right."

An unsettled part of Elliott calmed. Yes, Aiden had panicked about the age thing, but he knew he had, and he wasn't going to fire Elliott for fighting back.

"It's fine," Elliott said. "At the very least, we've put an image in his head that won't go away anytime soon."

They shared a short laugh, then blessed quiet fell.

Elliott leaned against the railing, breathing through his weariness. He had a long way to go before this night was over, and the effort of pretending to be an inanimate object again was draining him too soon.

The cool air whipped away the nagging voice at the back of his mind that whispered that they all knew he was more than Aiden's *friend* and that they thought he was lower than the dirt on their shoes.

The weight of it was heavier than he remembered.

Even the most staunch advocate of normalizing sex work would undoubtedly have bad days where they felt dirty or unlovable.

Self-acceptance was a battle that never ended, not a permanent state of enlightenment.

In twenty years, when he had the tenure he dreamed of, he'd probably still be reminding himself that selling sex didn't make him a bad person. It just made him resourceful, and willing to work hard for the people he loved.

Purposefully, he let his fingers relax on the railing, pulling himself out of his low moment with a forceful tug. Dinner would be better, with fewer people to be ignored by or jeered at, and the pleasant distraction of food.

"You okay?" Aiden had also braced himself on the railing. There was no lamp on the terrace, but enough light spilled from inside that Elliott could see the deep line of concern etched between Aiden's brows, replacing the stony poker face.

Elliott looked his fill, since Aiden would get his mask back in place as soon as they crossed the threshold again.

"Yeah," Elliott said. Aiden didn't seem convinced. "It's just been a long time. You know."

Aiden winced. "I really didn't want to have to drag you to something like this. If you want to leave—"

Elliott chuckled, feeling lighter already. "Dude, no, I'm fine. I wouldn't have come if I wasn't okay with it. Don't worry about me."

"All right." Aiden stared into his eyes longer than was socially acceptable, then moved his hand so that it bumped up against Elliott's on the railing, hot as a lamp left on too long. "But tell me if you change your mind. Honestly, I'm searching for a reason to leave."

"And not buy more raffle tickets for the children in need?" Elliott said. "Shame, Aiden. Ultimate shame."

Aiden rolled his eyes at him. "I'm already a gold-level donor. I think I've done my part for this year."

Elliott's hand slipped off the railing, and he barely caught himself before hitting the metal with his face. "Gold level?"

Elliott had read every name on the donor list—noting how few chose to remain anonymous—less than half an hour ago because he'd been bored of the conversation, and he remembered how many zeros were attached to the gold status.

Aiden shrugged like it was no big deal that he'd dropped that kind of money on a charity Elliott had never even heard of before today. "I like this group. They do good work."

"Yeah?" It came out as a breathy squeak.

Aiden's sudden smile lit up the terrace far better than any of the lights. "They're starting a reading program, sending storybooks to families who can't afford to buy them. It's great, and I think it'll be a big hit, if they have the money to advertise to people who need it."

Aiden had never spoken much about his charitable habits before, other than reminders of the football games he'd rescheduled a couple of dates for, but once he started, he opened like a busted dam. With Elliott as a willing audience, he outlined budget structures, mission statements, and long-term goals until he ran out and sputtered to a stop.

The only emotion that seemed to penetrate Elliott's shock was a frothy delight at Aiden's excitement about the project. "Wow."

"Sorry. I don't mean to go on and on."

"No, no, it's fine. Now I understand how Kevin must feel when I get emotional about the lost Temple of Artemis." A burst of laughter from inside was almost perfectly timed with Aiden's soft chuckle. "He might never totally get it, but he loves me, so he listens anyway, and makes all the right noises."

It was only when their rhythm lapsed that he realized what he'd said—what he'd implied. His first instinct was to open his big mouth and explain that he hadn't meant it like that, but he tamped it down. Obviously, Aiden knew what he'd intended to convey.

"So, yeah." Aiden's hand went to his bow tie, tugging it away from his neck. "They're a fantastic organization. Gold level is the least I can do."

"Still." Elliott's toe wiggled in his too-small dress shoes, a physical manifestation of the anxious curiosity he couldn't let go. "That's a lot of money."

"I guess, but it wasn't my biggest donation this year."

"What." Elliott was dimly aware of his hand tightening on the railing. "How do you afford that?"

Aiden's feet scraped on the concrete underneath him. "Easily."

Elliott stared at him, his brain short-circuiting at the dollar signs in front of his eyes.

Aiden sighed. "I have a trust fund from my parents. I invested wisely, and now the only thing I use it for is supporting nonprofits. My parents taught me well. They're donating to UCLA this year, actually. My cousin's an alumnus."

"Cool," Elliott said, blinking rapidly in the stiff breeze. "Would it be completely gauche and rude of me to ask you how much you're worth?"

Aiden's lips curved a little bit, his eyes shining with the teasing glint that Elliott only ever saw when they were alone. "Probably. But I'm not too worried about you only deciding to be with me for my money."

Then a number came out of Aiden's mouth that made Elliott glad he wasn't holding a drink. It would've fallen to the floor in elegant slow motion like the movies, a mess he'd have to clean up himself.

Elliott had always known there was a big wage gap between them. It was kind of the point of their arrangement. If Aiden had money to waste on companionship he could've gotten for free on a sketchy dating app, that was his prerogative and Elliott's privilege. Elliott still struggled with feeling like he was giving Aiden his money's worth, but maybe this new knowledge would help. Aiden obviously had more cash to blow on strippers and champagne than he let on.

The downside to this revelation was that Elliott felt like a pauper at a prince's banquet. And not in a Cinderella way. He didn't have to come up with a response, thankfully, because someone came out of the door to the building, saying, "Did you see that red carpet they have out there? So cringe, honestly."

"Hi, Jill," Aiden said, turning around and hugging her. "It gives the oldies a thrill, I think."

Jill Kent was just as model gorgeous as her brother and her uncle, in a sharp, angular way. Dangerously attractive, rather than pretty.

"They better not get too thrilled or they'll expire," she said, tossing a lock of dark hair over her shoulder with an irritated twitch, like she wasn't used to it bothering her. "What a way to die. On a tacky red polyester rug with half a glass of flat champagne in your hand."

"Could be worse," Elliott couldn't resist saying. "Could be a white shag carpet and a fake crab canape."

Jill shuddered. "God, you're right. I'll keep that in mind when I'm praying for death later on today. Who are you?"

"This is Elliott Meyer," Aiden said, saving him from his surprise at her bluntness, but pointedly keeping his hands to himself. "He's a friend from the gym."

That's how it is, is it? But Elliott didn't dwell on the meaning further than acknowledging that he had a certain role to play now. By the time he held out his hand for Jill to shake, his posture was different, slouchier. His other hand hung loosely at his side, taking up a larger space. "Hey. It's nice to meet you. You're the only thing I can get Aiden to talk about between reps."

Untrue. Most of what he knew about Aiden's family, Aiden had let slip while talking about something else. The divide between his family life and the one Elliott saw was wide.

"Nice to meet you, Elliott," Jill said, smiling, but her eyes narrowed suspiciously. "That's interesting. I've never heard of you. I don't think Shannon has either."

"Oh?" Elliott gave nothing away. It wasn't odd to keep a casual acquaintance in the weight room. That acquaintance being invited to dinner? Suspicious.

"Where is Shannon, by the way?" Aiden interrupted, saving Elliott from prolonged small talk. "Wasn't she coming with you?"

Jill made a face. "Sick as a dog. She's been in bed since last night, so I told her that if she showed up here and infected everyone else with her plague, I'd make her regret it. It says something about how sick she really is that she didn't even argue with me."

Aiden winced, and Elliott could almost see the new entry in his mental datebook titled *Call Shannon to make sure she's still alive.* "That's rough. I know how bad she is at being sick."

"You're telling me. It's a good thing it only happens once every few years. If I had to listen to her whining every flu season, I'd put her out of her misery."

Elliott snorted. "You're both lucky. I come from a whole family of bad patients."

"Oh, yeah?" Aiden asked, crossing his arms over his chest.

"Dad got injured on duty once and we nearly had to strap him to the bed to keep him still. He hated feeling useless. And my mom—"

Elliott cut off like a tap being closed as he remembered it wasn't just him and Aiden. Jill was there, her dark eyebrow raised.

But Aiden bumped his shoulder, arms still crossed, yet smiling. "Your mom?"

"She was worse. I used to taste every meal to make sure the nurses hadn't snapped and poisoned her." Elliott managed to grin over Aiden's choked laughter. "And that had nothing to do with the fact that nine-year-old me loved Jell-O and political intrigue."

Aiden laughed again, shaking his head at the floor. Elliott felt his lips curve more too, a rush of gratitude infusing him—he'd never told that story to anyone. That had been before they'd known how bad the cancer was, a time him and his dad rarely spoke about.

"Thankfully, no hospitals have been involved, but I'm tragically unaccompanied." Jill sighed. "Which would be considered more pitiful by the Second Marriage Matchmakers Club? Going to something like this alone or going with my sister? Not that I give a crap what they—"

"Going with your sister," Elliott said. "Definitely."

Jill's sculpted eyebrows shot up. Out of the corner of his eye, he saw Aiden's do the same thing. "Why? Isn't it better that I find someone, even if they aren't a viable romantic prospect?"

"Nope. Go alone, there's a chance they'll actually believe you when you tell them you don't want to bring a date. Bring a gay best friend or a big sis and there's nothing to stop them from thinking you're trying to fill the significant-other-shaped void."

"I guess it's for the best, then," Jill allowed. "What about Aiden, though? Should he be worried they'll come after him for bringing his presumably straight gym friend who probably doesn't know which fork to use?"

Elliott rolled his eyes. He did know which fork to use, but he wasn't living in *The Princess Diaries*, so no one cared. "Nah. He's a man, didn't you know? He's dedicated to his career. He's got all the time in the world to settle down with a nice girl."

"Ugh, stop it," Jill said, waving her beaded clutch in his face. "You sound like my great aunt. If I thought I could get away with it, I'd tape the definition of a double standard to her face so she'd have to look at it the next time she dragged me to the 'powder room,' to get 'pretty for the boys.'"

Elliott grinned at her air quotes and her childishly stuck-out tongue. "You can lead the baby boomer to water, but you can't make them progress."

Her eyes flicked between him and Aiden, and Elliott saw how many questions she was bursting to ask. He also saw the moment when she decided to let it go—for now.

"Well, in that case, don't escort me in," she ordered, as if Elliott would even try. "I'm going back there, and I want all those old biddies to see me without a man on my arm."

"You go, girl."

"I certainly will. And I am not going to tell the kitchen that Shannon won't be here to eat her dinner. They always serve three bites of steak and a single string bean, and try to tell me that's dinner."

"You deserve it," Elliott said.

"Yes, I do," she agreed. "You should probably come inside too. If you come in late for dinner, they'll think you're pulling an Uncle Innes at the Autism benefit concert last fall."

Elliott's face instantly prickled with heat. He was glad for the dim light on the terrace because as he went stiff, he could feel Aiden doing the same thing beside him.

Elliott remembered that night. Innes had fucked him in a broom closet that wasn't nearly as soundproofed as Elliott had thought, and when they'd walked into the concert late, nobody had been watching the performers. Until that night, he'd foolishly believed he couldn't be embarrassed by anything anymore.

After, they'd fought worse than they ever had, because Innes had tried to give him a cash bonus to soothe his bruised pride. He hadn't known it, but it'd been the beginning of the end.

"How do you know about that?" Aiden choked. "You weren't even there."

"I have my ways," she crowed, curling her cherry-red lips. "Or, really, my friend Heather has her ways of being in the right place for the best gossip, and she tells me all the good stuff."

"Fantastic," Aiden drawled, and Jill laughed at him as she walked away.

"Do you want to go in?" Elliott asked when she was out of earshot. He felt brittle—because he was cold, not because of how tense Aiden had gotten after Jill's flippant reminder of his sexual history. Aiden could tell Jill whatever he liked. He was paying handsomely for the privilege.

"Yeah," Aiden said, then he reached an arm across Elliott's lower back before he seemed to realize what he was doing and dropped it, wincing as Elliott failed to bite back a humorless smile.

"It's okay," Elliott told him. "She doesn't have to know if you're not comfortable with it."

Aiden sighed, dragging a hand through his hair and messing up the careful style. "It's not that I'm not comfortable. It's just that I don't date much, and she'll make any relationship into something it's not. Then she'll tell Shannon, who'll tell my mother, and it'll snowball into you spending a day learning how to make the Kent family seven-layer lasagna, and I don't want to put you through that kind of torture—"

"It's fine, honestly," Elliott said, laughing and already thawing out. "I can be your gym buddy for today. I'd help you with your squats *any time.*"

Aiden rolled his eyes, just like Elliott had known he would, and the tension between them evaporated. When they went inside and sat down to dinner a couple of minutes later, they shared amused looks over Jill's eager grip on her knife and fork.

It was odd to realize that if Aiden wasn't Elliott's boss, he could have been Elliott's friend. They spent the majority of their free time with each other. They shared a lot of the same opinions, some of the same interests, and they never ran out of things to talk about. The great sex was just a bonus.

Elliott had never had a friend with benefits, but if he and Aiden had met the normal way, at the gym for real or at a bar, that was what they might've become. He couldn't imagine that this parallel universe version of himself would have much time for dating either, so they wouldn't have been boyfriends right away. Probably wouldn't ever have been.

Elliott shook himself out of his head. They *definitely* wouldn't ever be boyfriends. Real life was way too complicated for him to go backward in Aiden's view from The Guy He Paid for Sex.

Dinner was over way too soon, and dessert—after about forty-three years of gushing speeches from the organizers—was even shorter. He could at least be grateful that the three dice-sized cubes of soggy toast they were calling "deconstructed bread pudding" hadn't made him uncomfortably full. Jill was looking particularly smug about having six whole cubes to herself. After he'd finished, and the incredibly efficient waiters started darting in and out to get their plates, he got bored.

There were only so many patterns he could arrange the spilled salt on the tablecloth into without getting obscene, and the conversations going on around the table were either incredibly boring (golf swings) or nothing he wanted to get involved in (Republican politics).

One good thing about the event was that the music they'd picked was attempting to be young and hip, so it was mostly one-hit wonders from the 1990s and the early 2000s, which was a nice change from the usual. He liked old-timey jazz as much as the next guy, but there were only so many times someone could listen to the same soundtrack at every boring party before they wanted to stab their eardrums at the sound of Frank Sinatra.

On the dance floor across the ballroom, two girls in fancy dresses were dancing to "Mambo No. 5." They were just old enough to be trusted at the grown-up party, but not old enough to stay trapped at the grown-ups table, so they spun around instead, giggling and silly. They were cute. Elliott wished he had moves like that.

"Hey," Elliott said, leaning over to Aiden, who was staring intently at his phone. "This might be a long shot, and feel free to say no, but do you want to dance?"

Aiden blinked at him in surprise. He turned around in his chair toward the largely empty dance floor and the two girls now flailing in an incomprehensible synchronized move. His lips twitched with amusement. "I'm not a very good dancer."

Elliott sat up, excited, because that wasn't a no.

"Is anyone?" he argued. "It's not supposed to be elegant. It's fun. Get your heart rate up by thrashing around to the beat."

Aiden shook his head, then looked at the dance floor again, which had gained a pair of old people doing the foxtrot, ignoring the peppy beat completely.

"I can't promise any thrashing," he said, hesitantly. "But I can step and snap beside you while you do it."

"Awesome." Elliott stood up from his chair, wincing at the loud screech. "Come on, we gotta show these kids how to Dougie."

"What the hell's a Dougie?"

"No clue, but I'm better at it than a ten-year-old."

"You're kidding," Jill said when she saw that Aiden had stood, then she followed his lead.

"What?" Aiden asked, suspiciously.

Jill ignored him and pinned Elliott with her glare. "You got Aiden—*Aiden*, my brother—to dance."

Elliott turned to Aiden, who was going pink and looked exasperated. It hadn't even taken that much convincing.

"You're welcome to join us," Aiden said, raising his chin in the way he did when he was embarrassed or on edge.

"You know what," Jill said. "I think I will."

She stalked past them both, smiling widely and confidently at the older couple, whose rhythm didn't falter as the song drew to a close. The next one began right away, and Jill grooved, despite her little black dress. It wasn't really made for dancing, but she made it work, moving to the beat with her shoulders and arms.

Elliott hooted from the edge of the floor, then happily cha-cha'd over to her, with Aiden not far behind.

It wasn't like in the movies. More and more people didn't suddenly come running to the dance floor, free from the bindings of the social order, thanks to a couple of quirky kids and their crazy dance moves. A few people came and went as they danced, some laughing with or at them, some ignoring them, but they were on their own for the most part.

Aiden hadn't lied about not being much of a dancer. He wasn't terrible, but his rhythm was off, and for someone who was so good in bed, he was terrible at moving his hips. Elliott almost told him this before he remembered that Jill still thought they were just friends. Maybe.

Elliott was pretty sure she was way too smart to think nothing was going on. Her eyes narrowed whenever Elliott danced too close to Aiden, but she didn't call him on it, possibly because she couldn't put her finger on their real relationship status. Friends who banged? Fuck buddies, no friendship required? Boyfriends? Jill certainly wouldn't be able to guess the truth, not without some outside help.

Elliott made a vow not to be around if Jill found out the whole situation. Aiden could deal with that hot mess on his own, no matter how much he was paying him.

The two little girls never sat down, not even after Elliott, Aiden, and Jill collapsed back into their chairs. Jill and Elliott complained about their burning thigh muscles as they held lukewarm water glasses to their cheeks, but since Aiden had categorically refused to get low, he was fine, if a little sweaty. Elliott himself was probably red as a tomato, while both of his Kent companions had simply gained a dewy glow. Stupid fantastic genes.

Jill left first, citing an early trip to get back to her college campus. She kissed Aiden on the cheek before she left and then, after a moment's hesitation, kissed Elliott's too.

"It was nice to meet you," she said. "The most interesting thing that usually happens at one of these is the Second Wives Club drinking too much and oversharing about their step kids."

Jill really was cool. She was exactly the kind of person he might have been friends with, if he allowed himself friends. Maybe in another life . . .

"Thanks," Elliott said, thumbing the remains of her red lipstick off his cheek. "I had a blast."

When had he last had so much fun at a party? Thinking back over the events he'd suffered through, the answer was, unsurprisingly, never. And it had everything to do with the company he was keeping.

The air-conditioning in the car was really unnecessary, but Elliott was too tired and happy to care or bother the driver.

"We can drop you off first." Aiden was already undoing his bow tie and the top stud on his shirt. His face was half-lit by the choppy shadows that fell into the car as they drove, but he looked as content as Elliott felt.

"Cool."

Elliott checked his phone. It was midnight. Early by his standards, but he'd probably go straight to bed, and maybe he'd be as happy in his dreams as he was awake.

"Unless you—" Aiden said, then he broke off.

Elliott glanced up from the glowing screen to see him staring out the window. "Hmm?"

"You could stay at my place, if you like," Aiden offered, turning his face a little, but not far enough that he met Elliott's eyes.

Elliott blinked against the cold air blowing from the front of the car, stinging his eyes. He watched Aiden's profile, trying to get a read on his request. "Should I?"

Aiden shrugged, tossed a glance over his shoulder, then turned his eyes to see the road ahead through the darkened windshield. "Your call. You could come over tomorrow afternoon as usual, or you could spend the night and I could cook you breakfast in the morning instead."

Elliott pondered the question carefully. He didn't stay the night very often, and when he did, he was gone before Aiden woke up. Breakfast had never been a part of their equation.

"Really?" Elliott asked, aiming for teasing nonchalance. "I thought that was the kind of thing that would fall into the cons list of relationships. The morning after." He shuddered theatrically.

"No," Aiden said, finally finding Elliott's eyes in the partial darkness. "Breakfast is a good meal to share if you like the person you share it with. There's none of the anxiety that comes with other meals. Dinner means expectations, usually, no matter how long you've been dating. Lunch is fine, but it always feels like filler. You can't really relax at lunch. You have to go back to whatever it was you were doing before you interrupted your day halfway through."

"No work to rush off to on a Sunday morning," Elliott murmured.

"Exactly. You can take your time. The pressure's off, you've probably already done what was making you nervous." Elliott laughed softly and Aiden smiled. "Breakfast is honest. I think it's harder to hide in the morning, when you're still waking up and you haven't shown anyone outside your face yet."

Aiden's face hid nothing just then. There was a wistfulness that Elliott could plainly see, and a little touch of sadness that was overtaken more and more by hopefulness as Elliott watched. Not a grand sort of hope, for a romantic victory against all odds. A quiet hope, for a small thing that wouldn't change anything. For a peaceful Sunday morning with a person he liked to spend time with. Elliott knew the feeling.

"I thought you didn't cook," Elliott said.

Aiden rolled his eyes. "I can scramble a couple of eggs. I'm not completely helpless."

If Elliott went home with Aiden now, he'd still be technically on the clock, for only a few more hours than he normally logged in a week, but it would probably be more like hanging out. He could see himself waking up on the guest side of Aiden's bed, his hair crazy from leftover gel. He could imagine what it would be like to have breakfast and chill over some coffee before he headed back to his dorm.

He agreed with Aiden about mornings, though. The light would be brighter, the day newer, and Elliott worried that he'd be more transparent than usual. Then again, what did he have to hide from Aiden?

Looking at Aiden, Elliott remembered the contained glee in his eyes back on the dance floor when he'd recognized a song and started to relax, revealing his embarrassingly thorough knowledge of the lyrics.

After their rocky start, they'd packed a hell of a lot of fun into just a couple of hours.

Aiden must have agreed, and maybe that was where this request was coming from. Maybe, like a kid refusing to go to sleep on Christmas Day because the fun would be over for another year, Aiden wanted to stretch it out.

"Okay," Elliott said, his stomach tight from happiness. "I'll stay."

"All right," Aiden said, smiling again.

Elliott grinned back. His contentedness felt too large for the small car, so he lowered the window. As they sped toward the rest of their night, Elliott was freezing and windblown, but so very happy.

Chapter  8

E lliott woke up slowly and naturally. He had no idea what time it was, but he'd spent enough nights at Aiden's that he wasn't confused for more than a couple of sleepy seconds before he knew where he was.

Aiden's bed. His California King mattress and cool, white sheets with an astronomical thread count. Easily the most comfortable thing Elliott had ever slept on, especially when stacked up against his dorm's poor offering and his well-worn mattress at home.

Elliott looked up at the ceiling and stretched, spreading his limbs and tendons to their limits and groaning at the sweet burn and breathtaking ache. He went completely limp when it was over, relishing the aftershocks like he'd just had the best orgasm of his life.

He didn't normally lounge on Aiden's bed. On the rare occasions that he had slept over, he picked up on Aiden's signals in the morning and got out of there quickly so there wasn't any awkwardness. This time, he was going to take full advantage of having the bed all to himself and an invitation to relax for a while.

At least, he was pretty sure Aiden had been serious about cooking him breakfast. He couldn't know for sure until Aiden came back from wherever he'd run off to, but he'd sounded genuine.

Last night had been . . . weird, he decided, flopping over onto his stomach in the middle of the bed and inhaling the clean laundry scent of the pillow until he felt light-headed. It smelled like Aiden. He hadn't even known he could recognize Aiden's scent until that moment. Another weird thing, but, like the night before, with the dance, and the drive, and the sex with the lights off afterward, it wasn't bad-weird. He would've gone so far as to say it was good-weird, rather than merely weird-weird.

He was so comfortable he felt a little bad about it. Phantom guilt was crawling out of nowhere, trying to make up reasons why he shouldn't be doing what he was doing, because nothing sane or legal was allowed to feel so good.

Without retrieving his phone from his far-flung pants, he could still guess what time it was. The light coming in the window was pale, and his Don't Sleep Your Sunday Away Dumbass! alarm hadn't gone off, so it wasn't past noon. More like nine or ten.

Wherever Aiden was, he wasn't sleeping in, enjoying his own Sunday morning in his sinful bed. Elliott started to worry that he'd chased Aiden out without realizing it, but he didn't think he was prone to snoring or starfishing. Aiden had certainly never complained before.

He didn't have to wait very long for his answer, because Aiden walked through the door, cautiously peeking around it.

"Hey," Elliott said, pushing up on his elbows.

Aiden flashed a small smile that was gone in an instant. "Hi. Sleep well?"

"As always. You?"

He shrugged, and Elliott noticed that he was wearing a worn-thin cotton shirt with a cut-out collar, and his throat and shoulders were glistening with a fine sheen of healthy sweat.

"I kind of hate you," Elliott blurted, his brain-to-mouth filter still waking up for the day. Aiden only raised a questioning eyebrow, so Elliott rushed to explain. "I just— Who works out this early on a Sunday?"

Aiden rolled his eyes, sat down on his side of the bed, and started taking off his running shoes and socks. His back, with its thin, sweat-darkened shirt, was within inches of Elliott's twitchy fingers.

"I hate myself a little, to be honest," Aiden said, over his shoulder. "I would've liked to stay in bed, but my conscience won't let me sleep or just relax past 9 a.m., so I might as well do something productive."

"Oh, to be so afflicted," Elliott said, eyeing Aiden's sleekly bunching muscles. Aiden huffed, then they lapsed into a still, sleepy silence as Aiden toed off his shoes. Suddenly, it seemed like all the domesticity they'd been ignoring by complying with Aiden's "low maintenance" request was catching up with them. Elliott lounging under the covers while Aiden went about his Sunday, exercising and probably starting the coffee pot. It was only going to get more couple-y from there if Aiden made good on his promise to cook breakfast.

It made Elliott a bit itchy, if he was honest, but the customer was always right. And it wasn't exactly a hardship to eat eggs and hang out.

Elliott scratched his scalp, dislodging more of last night's styled hairdo. He was comfortable here, in a room they'd christened with fast sex that had made their legs shake and faces clench in unflattering masks, then slow sex, painstakingly built to a roaring fire. He had no clue if he was likely to remain so comfortable if he stayed, or whether Aiden would. The best course of action, he decided, was not to sit in awkwardness as he wondered.

Flipping over onto his back, he pulled himself closer to the edge of the mattress and put a hand on Aiden's knee, right next to his own face. Aiden stopped rolling his socks up and looked into his eyes.

"Do you want me to go?" Elliott asked, keeping his voice as neutral as possible.

Aiden tilted his head to the same angle as Elliott's, then shook it slowly. "No. You can stay."

"If you're sure."

"I'd tell you if I wasn't." Aiden leaned over and kissed him, tempting his lips in slow, shallow pulls, while one of Elliott's hands fluttered on Aiden's thigh and the other came up to card through his fluffy-damp hair.

Elliott hummed into Aiden's mouth, his feet going restless on the bed, slicking down the covers just to feel the cool burn of the friction. His lips followed Aiden's when they pulled away, clinging to their gentle, wet press.

"Okay," Elliott said, his voice rough from more than sleep. "I'll kick around for a while, since you asked so nicely."

"Good." Aiden smirked down at him with a mischievous twinkle in his eye. "Does that mean if I ask you nicely, you'll brush your teeth too?"

Elliott squawked with outrage and scrambled up to his knees, slapping at Aiden's ass as many times as he could until Aiden was safely out of reach behind the bathroom door. Elliott nearly fell face-first onto the carpet, but saved himself at the last minute.

He gathered up last night's party clothes while Aiden showered, then finally retrieved his phone. He opened it up, and his thumb hovered over the bright red icon on his banking app.

Why would he check it now? It was habit, of course, to want to see the numbers in black-and-white for both comfort and motivation. But why now? He wasn't in need of either of those things, and it wasn't as if he could affect a change immediately.

He wouldn't get paid for another few days. He'd do the math and decide how much he could save versus how much he could send at that time.

For now, he tucked his phone back into his pants pocket and folded it with the rest of his things, then got in one more half-hearted smack at Aiden's impressively hard butt as he passed him to have his own shower. The noise wasn't as satisfying through a thick layer of towel.

When he was finished with the many punishingly pressurized jets of the shower—and the extra toothbrush, because he was a considerate guest—he had a few minutes to himself to stare into the steamed-up mirror. He looked a little tired. He hadn't had a drop of alcohol to drink, but he was a bit hungover regardless from the late night and the water and salt he'd sweated out under the bright lights on the dance floor.

For a hot second, he considered begging off and going home for some beauty sleep, but he had plenty of reasons to stay. Oddly, the most important one wasn't that he'd get paid for his time. This morning felt more like his off-hours.

Finding some soft Sunday clothes to borrow wasn't difficult. It was harder to find ones that fit, but eventually he found flannel pj pants that had a drawstring, and he gave up entirely on finding a shirt that was tight enough for him, going for the opposite effect instead.

Always working, he congratulated himself wryly, as he deliberately chose a shirt with a wide neck that would do nothing to hide his collarbones or at least one shoulder. Aiden didn't have a neck thing, necessarily, but he wouldn't say no, and who was Elliott but an exemplary employee who went the extra mile?

When Elliott entered the kitchen, Aiden, who was at the stove and also in pj's, raised an eyebrow, but didn't otherwise comment on his revealing choice of outfit. He didn't immediately start drooling, either, but Elliott wasn't worried.

"Hope you don't mind," Elliott said, gesturing at the borrowed clothing. "I didn't really want to wear my rented stuff from last night."

Aiden nodded at the contents of the pan he was poking with a rubber spatula. "Makes sense. You should be comfortable on the weekend."

"Exactly." Elliott walked over to the marble-topped counter and hopped up onto it, perching on the edge and peering into the steaming pan.

"Hope you like scrambled," Aiden said, tilting it so that Elliott could get a better look at the squidgy yellow mass of egg. "I never could get the hang of any other way to do it."

"Nah, scrambled is good. Easy and quick is the best way to do pretty much anything."

Aiden paused his scraping of the bottom of the pan and gave Elliott a mischievous squint. "You sure about that?"

Elliott grinned and swung his feet back and forth in front of him. "Okay, fair point. You win this round, Mr. Prosecutor."

"Thank you, Your Honor. The prosecution requests a recess while breakfast is served."

"Granted. You need help?" He didn't know the layout of Aiden's kitchen well enough to be very efficient, but he could try. He braced his hands on the counter, sliding closer to the edge.

Aiden waved the eggy spatula at him and shook his head. "No, I'm fine. You stay there."

Elliott drummed his fingers against the counter as Aiden grabbed some plates from one of the many cupboards and served up the contents of the pan.

"You had eggs in your apartment, eh?" Elliott couldn't resist needling. "I thought you didn't like to take up fridge space with food that required assembly."

Aiden stilled for half a second, then admitted, "I had them delivered. They got here while you were in the shower."

Elliott didn't bother to keep his laughter inside. Aiden could take it, and his unwillingness to store a normal amount of perishable food in his kitchen was hilarious to Elliott, who didn't really have a choice, without a kitchen of his own.

"Yeah, yeah," Aiden said, rolling his eyes, then reaching next to the fridge for four pieces of fresh toast, which he dropped swiftly on their plates, before rubbing his fingertips together. "But I did have bread and even some butter. Toast is not too much of a hassle for me, if you can believe it."

They ate in the brightly lit kitchen, Aiden standing by the stove and Elliott sitting, slumped on the counter in a way his back would probably complain about later. The eggs were no better or worse than the ones he made for himself and his dad when he visited home. Aiden rinsed their plates in the sink, refusing again to let Elliott help.

"So." Elliott slapped his hands down on his knees, thumping his heels on the cupboards underneath him. "It's Sunday morning. Aiden Kent is awake, fed and watered, and looking for something to do with the rest of his weekend. What's the usual plan?"

"That depends," Aiden said, then he wedged himself between Elliott's relaxed knees, placing his hands on the counter on either side of Elliott's thighs. "Is Elliott Meyer also awake and looking for something to do?"

"Oh, yeah." Elliott widened his legs further and leaned back, dragging his foot up the back of Aiden's knee. "I'm awake."

The second kiss Aiden gave him that day was deeper, hotter, and had more tongue involved than the first. Elliott hummed into it, his spine arching into Aiden's body and arms, which wrapped around his lower back in an instant.

"I'm very awake," he mumbled into Aiden's mouth.

"Good. Stay that way, and don't move."

Aiden did the moving for him. He pulled Elliott's hips closer to the edge of the counter, then grabbed the waistband of his pajamas and tugged them down and off in a smooth motion that Elliott was jealous of. Next, he knelt and manhandled Elliott's legs until they were over his shoulders, framing his head as he looked up with a heat in his expression that told Elliott exactly what he was planning.

Elliott could barely breathe. It'd been a long time since he'd been on the receiving end of this. He fidgeted as Aiden kissed up the inside of his thigh, too impatient to sit and let it happen. His fingers twitched and plucked at the counter as Aiden drew closer and closer, his breath warm on Elliott's cock, then his lips—

"God," Elliott moaned when Aiden took him inside. The summer swelter of his wet mouth cradled him gently, then sent sparks of pleasure up his spine and down his trembling legs. His hips tensed and he fought against jerking forward with every suck and flick.

The counter was too high and the angle too awkward for Aiden to take much of him in, but Elliott didn't care. He didn't need pornographic deep-throat action to be helplessly turned on, and Aiden's skilled tongue kept yanking high whimpers and tortured sounds from Elliott's throat.

He didn't last long. Between Aiden's spit-slick hand covering the parts his lips couldn't reach and the gorgeous, humid suction, he was tensing all over and falling back onto the countertop in minutes, his hands and elbows squeaking on the slippery marble.

He panted there, dazed and drained, until he felt Aiden moving his feet around, slipping his pajama pants back on. He grinned, lolled his head to the side, and slurred, "I could've done that. Just gimme a second."

"It's okay." Aiden lifted Elliott's hips, just like he had to take them off, then snapped the waistband when they were in place, but not enough to actually hurt. Elliott grunted and pushed up slowly until he was sitting again.

"Come here," he said, tugging Aiden back between his legs. Aiden came willingly, resting his jaw in Elliott's cupped hands and accepting a chaste peck on the lips. "There's more where that came from," Elliott said. He made loud kissy noises, then poked Aiden in the stomach. "But now you have to brush your teeth again."

Aiden laughed, helped Elliott down off the counter, then left. A few minutes later, the sink turned on.

Elliott stretched out on the couch while he waited, checked his email, and got back to his dad, who'd texted him about another officer on the force who was retiring early to go raise goats in Oregon.

He rested his head on his hands, smiling up at the ceiling. He had reading to do at home, but nothing he couldn't handle. His body was still tingling and loose after a fantastic blowjob he didn't even have to return until he was finished with the afterglow. Not a bad way to spend an early shift.

Aiden lifted Elliott's feet and sat down beneath them, keeping them in his lap with a solid, warm hand around his ankle.

"Business as usual?" Elliott asked. "Book or movie?"

"Movie." Aiden squinted. "Sort of. On Sundays, I usually watch something a little different."

Elliott waited, his curiosity piqued, while Aiden turned on the TV and found what he wanted on Netflix. Elliott's eyes widened with disbelief when he stopped on a brightly colored kids' cartoon. Elliott had seen reruns of it when he was a kid.

"Cartoons?" Elliott said, staring across the couch at Aiden in a way that probably wasn't the most attractive.

"I like them." Aiden shrugged, almost managing nonchalance, but falling short with the embarrassed dip of his stubbled jaw.

"This is why you always want people to leave right away in the morning," Elliott guessed. "So that you can get your Nickelodeon fix."

"Not every morning. Only Sundays, when I don't have anything better to do."

"I could say something here about you having at least one better thing to *do*."

"Please don't. I already made that joke, remember?"

"Fine." He twisted around on the couch so that he was on his side, with a clear view of the TV screen. "I am entirely ready to feel guilty about this pleasure. Hit me with that nostalgia."

In some ways, the morning felt like playing hooky from school and work for no reason other than because he hadn't wanted to go.

Eventually, the ticking timer of how long he could convince himself to go without doing his *work* ran out, and he returned Aiden's favor on his knees to the soundtrack of zany circus music from the television. It was surreal, but not entirely off-putting. He loved it when Aiden started off pretending to ignore him. It felt like an in-joke between them, and the payoff when Aiden could no longer stay cool and collected was great.

He left soon after because he saw Aiden check the time twice within ten minutes, a one hundred percent increase from the previous hour. He didn't let it get weird and wasn't offended by Aiden not trying to convince him to stay while he did his laundry, because that was what Aiden paid him for.

Well, besides the obvious.

"And then we watched cartoons for, like, three hours. It was the freakiest morning after ever."

"I bet."

Elliott heard a *clink*ing on Kevin's end of the phone line. He didn't care that Kevin was doing his dishes while Elliott rambled about his weekend—omitting incriminating details—because he'd done the same thing before during other Sunday catch-ups.

Elliott drummed his fingers against the heavy hardcover textbook he could only ever read in his room because of its obnoxious weight, which prevented it from fitting comfortably in his bag. "He really didn't seem the type to go in for mindless entertainment geared toward millennials."

"What type did he seem?"

"Well, based on what we usually watch, I'd expected him to stick exclusively to thinky, arty Oscar winners, with the occasional smart action movie thrown in for something relaxing."

There was a pause, and a noise like something heavy being set down. "You watch movies with him a lot?"

"Yeah, all the time." That wasn't all they did, especially after the first couple of weeks, since they'd gotten through the backlog of Aiden's *To Be Watched* list. They mostly read together, or sometimes, Aiden ate dinner while Elliott talked his ear off about anything and everything.

"Uh-huh." Elliott could hear the smile in Kevin's voice, could picture his face perfectly. He immediately panicked, because that face never led to anything good. "How long have you been *watching movies* with this guy? I thought you said he was an awkward morning after."

"Oh." Elliott wished he could rewind and clap his hand over his flapping mouth. "Well, yeah, it was a bit awkward, but we aren't strangers. It's the same guy I told you about a while ago."

A moment of silence followed, in which Elliott would have been willing to swear Kevin's grin got more gleeful. "I thought it might be. He sounds cool."

"He is," Elliott admitted, hoping it would give his best friend some comfort. Kevin worried about him enough without Elliott telling him the entire truth: *Well, I thought he was going to ignore me before and after we fucked, then kick me to the curb when he was done, but he's actually decent and can hold an intelligent conversation about pretty much anything, which has somehow become sort of a kink for me.*

"So, is that a thing?" Kevin asked excitedly. "Are you having cozy movie nights with a guy, and you didn't even tell me?"

"Nooo," Elliott said, sitting bolt upright in bed. The heavy textbook fell off his chest, and he only just caught it, preventing his offspring-siring years from being cut short. "I mean, yeah, we watch movies, sometimes there's popcorn. Usually there's one or both of our dicks involved—"

"Ugh, PG-13, Elliott!"

"But it's casual. We're not dating, we aren't meeting each other's friends or family, and we're definitely not serious. At all. Ever."

Kevin sighed. "Okay, okay. Point made. Studly lawyer dude isn't marriage material."

"One, how dare you use the word 'studly' in my earshot. Second, I hate you for it and I want to throw up."

"Serves you right for putting your dick into my mind. God, that sounds wrong. And anatomically impossible."

Elliott grinned and lay back down on the bed, the textbook poking him in the hip to remind him that he should probably get back to it. "Hey, virtual sex is the way of the future."

"Yeah, but not with *you*."

"That goes without saying, bro."

"Hello?"

"In here," Elliott called, not putting down his book. He'd just gotten into a perfect reading position for the weight of this particular tome—on his back with his feet propped against the end of the couch so that he could balance the book on his knees without his arms getting sore. It'd taken him forever to get there. He wasn't about to get out of it if Aiden was going to take fifteen minutes to remove his lawyering clothes.

"I'm so sorry, Elliott," Aiden said, his voice getting closer to the living room. "I was in court today and we thought we'd be done by four at the latest."

"It's no big. I got some stuff done." Elliott turned to the next page. He was so close to the end of the chapter he could smell it.

Another big difference between his current entanglement and his last one was that he was a lot more productive. Innes had used his allotted time to drag Elliott off to clubs or parties before he dragged him off to bed. His evenings out had been a complete wash when it came to accomplishing things. Aiden, on the other hand, didn't care whether he read for school or pleasure, as long as they spent at least thirty minutes a week with their legs tangled up on the couch, melting the tension from his broad shoulders.

Aiden put his briefcase down on the coffee table next to Elliott's head but said nothing. There was a rustling—probably Aiden taking off his coat—which was distracting enough that Elliott glanced over.

"Holy business suit, Batman," he said, flopping the book down on his chest and taking in the full splendor of Aiden's clothes. "Damn. Why didn't I know you looked so good like this?"

Aiden paused in the act of shrugging the jacket off his shoulders and looked down at him with a quirked brow. "You've already seen me in a suit."

Elliott sat up, groping for his bookmark and shoving it in so he could abandon the book on the coffee table. "Yeah, but that was like . . . a rich and fancy suit. This is an everyday, go-to-work, bring-home-the-bacon suit. It's different."

"Is it?"

The suit Aiden was wearing could probably cover the cost of Elliott's entire wardrobe. It made Elliott want to set fire to his overstuffed closet and let it burn along with the piles of old tees and cheap button-ups.

"Oh, yeah." Elliott got up and stood in front of Aiden, then he smoothed his hands down Aiden's lapels. On the way back up, he slipped his fingers underneath them and started pushing the jacket off Aiden's shoulders. Aiden didn't resist, just glanced down with a little smile on his face while Elliott undressed him. Apparently, he wasn't too tired after his long day to skip right to the activity portion of their evening. There would be plenty of time for no-strings relaxing after Elliott got him out of that suit.

Once the jacket was in a pile on the floor, a thorough ironing in its future, Elliott got distracted by Aiden's tie. Up close, both the tie and the suit had more blue in them than he'd thought, making the medium gray more stormy. He played with the strip of fabric, letting the silky grain slip through his fingers and over his wrists. Elliott wasn't normally into being tied up, but it was on the Allowed list. They hadn't worked their way through many of the bullet points, so maybe it was time to drop some hints. He could think of a couple of things he could do with the tie he was fingering . . .

Aiden's hands came up and encircled Elliott's wrists, squeezing firmly, just shy of pain. Elliott looked up, surprised and even more turned on. Aiden's gaze was hungry and dark, his eyes glittering impatiently.

"Come on, Elliott," he said, loosening his grip on Elliott's wrists.

"What?" Elliott asked, his eyes widening in a way he knew made him resemble a Bratz doll. In a good way, he was pretty sure.

"Get on with it."

"Or what?" Elliott challenged, a devilish impulse spurring him on. "You'll spank me, Daddy?"

Aiden's whole body jerked and his hands tightened again. It was a risky move, calling him that, but Aiden would probably laugh it off and just make Elliott promise never to mistreat his erection like that again.

He didn't expect Aiden to go so utterly still and silent.

"Did you . . . like that?" Elliott purred.

Aiden huffed and gave a tiny shake of his head, his face spasming with some unidentifiable expression. But the tension was still there, squaring his shoulders, firming his jawline until it could cut glass.

"You sure?" Elliott pressed. "I've been known to behave pretty badly. I might need Daddy to teach me a lesson."

"Elliott," Aiden growled.

"What?"

From so close, Elliott could see Aiden's pulse beating in his neck, and feel the increase in his breaths. Aiden hadn't moved an inch, not to pull him close and ravish him, but not to fling him away in disgust either.

An answer from Aiden didn't seem to be forthcoming, so Elliott pulled his hands out of Aiden's grip and loosened the tie, getting it out of the way so he could reach the buttons of Aiden's dress shirt.

He hummed as he bared Aiden's collarbones and his upper chest. "I wish you'd told me you liked it. I would've called you Daddy ages ago."

Aiden flinched again, and his hands flew to Elliott's rib cage, pulling him in and burying his face in Elliott's neck. "That's not—" Aiden mumbled. "It's just . . ."

"Weird? Maybe," Elliott acknowledged. "We might both need therapy."

Elliott kept on unbuttoning Aiden's shirt, pulling the tails out of his pants to get to the bottom. As he reached for the button on Aiden's slacks, he planted a single biting kiss on Aiden's exposed neck, relishing the shudder it caused, and the squeeze of Aiden's tightening grip on his waist.

"I could stop," Elliott said softly, breathing into the shell of Aiden's ear. "I would, if you asked me. I'd never say it again. But first, you have to tell me to. Say to me that you don't like it, and you won't hear it anymore." He nipped Aiden's earlobe and let his hand travel down from the waistband of the suit pants. "Daddy."

With an animalistic growl, Aiden took Elliott's mouth in a wild, hard kiss. Elliott gave as good as he got, digging his fingers into Aiden's hair. He groaned when Aiden put his hands under Elliott's ass and lifted him, using his height and strength to carry him to the bedroom. They barely stopped kissing during the short journey.

Elliott bounced after Aiden dropped him onto the bed, then immediately lay back so he could undo his jeans. Aiden helped, yanking them down his legs as soon as he'd shed his own unbuttoned clothing. When Elliott threw off his T-shirt, Aiden turned him over onto his front and made him get on his hands and knees.

"Yeah," Elliott panted, blood pounding in his ears. "Give it to me. Come on, Daddy."

He heard the sound of the bedside drawer opening, then the squelch of lube on fingers. He didn't look up, just breathed with his head hanging down between his arms, fists clenching the comforter in anticipation.

With practiced ease, Aiden's fingers opened him up. They'd done this so many times by now, Elliott didn't even need to tell Aiden he was ready. Aiden knew by the pitch of Elliott's moans and the toss of his head.

Aiden entered him in one forceful push, without much more warning than the absence of his fingers in Elliott's hole. Elliott lost his balance and face-planted into the mattress, but recovered quickly so he could push back into Aiden's powerful thrusts.

Despite Elliott's best efforts, he still jolted forward every time Aiden's hips connected with his ass, and it didn't help that his arms and legs went weak with each glance of Aiden's dick over his prostate.

Elliott's elbows gave out when Aiden started stroking the space above his ass, running spread hands over the depressions beneath his lower back. Elliott was incredibly sensitive there, and he moaned into the blanket on each pass.

Aiden's low, continuous panting started gaining voice, accompanying each driving thrust of his hips with an open-mouthed groan. The sounds resonated in Elliott's ear when Aiden leaned down, scooping Elliott into his arms and yanking him up so that Elliott's back was against his chest. Elliott shouted at the deeper penetration, shivering as the slight breeze from their sudden movement lit up his leaking, red cock.

"Say it," Aiden growled. His thrusts lifted Elliott up, reaching deep each time. "Beg me."

Elliott's chest quavered with his neediness, his fingers clutching at Aiden's anchoring arms. "Please. I need it, Daddy, please, fuck—"

Aiden's hand unwrapped from Elliott's waist and fisted Elliott's dick with quick, twisting strokes. His thrusts picked up speed, keeping time with his hand. With a yell, Elliott was catapulted into orgasm, and he slumped forward, writhing while Aiden chased his own.

The onslaught of sensation was a lot; he was oversensitive and raw, every emotion closer to the surface of his flushed skin. He was about to ask Aiden to pull out before Aiden thrust hard one last time, then his only movements were full-body contractions as he came deep inside of Elliott.

Neither of them moved for a while after that. Elliott rested on his elbows, the blanket under his cheek damp with his heavy breaths. Aiden's hands dented the mattress next to his head, and Aiden was panting just as hard as he was. His skin tingled from the passage of air over the thin sheen of sweat on his back.

When their respiration reached a normal level and things started to get sticky and uncomfortable, Aiden pulled out. Other than a wince, Elliott didn't move much even then. He just stretched his legs out and groaned, not looking forward to getting up to fix the sticky and uncomfortable problem.

He snaked a clumsy hand between his chest and the bed, like he could hold in rippling unnameable emotion that made him want to curl up. His lungs shuddered with the euphoria of great sex and shared contentedness, but something in his chest twinged. The idea of getting out of bed to deal with cleanup while Aiden entered his normal undead state made him bury his face in the mattress.

The bed dipped next to him, and he started to roll over, but stopped when he saw Aiden stand, then shuffle over to the en suite. Elliott almost laughed at the zombielike slackness of Aiden's face.

But he wasn't about to make fun of Aiden for taking a turn at cleanup for once. Elliott normally didn't mind doing it. Aiden almost always made sure Elliott came his brains out, unless Elliott didn't want to, so who was Elliott to complain that Aiden never volunteered to deal with the aftermath? It was just a quirk Elliott was happy to have noticed.

Aiden came back after a few minutes, slightly damp all over, with a washcloth in hand. Elliott's breath hitched a couple of times as he let Aiden move him around, but he kept it under control.

"Shit," he said, after Aiden came back from tossing the washcloth in the sink. "I'm wrecked. Can I stay?"

"That's fine," Aiden said, climbing under the blanket while Elliott stayed on top, his body still weak. Then, Aiden leaned over, cupped Elliott's jaw in a damp hand and kissed him.

They kissed all the time. It was one of Aiden's favorite things to do, and there'd been a handful of nights that that was all they did. Sliding their lips together until they were chapped and bruised.

This kiss wasn't different. A kiss was a kiss was a kiss. Aiden still knew how to take charge, how to lead Elliott's tongue where he wanted it.

It made no sense that this time, out of all the other times their lips had kissed, Elliott didn't want to let go.

Chapter 9

Elliott was jerked out of near unconsciousness by the bus braking a little harder than normal. He lurched forward, which peeled his sticky face off the metal pole it'd been leaning on. He managed to stay upright, only to go right back to leaning on the pole, his eyes crusty, stinging, and half-open.

Hot. He was *so* hot. Was he wearing a coat? Yes. His thickest one, though March had come in like a lamb. A fuzzy, warm lamb, like the fuzz that was taking over Elliott's brain. His coat. Should he take it off? Probably.

He let go of the pole, nearly fell over again, then started tugging on the arms of his coat to take it off, but it was difficult to do when he couldn't keep his balance on the moving vehicle and— A new wave of nausea rolled over him. He hugged the pole, curling in on himself and breathing evenly to calm his churning stomach.

Nope. Not trying that again.

It was fine, because even though he'd been hot a few minutes before, he was cold now. His hands—or maybe his forehead?—had made the pole greasy with thick sweat. His face, which he'd plastered to the metal again, was still burning, but the rest of him shivered.

He blinked slowly and wondered how many germs were living on the pole two inches from his mouth. He was already sick, but the next person to use it would need hand sanitizer, or it would be his fault if they got infected.

"Sorry," he mumbled, and the lady in the seat closest to him pursed her lips, but looked a little sympathetic.

He hurt. Everywhere. His ribs were aching from heaving the whole morning until there was nothing left of the meager dinner he'd shoved in his mouth the night before. His throat burned from the acid, and his head pounded from how hard he'd wretched. Everything that touched his skin was as rough as the hooky part of velcro. Even his feet were sore. He just wanted to sit down, but the bus was crowded, there were people everywhere, trying to get home after work to start their weekend. *TGIF*, he thought, and it was so goddamned funny, but he couldn't breathe out of his nose properly to laugh.

He took his phone out of his pocket and blinked at the time, but his eyes were too foggy and gunk-crusted to see the tiny numbers.

Aiden would be home by now, though. He might be wondering why Elliott was late. He was late because . . . he didn't remember. He didn't really remember putting on his shoes to leave the dorm, or taking the elevator and making the walk to the bus stop.

Was he even wearing shoes? He looked down.

Bad idea. The world spun and he almost threw up again, but eventually the crazy turning stopped and he saw his feet. They had shoes. Good. They might be on the wrong feet, though, which he deduced was why his feet hurt.

"I'm fuckin' Sherlock Holmes," he said, and the lady next to him shifted uncomfortably in her seat.

He felt like shit. His body hated him. That lady hated him. The bus driver probably hated him too. His eyes filled with tears and he sniffed. Coughed. Winced at the pain in his ribs. God, his knees were too weak for this bumpy ride. Was he going to pass out? White sparkles had been interrupting his vision for the last half hour, so he wouldn't be surprised.

He'd be pissed, though. He'd have come all this way, only for his body to quit on him before he'd passed go and collected two hundred dollars from Aiden, who was waiting for him. Elliott took a deep breath and locked his knees, willing them not to fail. He just needed to get a little farther—

The robotic voice announced the next stop, and Elliott's feet were moving to the exit before his brain caught up with the fact that it was *his* stop. Well, Aiden's. But he spent so much time there these days that it felt like his.

When the bus halted, he stumbled off into the bright light outside. The sun stabbed him in the face, which made his headache flare, which made his nausea bubble up, which made him gag, and then he was puking into a concrete planter next to the road.

"Fuck," he moaned when he was finished. He spat to clear the grossness in his mouth, his arms shaking, and his hands propped on his knees to keep from face-planting into vomit and dried-out dirt.

He wiped his face with his hand, wishing he'd remembered to bring a box of tissues with him when he'd left the house. His hand was barely effective, smearing the mess more than cleaning it. His old track pants and his thin T-shirt with dark sweat stains at the armpits and neck felt grotesque against his skin. He wanted to curl up in a ball and die, so he did one of those things. Leaning against the planter, he sat on his ass on the hard, dirty sidewalk and pulled his legs as close to his chest as his gurgling stomach would allow him.

He might have fallen asleep, but couldn't know, because all the sleeping he'd done that day had been taken over by dreams, the subjects of which had been bizarre, apocalyptic versions of things he did in real life.

So, when he heard Aiden's voice calling his name, he couldn't tell if it was actual Aiden or Dream Aiden.

Elliott opened his eyes.

"Elliott?"

He sure sounded real. And loud.

"Hunf?"

"Do you know where you are? How did you get here? What happened?"

"Oh," Elliott said, his tongue flopping in his mouth, thick and sticky. He opened his eyes fully and peered at Aiden. He looked worried. He also looked good in the sunlight, which Elliott hadn't known before because they usually went places after dark. The sun was setting later now that it was getting closer to springtime, but they still hadn't—

"Wait," Elliott said—or croaked, more accurately. "The sun."

"Yeah," Aiden said gently, like he was talking someone off a rooftop. "It's shining."

Too brightly. It made Aiden squint now as he crouched down next to Elliott.

What the hell time is it?

"It's four thirty in the afternoon. What are you doing here, Elliott? You look terrible."

Elliott blinked slowly, the cogs in the brain sticking and struggling to turn. He was too early. Why was he early? Had he checked the time before he'd left his dorm?

"I'm sick," he mumbled, hoping that would answer all of Aiden's questions, even the ones he couldn't remember.

"You look it," Aiden said. "Come on, let me help you up. You should get inside."

Elliott whined and let his head fall onto his knees. "Don' want to."

"You have to. The sidewalk isn't very comfortable, is it? There's a couch upstairs. Or maybe the bed. You can use the shower."

Elliott flinched from the thought of the tiny, razor-sharp droplets on his feverish skin. "No shower."

"Okay, okay. No shower," Aiden soothed. "But the bed will be comfy, right?"

"Yeah. 'S hard, though."

"I know. It'll be worth it, I promise. Up you get."

Elliott let Aiden unfold him and lift him to his feet. Collapsing against Aiden's shoulder, he breathed in through his nose to keep from throwing up again. Aiden guided him silently up the short distance to the apartment building's entrance and into the elevator, which was seriously not fun. Not only did it move too fast, it also smelled like a lemony cleaning chemical and the perfume of the lady who got off a few floors before they did. Elliott buried his face into Aiden's soft shirt to drown out anything else, huffing the familiar laundry detergent and praying that his stomach didn't decide to ejaculate any more of its contents.

They made it to Aiden's apartment before his resolve gave up the ghost. As soon as the door was unlocked, he bolted to the hall bathroom and heaved over the toilet fruitlessly. There was nothing to come up but saliva and bile, but *still*, his ribs and stomach contracted over and over.

When the urge to vomit subsided, Elliott laid his head on his arm, leaning into the toilet bowl. He breathed, his eyes watering, his nose running, his mouth still producing so much drool that he could barely keep swallowing it away.

He sobbed, then whimpered at the sore muscles that it tugged. He just wanted to not be sick anymore. He wanted to stop throwing up. He wanted to get up, but he didn't trust his knees.

He wanted his mom.

His eyes watered harder, and tears dripped onto the gray tile beside the toilet. Elliott watched them fall—*plink, plink*—knowing she wouldn't appear. She wasn't alive to make him soup, or let him sleep in her and his dad's bed with his favorite pillow and blanket. She couldn't put her cool hand on his sweaty forehead, because she was gone. Even the place she used to care for him was different. The couch he used to sleep on whenever he was sick was gone, lost to basement mold, and the gigantic crack in the wall of his old bedroom would have made him too uneasy to sleep there.

He didn't even have his dad to try his best to fill her gaping absence. He was back home, safe and happy, but far away. He didn't even know Elliott was sick.

Elliott sniveled for a while longer, trying to wipe the tears away, hiding his face under his arm. When a sock-covered foot stepped into his vision, he didn't look up.

"Arms," Aiden said, his voice barely carrying over the echo of Elliott's rasping breaths.

Elliott didn't do anything until Aiden tugged at his shirt. He lifted his arms at another gentle prompt and his shirt came off, a soft blanket replacing it. A warm, wet washcloth was dragged across his face, under his swollen eyes, his sore nose, and his chapped lips.

"Blow."

He honked into the cloth.

"Drink."

He drank tepid water from a glass, grimacing at the taste in his mouth—sweet and metallic.

"Let's get you to bed," Aiden said, and Elliott groaned. More moving. Joy.

Aiden had turned back the covers on Elliott's side, and he slipped gratefully in between the cool, soft sheets. Aiden made him take off his pants before he could really snuggle in, but it did feel a lot better.

Aiden disappeared for a while as Elliott shivered in bed underneath two thick blankets, returning with another cup of water, a bottle of pills, and a big plastic bowl, which he set on the floor next to Elliott's head.

"Just in case," he said, and Elliott smiled a little bit for the first time in hours.

"Thanks," he slurred.

"No worries." Aiden sat down on the bed next to Elliott's legs, slowly, so the bed didn't wiggle too much. "Elliott, why did you come here? What would you have done if I hadn't come home early from work?"

Elliott squinted at him. "We had a date."

Aiden frowned. "Yes. On a normal Friday, we do. But you look like death."

"It seemed like a good idea at the time. I'm going to blame the meds." They hadn't seemed to work earlier, but his fever had probably come down a bit, since he could tell now what poor choices he'd made. He wasn't the type to call in sick for a little sniffle, but he was a walking petri dish, and Aiden wouldn't want to catch what he had.

"Seriously, you look awful. You probably shouldn't even be here, you should be at a hospital."

"No hospitals," Elliott said, turning his face into the pillowcase. "I don't like them. I won't go, even if you try to make me."

"All right," Aiden said, sounding frustrated, though Elliott couldn't see him. "I won't make you go unless it's in an ambulance."

"I won't need it. It's just a bug."

A more rational part of him knew that he would probably be better off going to the ER for some fluids. The larger part was so exhausted that a fight-or-flight response kicked in at the very thought.

The last time he'd been to a hospital had been to see his mom while she'd been wasting away from the havoc the cancer had wreaked on her brain. He remembered the hard plastic chairs, the constant murmur of the PA system, the taste of Jell-O for every meal because his dad was too busy to notice. All in all, he had too many sense memories associated with the smell of disinfectant and grief to willingly step foot in a hospital if he wasn't dying.

"I'm tired." He wished he was more comfortable in the cozy bed with its soft blankets, but comfort was relative when he was this sick. It was better than a dirty sidewalk, and his brain felt a little less cooked from fever.

"I bet." Aiden lifted his hand, like he was about to brush Elliott's shoulder, but seemingly thought better of it. He made Elliott sit up again to take a couple of pills to get his fever down, then stood up, heading for the door and flicking off the ceiling light. "You should sleep. I'll be outside if you need anything."

Elliott nodded and winced at the rough drag of the pillow on his blazing cheek. Just before the door closed, he lifted his head up again and blurted, "I'm sorry."

Aiden smiled sympathetically at him. "It's fine. I can handle a bit of nursing."

"No, I mean—" Elliott rolled over onto his back, rubbing a hand through his sweaty, gross hair. "I'm sorry we can't— You know. Gimme a few hours and I probably can."

Aiden's lips pursed, and Elliott had never seen him look so disapproving. "Seriously? You think I'd try to have sex with you when you can barely keep your head up?"

"No, it's not so bad, I'll just sleep it off—"

"Elliott," Aiden interrupted, his voice brooking no argument. "Drink some water. Go to sleep. We'll talk about it later."

Elliott nodded and flipped back over to face the side of the bed with the bowl near it, just in case. Aiden's tone suggested that he wasn't intending to talk about it later, but Elliott wasn't about to let that happen. The only reason Elliott could afford to even consider going to the hospital for fluids and antibiotics was because Aiden was paying him for sex and for the benefits of a monogamous relationship without the drawbacks. Elliott was too tired to stress about it now, but after a few hours of shut-eye, his conscience would be screaming at him to even the scales.

His eyes drooped and the quiet darkness combined with the medication took effect, dragging him down into sleep. He'd pay Aiden back for the use of his bed and his plastic bowl. In a while.

"Well, you look better," Aiden said as Elliott came into the living room.

"Yeah," Elliott said on a yawn. He crossed his arms, a little chilly with only a towel around his waist and damp hair from his shower. "Still feel like crap, but not a metric ton. More like a modest few steaming pounds."

"Vivid. Thanks for that," Aiden said, putting down his book. "Your clothes are in the dryer. They should be done by now if you want to grab them."

"Sweet."

Elliott wandered over to the laundry closet and snagged them, rubbing the warm, dryer-scented clothes all over himself before putting them on. When he came back to the living room, Aiden handed him a huge blanket in bright turquoise. Elliott let out an orgasmic groan when the fuzzy fabric slipped over his shoulders and hugged him in a polyester cocoon.

He sat down at the other end of the couch in his blue-green shroud, but Aiden patted the seat next to him.

"I'm warmer if you want to cuddle up."

Elliott did. Good *god*, did he. He was a pretty tactile person on the best of days, but when he was sick or sad—Kevin could attest—he turned into a magnet for body heat and hugs. But was it fair to Aiden, if he wasn't guaranteed a happy ending out of it?

Aiden sighed and flapped his hand at him. "Come on. I got the flu shot this year; you're fine."

Elliott was skeptical, but not enough to overpower his mighty need for cuddles. He shuffled down the length of the couch, dragging his blanket, and burrowed under Aiden's outstretched arm. He fit just as well as he usually did, but there was a different vibe to their close contact this time. Elliott rarely forgot that their encounters, more likely than not, ended in sex. Not because he didn't enjoy bugging

Aiden about his work day while he ate dinner, or complaining about how unrealistic movies portraying ancient Romans were.

It was only that Elliott found Aiden so mind-meltingly attractive that he was always one pants-adjustment away from hitting Pause on the TV and dragging Aiden to the bedroom.

Right then, though, Elliott couldn't have been less interested in getting it on. Aiden could've been back in his tux, with those skinny suspenders doing terrible/wonderful things, or mouthwateringly postworkout like last week, and Elliott still couldn't have summoned genuine excitement.

A job is a job, he thought . . . and his stomach dropped. His chest got tight and he snuck an arm out of his warm blanket nest to snake around Aiden's waist. Aiden, reading again, automatically rested his hand on top of it, brushing his thumb over the skin above Elliott's elbow.

A job was a job. Except this wasn't just a job anymore. Elliott had taken it home with him, so to speak. He'd allowed Aiden to become someone he let see him at his lowest: sweaty, pukey, and crying on the floor of a bathroom that wasn't even his.

Elliott wanted to slap himself for not realizing earlier how far from a job his time with Aiden felt now. It was inconceivable, really, considering how many times he reminded himself every day that he was selling his body and his time as a commodity, but not his soul or his pride. He thought of Aiden as his employer every time he whipped out his debit card to pay for a carton of chocolate milk to take to class. He tried not to forget that they weren't actually boyfriends, but while he'd been busy telling his brain that, he'd forgotten to tell his emotional muscle memory not to slip into tenderness territory.

He inspected Aiden's face from under the hood of his blanket. Aiden was reading the last book in a trilogy he loved and didn't even glance over, so Elliott could look his fill. Without the haze of *want gorgeous gimme*, Elliott's eyes raked over the parts of Aiden's face he'd seen a hundred times before.

He hadn't hit thirty yet, and the lines beside his eyes and between his heavy eyebrows were already deepening from him frowning in concentration all the time. His scruff, grown out slightly for casual Friday at the office and a lazy evening at home, had a little bit of red in it. His upper lip had a deep dip in the center, made even more obvious by the five-o'clock shadow.

Elliott wanted to run his fingers across it. Not, for once, to guide Aiden's lips closer to his, but because it looked soft, and his thumb wanted to know the curve of it. Because it made his chest shudder to imagine that he could know Aiden's face by touch only.

Shit, he was in trouble.

He shut his eyes against his growing anxiety. More hydration was needed, apparently, because the room was getting a little wobbly. Breathing in and out, he ignored the way his heart rate calmed a few notches with the regular turn of a page of Aiden's book. He was too out of it to get weepy about attachment issues that were probably only Florence Nightingale Syndrome.

He drifted, consciously not thinking about any one thing too hard. When he opened his eyes next, it was because his still-damp hair was being stroked away from his face, softly and rhythmically, both waking him and putting him in a trance. He hummed, leaning into Aiden's fingers.

"Are you hungry?"

Elliott looked up. His face was only a couple of inches from Aiden's, and there was nowhere he'd rather stare than into Aiden's dark eyes. He hadn't known they were kind eyes before he'd stared into them like this a few dozen times, but now, he wouldn't describe them as anything else.

Aiden was smiling faintly, deepening those premature crow's feet. Elliott wanted to kiss them, and make Aiden smile more so his happiness could take the blame for his wrinkles, not his stressful job.

"Not really," Elliott admitted. He still felt vaguely nauseated and his nose was stuffed up, which would make it hard to eat with dignity. "I should probably eat, though. The last thing I had was half a pack of saltines before I went to bed last night."

"Were you sick yesterday too, then? It's good that you were able to force something down."

"No, it hit really suddenly this morning. I just like saltines."

Aiden laughed, and Elliott's body jolted. The roiling of his stomach at the sudden movement was totally worth it for that laugh.

Fuck. Since when was Aiden's laugh so important to me?

Aiden looked over his shoulder, grimacing in the direction of the kitchen. "I don't have much to offer you in the way of food, but I could get delivery?"

Elliott blamed his rush of gratitude on his empty stomach and whacked-out body. "You don't have to—"

"I want to," Aiden insisted. "It's not an imposition, I need to eat dinner anyway."

Elliott frowned and squinted at the TV across from them. He'd barely been aware of the passage of time *before* he took a nap in the middle of the day. Now, he wasn't sure if he could correctly guess the date, let alone the hour. After some blinking, the green glowing lights came into focus.

9:37 p.m., they read.

He looked back at Aiden, raising an eyebrow. "Dinner?"

Aiden shrugged. "Late-night snack."

"Yeah, okay," Elliott relented. He had to do the responsible thing and get some calories in him, even though his insides still felt like the fiery pits of Mordor. "Whatever's fine, I'm not picky."

Aiden disappeared into the kitchen for a takeout menu, and Elliott listened to his voice modulate into *talking to a stranger* mode. Elliott rubbed the fuzzy blanket over his knees so long that it started to crackle with static. He kind of wanted to turn out all the lights and see if he could make it sparkle with lightning bolts like he used to do when he was a kid.

Aiden came back before he could give in to the temptation. "It'll be twenty minutes," he said, sitting down.

"Speedy."

"Yeah, not too many people ordering chicken noodle soup this late at night, they said. Not sure why. After nine o'clock is when I always start to crave comfort food."

Elliott nodded. "Midnight mac and cheese. I've been there."

Aiden grinned at him, then stroked his thigh under the blanket. "So, now we wait. I bet you'll be tired again after eating, so if there's anything you need to do, I'd recommend doing it."

"Well, now that you mention it," Elliott said, his voice dropping a couple of pitches almost without his say so. "I wouldn't mind doing you."

Aiden stopped rubbing Elliott's thigh and looked at him straight on, his eyebrows crimping in . . . disapproval? Disappointment, maybe.

"Elliott, I thought I told you I'm—"

"I feel a lot better, really," Elliott insisted, throwing the blanket off his shoulders even though his sensitized skin was screaming for him not to. "I'm totally fine, and we've got twenty minutes to fill. You can just sit there. I'll do all the work."

Aiden grabbed the blanket and wrapped it around Elliott's shoulders again, keeping it in place when Elliott tried to shrug it off.

"Why would I want to do that?" Aiden said, like a dad keeping his cool while convincing an obstinate child.

Elliott thrust a hand through an opening in his blanket prison so he could tug at his hair. "Because that's—"

He faltered. His daily mental reminder of his standing no longer seemed acceptable to his sense of self-worth. He said it anyway, because it was more truthful than hurtful.

"That's why I'm here. It's why you pay me."

Aiden froze, then his grip loosened on the blanket. Elliott stared down at Aiden's hands to avoid his gaze. *Stupid*, his inner overbearing cheerleader chided him. *You'd be better, stronger, if you looked him in the eye and owned it, like you usually do. He pays you for sex. It's fact, not an opinion.*

Aiden's hands dipped under the edge of the blanket. Elliott's heart slammed in his chest, because he was sure for a second that he'd somehow done a good enough job of convincing Aiden that yes, he was in an okay headspace to blow him today, and his brain wasn't screaming at him to abandon the mission so he could go hug a hot water bottle instead.

But rather than removing a layer of protection from him, Aiden slid his hands up Elliott's chest, over his neck, coming to rest on either side of his jaw. When his face dipped closer, Elliott tensed despite himself, but Aiden's lips landed on his clammy forehead and stayed there, a firm press of dry lips on his skin in an unofficial but well-known symbol for caretaking and affection without heat.

When Aiden's lips started to pull away, Elliott grabbed Aiden's wrists to keep them in place, and to still the faint trembling in his own fingers.

Aiden brushed his mouth on Elliott's cheeks next, closer to the corner of his eye than his mouth. His stubbled face rasped Elliott's skin as he sat back, and Elliott could feel its burn long after it was gone. Aiden's thumbs stroked Elliott's jawbone as he looked into his eyes.

"I think you know that's not true," Aiden said. His throat bobbed once his words were out in the air.

Elliott swallowed himself, trying to find something to say that would hide all his hopefulness and not disagree with Aiden outright.

"You're— It's—"

"You're here for more than just sex," Aiden said, fiercely, taking his wrists back and grasping Elliott's shoulders like he was about to shake some sense into him. "I don't think it's ever just been about sex between us, not from the beginning. It definitely isn't now."

Oh, no. Aiden had fallen into the boyfriend trap too. Somehow, despite their best efforts, they'd managed to trick themselves into forgetting what their relationship really was. It wasn't love. Elliott didn't have to have ample experience with the emotion to know that he didn't love Aiden.

But given time and a forceful shove, he could. If he didn't walk away, it would get there, and he'd be in trouble.

But right now, he was too weak from hunger and fever to resist even a hint of affection, and changing his and Aiden's trajectory was impossible. When he was well again, he'd beat back the soft and squishy feelings with a shovel, but until then, he'd let himself have this one selfish day.

Aiden apparently took his silence as a sign that he'd won. He gave one of his barely there smiles and rearranged the blanket, then settled back into his normal spot at the end of the couch, leaving his arm open for Elliott to cuddle up.

"It's fine," Aiden said, doing his best puppy-dog eyes. "Sit on the couch with me and let me feed you soup and fluids and Advil until you feel better."

Elliott slumped over, resting his head on Aiden's thigh. "I've never taken a sick day in my life," he grumbled. "I'm kinda pissed about breaking my record."

"Don't consider it a sick day, then. Think of it as a day when I would rather cuddle on the couch."

Elliott curled up into a smaller ball. "We do that all the time anyway."

"Exactly. And I always enjoy it. Why can't I just want that today, and nothing else?"

Because that wasn't how it worked.

There wasn't a good reason Aiden couldn't want that. The problem was that there were some excellent reasons why Elliott wasn't allowed to want it. The foremost being that he should've been swimming back to his safe, apathetic, pragmatic shore. Not deeper into the murky waters of whatever his feelings were for this surprising man.

Above him, Aiden picked up his book and rested his hand on Elliott's elbow. Reflexively, Elliott caught it and tugged it around his chest so he could hug Aiden's whole arm to him, their fingers curled loosely together.

Tomorrow, he'd deal with everything. He'd take stock, take a big step back and see if he could still do this with a professional distance between them, or if it was too late and he'd have to quit.

The thought made his teeth clench. Not only because of the money, but because of the inevitably messy end they would face if Elliott decided to make his living with another man.

If their connection was truly as strong as it felt, Aiden might give an open relationship a go. He'd say he was fine with it, and at the time, he'd most likely mean it. That open-mindedness would probably last just long enough for Elliott to get his heart broken when Aiden changed his mind. But that was for future-Elliott to worry about.

Tomorrow, he promised. Or maybe the next day.

He listened to Aiden's book scrape to the next page. He stroked his thumb down Aiden's palm.

Soon. But not yet.

Chapter  10

"**N**o!"
"I swear, Elliott, if you don't give me that right now—"
"You'll never take me alive!"

Elliott tore down the long hallway of the apartment, skidded in his socks, but managed not to hit the wall before he switched directions and ran for the living room. Aiden wasn't so lucky, and Elliott cackled when he heard a dull smack and an *oof*. He pressed on mercilessly, vaulting over the back of the couch and bouncing along the cushions, his prize lifted high above his head.

"Give it back," Aiden said, far too close behind him for comfort.

"Nuh-uh, you brought this on yourself when you left your baby photos where I could reach them." Elliott jumped to the love seat and turned around, one hand keeping the album up by the ceiling, the other stretched in front of him, warding Aiden off as he marched closer, panic in his eyes. "Rookie mistake, buddy. I can't *not* see, now that I know there's pictures of tiny Aiden here."

"That isn't going to happen," Aiden said ominously, advancing with his arms spread wide in case Elliott made a break for it. "Those pictures were put in an album instead of a frame for a reason."

"Exactly. I'm guessing that the reason is that you were an adorably funny-looking kid before you grew into that face." Elliott tapped his chin with a finger. "Yup, I can see it. The eyebrows, the ears, they would've been pretty goofy looking— Ah!"

Aiden had lunged forward and grabbed him around the waist, flipping him and dragging him down to the couch. Elliott tried to keep the book out of reach, but he was off-balance, his feet on one side of Aiden's lap and his ass on the other, cramped in the small space between the arms of the love seat, so he cut his losses and opened it to a random page.

"Oh my god," he said, staring at the four color photos of Aiden surrounded by his sisters, the family dog, and his parents. "I was right. You were so goofy."

Aiden sighed and stopped reaching for the book. "Well, that's it. The illusion is ruined. Might as well look all you want. It won't make a difference now that you know I'm actually part troll."

Elliott burst out laughing and pulled Aiden closer so that he could rub his face in the hollow where Aiden's jaw met neck. He was still a little worried about being contagious, since he was only two days out of the worst of his cold, but Aiden had spent all of Saturday and this morning trying to convince him that he didn't mind. And Elliott probably wouldn't have been able to stop himself from nudging away that pout even if he'd still been throwing up every few hours.

"But a very cute troll," he offered, patting Aiden's cheeks. "I mean, that hair. It's so fluffy, I just want to pet it."

Aiden sighed again and took the album, flipping it to the first page. Elliott devoured every picture, smiling and cooing at hours-old Aiden in the hospital and his squished, jaundiced face, teasing him about how brave his parents must have been to take him home with them when he was clearly a changeling. He burst out in giggles multiple times at the evolution of Aiden's hair, all the way to the end of high school, when he'd finally figured out how to make it look as attractive as the rest of him.

Elliott pointed to a picture. "And that's Jill?"

"Yeah."

"What's the age difference between you?"

"Six years. And eight between her and Shannon, our older sister. Our parents insist that Jill was planned, but she counted back nine months once and she has her suspicions about their romantic second honeymoon to Paris. I try not to think about it too much."

"Understandable. I did the math and I can never enjoy St. Patrick's Day the same way again." Elliott turned another page and saw a photo of Aiden and his parents, all smiling brightly. "They seem nice."

"They are. I think I'll keep them."

Elliott looked back at the picture, and saw the same quirk of Aiden's lips on his father's face. He turned another page, and his fingers froze on a picture of a teenaged Innes, lounging on a porch with his feet propped on a playfully scowling Aiden. He stared at the photo for a long time. It was surreal to see someone he used to find so impressively larger-than-life just being a normal person who horsed around with his family.

"We were pretty close when we were younger," Aiden said softly, and Elliott tore his eyes away from Innes's bizarrely relaxed posture. Aiden's eyes were unfocused even as they roamed over the picture. "There's only eight years between us, almost like with Jill, so he felt more like an older brother than an uncle. The difference is that his parents never let him forget he was a mistake."

Elliott winced. Regardless of Aiden's feelings regarding Innes, it must have been hard for him to know his grandparents were so flawed. Elliott hadn't known his grandparents, since they'd passed before he was born, one set on American soil, the other back in the old country. As a kid, he'd imagined them as smiling, wrinkled elves who would've given him cookies and patted him on the head, but real grandparents were just human. Some were cruel or too careless with their words.

"You aren't close now," Elliott said. It wasn't a question. Aiden's office was only one floor away from his uncle, and yet they rarely saw each other.

Aiden shook his head, his lips turning downward. "No. He's my family, so I'll always be loyal to him, but he became . . . cynical. Constantly being compared to my dad, being gay and aggressively out when his parents were alive to disapprove, some other stuff. It all compounded and made him harder. I think he'd rather die than feel inadequate again, so he builds himself up as this vain playboy with a mean streak that gets him what he wants. I miss him. The old him. I decided I wanted to go into the family business when I was nine years old because, at fifteen, Innes already knew that was what he wanted to do, and I wanted to be like him. My mom too, obviously, but mostly Innes. It wasn't long after that that he really changed for the worse, but it took me a while to stop wanting to impress him, and by that time, I was already planning on law school." Aiden shook his head, reached for the next page in the album, and started to turn it. "I'm sorry. This must be weird for you."

Elliott blocked Aiden's hand and the Ghost of Innes Past continued to smirk at them. "It's fine. I figured he didn't pop out of the womb with a sneer and a holier-than-thou attitude. It's kind of nice to know that he got it from his tragic supervillain backstory, rather than it just coming naturally to him."

Aiden shrugged, and his eyes sharpened. "I'm not excusing his shitty choices. My dad had the same parents he did, and he turned out fine."

"Lucky."

"Yeah."

Aiden tapped a finger on the stiff page of the album. Elliott could see a question forming in the tension in his face. He was pretty sure he knew what was coming and wasn't looking forward to answering, though he was surprised it'd taken Aiden so long to bring it up.

"Elliott, could I ask you something?"

"Yeah." Elliott counted up to five and back down to zero in his head, his fingers twitching almost imperceptibly with each number.

"Why did you break it off with Innes?"

Elliott frowned. He'd been expecting Aiden to ask why Elliott had been with Innes in the first place. The answer to that one would've been easy: because Innes had been in the right place at the right time with the right tax bracket.

"Oh, that," Elliott said, trying not to squirm in his seat. "Why do you want to know?"

"You don't have to tell me. I just wondered, since you always seemed like you got along, up until you didn't."

Elliott couldn't hold in a rough laugh. "I don't know if we ever really *got along*. I didn't like him—"

"Nobody likes him."

"But we were compatible, mostly."

In bed, they'd been evenly matched. On some days it was twenty percent grappling, eighty percent sex. Other days, it was closer to fifty-fifty, though it hadn't started off that way. Innes had liked Elliott's innocence, at the beginning, then he'd liked knowing that he'd contributed to changing Elliott's world view and tinting it a little less rosy pink.

"But it's true, we worked, up until we didn't work anymore, because Innes asked for something I couldn't give him." Elliott felt Aiden tense beneath him, and it took him a few long seconds to realize what Aiden was thinking. "Nothing like that! God, Innes is the worst, but he didn't pressure me into anything weird."

Aiden's body returned to a posture that counted as relaxed, for him. "Good. So, what did happen? If you don't mind telling me."

"It's not that dramatic. Innes asked me to accompany him to a benefit at UCLA. Your family was considering setting up a scholarship fund."

"Yeah, I've been informed. My mother is taking care of it, but they told us last year." Aiden's eyebrows crashed down in a frown. "Wait. Wouldn't that be—"

"Awkward. Yeah. Innes asked me to go with him to this thing on school property, with the dean of my whole department in attendance. I couldn't believe he asked me in the first place, but then he had the balls to be pissed off when I said hell no. I tried to explain that it was too close to home, but he seemed to think that there wasn't any greater risk in that than an event somewhere else in the city."

In retrospect, Elliott's panic about the truth of that had made him react more strongly than usual, but Innes had still pushed his buttons.

"And that's what it came down to," Elliott said. "He must have known that he was asking for something I couldn't give. He acted like he was all miffed, but he was relieved, I think."

"Relieved?"

"It wasn't just the school thing, to be honest," Elliott said, watching his own fingers as they toyed with the buttons at the neck of Aiden's soft shirt. "Our arrangement started to bore him, or at least that's what I gathered from him trying to spice things up."

"Do I want to know?"

Elliott snorted at the wrinkled distaste on Aiden's face. "Probably not. It wasn't that bad. He just started asking for things I'd already said I wasn't interested in, and offering cash incentives so I'd change my mind. I hated that. It was like he was trying to buy more of me than I was already giving. We also started annoying the shit out of each other.

He was basically finished with me, but he doesn't like to be the first one to tap out, so he was trying to find ways to make it more exciting."

"He hates to lose."

"Lawyer," Elliott teased.

Aiden smiled ruefully. "Exactly. It's what makes the good ones great. It's why I'm not going to be one of the Kents in Kent, Kent & Morris for at least another fifteen years."

Elliott raised an eyebrow at him. "You don't hate losing?"

Aiden shrugged. "Not any more than any other person does. I love to win, though. It's what makes me work hard to get clients I can't stand out of jail time for embezzlement they're definitely guilty of."

"Noble."

Aiden rolled his eyes. "Someone has to do it. And it might as well be a guy with the track record to be able to charge them a ridiculous fee."

Elliott laughed. "Nice. So you are a little bit noble."

"I try." Aiden's smile faded, and he stared at Elliott beseechingly. "I stick to a moral code outside of work and hope that it balances out all the not-so-virtuous things."

"I think it does," Elliott said. "I think if you weigh it all up, you're still a good man."

"I hope so," Aiden said, his eyes unfocusing. "It keeps me up some nights."

"So, why don't you quit?"

Elliott hadn't meant to say it. He had some stake in hoping that Aiden stayed employed, but the blankness of Aiden's face had made it pop out without any hope of a filter.

"I couldn't do that."

"Why not? You've already said you don't need to work, trust-fund baby."

Aiden shook his head, adjusting minutely in his seat. "That's not it."

"Then, what? What's keeping you from throwing in the towel when it obviously makes you miserable?"

"It doesn't make me miserable."

"Oh? Then there's a secondary reason for your misery?"

"You," Aiden said, slanting him a look. "You cause me misery."

"Oh, ha, ha. I'm being serious. Why haven't you done something else, or tried to change your specialty?"

Aiden's hands curled into fists on the edge of the photo album, and he studied Kents gone by for a long minute. "It's not about what I want. I'm thinking of my family too. My mother, mostly. I'm the only one of her three children who showed any interest in following in her footsteps. She was so happy when I told her my plans, and that made me happy as well."

"But not anymore."

"No. But I still couldn't leave the firm, not with her support behind me, and there's no room for me to try something else while I'm there. I don't think it would work anyway."

"That sucks."

It was all Elliott could think to say, but it felt insufficient. He was glad that it at least pulled a tiny smile from Aiden's lips.

"I know." Aiden's forehead creased. "I'm nearly thirty, headed for another ulcer—"

"Another?"

"And one of the only things that makes me happy is a relationship I have to pay for."

Elliott knew what Aiden meant. There was no offense for him to take, because it was the truth, and for once, Elliott only heard the positive.

"I make you happy?" he asked, in a voice that sounded timid to his own ears.

Covering Elliott's hand with his own, Aiden said, "Of course. I've told you that before."

Elliott closed the album and let it slide to the floor beside the love seat (or couch with delusions of grandeur, as Elliott liked to call it).

Aiden's hair was soft and clean after his shower that morning, and it lacked the sticky-crisp product that usually made it stay in its normal style. Elliott brushed some of it away from Aiden's forehead, letting it slip through his fingers as he framed Aiden's face with his palms, then he stretched up to lay a chaste kiss on the worried line of Aiden's lips.

The next real kiss felt new.

It was the first they'd had all weekend, since Elliott hadn't felt well enough for more than binge-watching TV shows and complaining about having to eat nothing but toast and soup. This morning, though, his energy levels had surged, and he'd felt more human than he had in two days. When he'd woken up next to Aiden, he'd looked at Aiden's body, open and relaxed in sleep, and wanted.

It had been a comfortable want that had previously been uncomplicated and easily acted upon. This morning though, after admitting to himself that he needed to step back or risk fucking everything up, it had been anything but simple. That didn't mean it wasn't good. They still fit together perfectly, warm lips sliding together sweetly.

An energy fizzed between them that hadn't existed before. It simmered inside him and made him clutch tightly at Aiden's shoulders, then swelled until he got scared of it. Was he imagining things? Or maybe *he* was feeling this stuff, but from Aiden's perspective, it was business as usual.

Aiden broke the contact, sucking in air, but he brought Elliott's body even closer, bending his spine with a strong arm behind his back, curling Elliott up even more.

"Elliott. Fuck," he breathed into the space between their lips, then they crashed together again.

The speed and biting fervor were at odds with their languorous weekend, an intoxicating contrast that made Elliott's head spin. It also made the new affection shiver in his chest, because he could swear Aiden felt it too.

Aiden's hand slid down his back, slipping his fingers under the band of Elliott's borrowed flannel pajama pants. They stilled there, pressing into the skin at his lower back, not demanding or pushing, but claiming those few inches as territory gained by this one, hot kiss.

"Aiden?"

The familiar woman's voice came from the front door. Elliott and Aiden froze.

"Are you here? You'd better be decent, because I'm coming in."

Elliott looked down at himself. He was basically clothed. The only part of him that he needed to cover was— Elliott jumped as the reality of their position caught up with him. They lurched away from each other just as Jill came into the living room, and Aiden's hand was still sliding out of Elliott's pants when she saw them and stopped dead.

Aiden and Elliott quit trying to extricate themselves. The damage was done. Gym buddies didn't cuddle with their hands in each other's pants.

"I fucking knew it," Jill hissed.

Elliott winced, then reclaimed his legs and stood up, tripping over the photo album as he hiked up his pants. He needed to get out of there. Aiden would—probably—survive Jill's wrath, but Elliott had no such guarantee.

He flinched when Jill let out a squeal, then he took a step toward her and the front door. He didn't get far, because Aiden grabbed his arm with an urgent, "Wait," as Jill started jumping in place.

"I knew it, I knew it!" Jill said, a wide, mischievous grin on her face. While Elliott blinked at the abrupt shift, she slapped Aiden's shoulder hard enough that the sound cracked in the high-ceilinged room. "Why the hell didn't you tell me, you asshole?"

"I—" Aiden stammered. "There was nothing to tell. This . . ." He gestured between them while Elliott watched helplessly, wondering why he hadn't left yet. "It's a recent thing. It's changed since the fundraiser."

He looked at Elliott directly as he said it. Elliott's stomach leaped into his esophagus. They hadn't talked about it, but things had been different between them since the night of the fundraiser and the morning that had followed. Elliott hadn't acknowledged it until recently—it had freaked him out too much—but Aiden was basically telling him now that he'd felt the same shift.

He was staring into Elliott's eyes and telling him that they could be more.

Elliott looked away. He fixed his eyes on Jill and tried to ignore Aiden's burning gaze until he could think straight, without panic and gut-reaction happiness clouding everything.

"Uh-huh. Sure," she said, her eyebrow rising in a manner so much like Aiden that Elliott wanted to laugh. "And when were you going to tell me that *this*"—she flapped her hand in an exaggerated version of what Aiden had done—"had 'changed'?"

"Maybe never?" Aiden's voice was tight, his words clipped, maybe by Elliott's refusal to make eye contact. "It isn't a big deal."

"Not a big deal?" Jill let her purse fall to the ground with a *thunk*, then crossed her arms over her chest. "Aiden, the last time you had a significant other that lasted longer than a single night, you were in college, and you went to Chili's for all three dates."

There was a quick intake of breath, then a short pause. "That's an exaggeration," Aiden said, sheepishly.

Jill's lips twitched, and she stepped closer, grabbing Aiden's hands. "Maybe, but only a bit. Aiden, I know you. You don't keep things like this from us, not for long. I'd bet money that you were going to tell us about him at the party this Saturday."

Elliott's heart pounded, and he finally snuck a glance up at Aiden. That couldn't be true. How could Aiden have expected them to go from almost-friends who have sex appointments to meet-the-family serious relationship?

When he saw Aiden's face, though, he knew the answer. He hadn't. Aiden didn't seem embarrassed or hopeful. Just resigned. Disappointed that it was never going to happen.

"Jill," Aiden said, looking down at her hands. "It's complicated. I want to tell you everything, but in this case, I need some privacy. Don't be mad?"

She stared at Aiden in silence, then withdrew her hands, wrapping her arms instead around his shoulders. She was tall enough that her head rested comfortably on the top of his shoulder.

"All we want is for you to be happy," she said. "We thought that if you were happy on your own, then that was fine. But we could see that you weren't. You're not like me, preferring your own company to anyone else's. You don't want anyone to know, but you don't do so well on your own. You always did need a teddy bear to hug."

"Thanks," Aiden muttered, a smile softening his sarcasm. Elliott tried to keep his eyes on the ground instead of the tender moment, but it was hard not to look to Aiden, who was watching him over Jill's shoulder.

Elliott bounced on the balls of his feet, indecisive. He wanted to stay, to ask Aiden if anything was going to change. But he sure didn't want to have a conversation where he was forced to make a choice between his next paycheck and whatever they had between them.

Jill pulled away, then poked Aiden in the chest, hard enough that Aiden rubbed the spot.

"You've been different lately. Even Mom and Dad can tell." She suddenly turned to Elliott and pointed at him accusingly. "I was really hoping you were the reason why."

"Well, I don't know if . . ." Elliott stammered.

"Don't even. The timeline fits."

"How the hell do you know the timeline?" Aiden didn't sound put out anymore. Just baffled.

She tapped her finger on her chin, smirking knowingly. "I'd say . . . January, right? Or the beginning of February?"

Elliott and Aiden looked at each other. She was right, but did that mean they had to tell her so? Elliott didn't know Jill well, but from what he'd witnessed, she'd probably get insufferable.

"How did you guess that?" Aiden asked, with an indulgent roll of his eyes.

"That was when you stopped calling us twice a week. We assumed you were busy, but we didn't think you were *getting* busy until the fundraiser, and I saw you watching Elliott's ass like a piece of meat—"

"Yes, okay, Jill. Your incredible observational skills are appreciated. Shut up now."

Jill sighed gustily, but she was smiling too much for genuine annoyance. "Fine. Shutting up. Except that I did come over for a reason. Catching my brother rounding the bases was just a horrifically scarring added bonus."

"And whose fault is that? Yelling 'I'm coming in' isn't exactly adequate warning to—"

"Doesn't matter. Since I was home for the weekend, Mom told me to come visit you. Her motives were as transparent as they were selfish. She really wanted me to pressure you into confirming you're coming to the birthday party at Mom and Dad's this weekend."

"Who's this one for?"

"Jim's kid."

Aiden groaned so painfully that Elliott actually jumped an inch. His lips twitched in an unwilling smile at the picture Aiden's misery made: His shoulders slumped belligerently. His face wrinkled like a toddler's did in the minutes before a meltdown. His head dropped back to look at the ceiling as if asking a higher power, *Why must I have family members? Why must they have children? What have I done to deserve this?*

"Should I take that as a no?" Jill asked, sweetly.

Aiden groaned again, then let his face fall into his hand. "No. I like Jim."

Jill hummed her agreement.

"I should go. God, I don't want to. I hate birthday parties."

"Well, lucky for you, no one's asking you to enjoy it. All they're asking is that you show up long enough to eat some cake and sit through the parents trying to make the kid read all the cards."

"Yikes. It'll be awful."

Jill nodded sagely. "Undoubtedly. But you kind of have to go."

"I know. Tell Mom I'll be there, but I will leave the moment anyone breaks out a piñata. I have to draw the line somewhere."

"Will do. But hey, look on the bright side. At least this time, you won't have any of the aunts asking you if you're seeing anyone." Her eyes swung over to Elliott.

Elliott took an involuntary step back. "Whaaat? No, thank you."

"Oh, come on," she pleaded. "However new this is," she waved her hand even more crazily this time, "you've still known each other for a good couple of months."

Try a couple of years.

"Your mother isn't expecting me. She won't be prepared for an extra," he countered.

Jill held firm. "Our dad makes enough to feed an army. We'll have leftovers for days, even with you there."

"I'd feel like I was intruding,"

"You wouldn't be. In our family, plus-ones are always welcome."

"Do I get a say in this?" Aiden cut in.

"Yes!" Jill grabbed Aiden's arm and made him face Elliott, pulling her best pouty face. Elliott was impervious. She had nothing on Kevin. "If you don't go, Aiden will be all alone. You don't want that, do you, Aiden? Tell him you don't want to be alone."

Jill's pout seemed to work better on Aiden than it did on Elliott. He looked at Elliott helplessly as she hung off of him, her lip trembling without any attempt to make it seem genuine.

Elliott felt like he was in the last round of a game show. The wrong answer to the One Important Question—in this case, whether he would cross from professional territory into very personal—would see him lose all the progress he'd made. His progress being the new vibe between him and Aiden, and the yarn Aiden was spinning about how long they'd been *together*. If he said no, would Aiden be offended and cut him loose, ending any potential for a relationship?

If he said yes, could he go back from there to the safety and comfort of three appointments a week and a monthly direct deposit, no icky feelings involved?

If he said yes . . .

If he said yes? What the hell was he thinking even considering it?

He was thinking . . . that he wanted to see what Aiden was like with his family. He'd seen him with Jill, glimpsed a side of the whiny, sensitive child he might have been before he grew up to be a generous, self-possessed man. He'd get to see how Aiden fit into the family. The middle child, the only boy, the one to continue the family business. The bisexual one, but was that a big part of his identity in his family? It seemed like he kept his dating history pretty much to himself.

When it came down to it, Elliott was still working a job. If Aiden wanted him to go to a birthday party, that was his prerogative. It didn't matter if Elliott did or didn't want to go. That he desperately *did* was just a bonus.

And if Aiden's wide eyes over the top of Jill's head were anything to go by, he wanted Elliott there.

"Okay," Elliott said. "I'll come if it's on a day I can make it."

"Yes!" Jill shouted, dropping the puppy-dog eyes. "It's on Saturday. Be there."

"We will be," Aiden said, dodging her flailing fist. "But please don't make a big deal out of it."

She rolled her eyes at him as she picked up her abandoned purse from the floor. "Are you kidding me? That's not really an option you have. While I might be completely circumspect, Mom and Dad are going to flip when they find out you're bringing someone to meet the family." Her smile turned playful. "God, we thought we'd have to convince you to pay someone to date you like Uncle Innes does. I told them you hadn't quite reached that level of pitiable sleaze."

Aiden tensed, and the nausea Elliott had fought off all weekend came crashing back. It was the gala all over again. He wanted to disappear into the floor.

"Let me guess," Aiden said, his voice tight and neutral. "Your friend's gossip again?"

"Of course," Jill said, flippantly. "Heather knows all and shares all. Lucky for me. But I don't share half of what she tells me about Innes with Mom and Dad. There's just some things Dad doesn't want to know about his kid brother, even if Innes is middle-aged now."

Thirty-six is not middle-aged, Elliott wanted to say, but he didn't dare. It was a pointless distinction anyway. The only reason it was important to him was so he could tell himself that no, he hadn't had sex with someone as old as his father. Not quite.

Aiden had frozen, his eyes fixed on the ground. He looked almost as ill as Elliott felt, and that was enough to make Elliott wish for his blanket cocoon again.

It made sense that Aiden would be disturbed. How embarrassed would Aiden be if his sister found out that not only was he doing what she'd just insulted, but that he was doing it with the same person as her "sleazy" uncle?

They were living in a goddamned soap opera.

"Will Innes be there?" Aiden asked, apparently recovering himself.

"At a family birthday party? Are you kidding? He hates them more than you do. He'd rather contract a virulent toe fungus than be around that chaos. Everyone else will be though."

Aiden's lips turned down in a pout that wasn't nearly as dramatic as Jill's, but couldn't be mistaken for a manly scowl. "Why does he get to skip out and I don't?"

Jill stepped close to him, her purse on her arm, and clapped her hands on Aiden's cheeks. "Because you're a pushover, Aiden. And Jim will be ecstatic to see you, even if little Riley won't."

Aiden mumbled something about little Riley that didn't sound complimentary.

"Well." Jill dug her sunglasses out of her bag. "I was going to make you take me out for lunch, but I don't want to interrupt anything."

"You already did," Elliott pointed out.

"Take this as the kindness it is, Elliott, and don't question it," she tossed over her shoulder as she made her way to the door. Before it closed, she yelled, "Welcome to the family!"

The silence she left behind her was dazed. After a few quiet seconds, Aiden blew out a long breath. "I'm sorry," he said, with a pained expression.

"For what?" Elliott was still numb.

"I didn't know she was coming, I swear."

"I know."

"She can be a bit much. You don't actually have to come to the party if you don't want to, that's completely outside of what you agreed to."

"Do you really want me there?" Elliott asked. There was no other question he'd rather ask, and there was nothing more important than an honest answer.

"Yes," Aiden answered right away.

Elliott released the breath he'd been holding. "Okay, then. I'll go with you."

Aiden looked like he might argue again, like he wasn't sure if Elliott wasn't forcing himself into something, but Elliott's face must have changed his mind. "All right, then."

Some of Elliott's tension leaked away, but he didn't quite relax. Too much had changed for that to happen. With all the revelations, he felt like he'd been awake and sprinting for twelve hours.

Jill had reacted better than he could have hoped. Still, Elliott wished he could go back in time and hide in a closet before she came in. A lot of things seemed trickier than they had half an hour ago.

Elliott was going to meet the family. The family of Aiden, his lover/employer. His employer who might have the same beginnings of feelings—*liar, liar*, his conscience whispered—that he did.

Jitters shook outward from Elliott's stomach. Their consequence-free bubble of a weekend was over. There would be no more ignoring things until they went away. That time was past. Wasn't it?

"Elliott," Aiden said, softly. "We should probably talk about—"

"Yeah, I know." Elliott ran stressed-out fingers through his messy hair. "But could we just . . . not?"

Aiden frowned, giving Elliott the side-eye. "What do you mean?"

Elliott stepped up to Aiden and took his wrists in his hands, running his thumbs over Aiden's pulse points like worry stones. "Are you happy?" Elliott shook his head and rephrased. "Is there something that you absolutely need to change about us, how we've been working. Like, right now?"

Aiden hesitated, looking from Elliott's hands to his face. "Well, no. Not urgently, but aren't things a little different?"

Elliott nodded, even as his heart rate spiked. "They could be. But if you're happy, and I'm happy, and we make each other happy, can we leave it? And not talk about it?" Aiden blinked and drew breath, but Elliott pressed on. "Just for a little while. I need some time. This is—" He swallowed, grappling with his panic. "—a lot. I'm not prepared for—"

"Elliott, it's fine," Aiden soothed, flipping his wrists around and grasping the tops of Elliott's forearms firmly. Elliott leaned into them, swaying closer to Aiden's body but not pressing in yet. "Don't worry about it. You take the time you need, I don't want to pressure you into anything you're not comfortable with. This is odd for me too." He smiled ruefully. "I swear, I didn't want more than what I asked for when we started this. But I didn't know you. I didn't think—"

"Stop," Elliott interrupted, pulling his hands from Aiden's to cover his ears. "Stop, stop, stop. Please."

Aiden lifted his hands in surrender. "Stopping, sorry."

Elliott gave in to the urge and wrapped his arms around Aiden's waist, resting his cheek on Aiden's shoulder and murmuring into the soft fabric covering his warm skin. "This is happening. Something's changed, and I'm not ignoring it or denying it, but give me some time to deal with it. Let me bring it up when I'm ready. Okay?"

"Of course." Aiden took Elliott's face in his hands and kissed him, just once, gently. "I'll wait patiently."

It was reckless, Elliott acknowledged as he lunged in for a deeper kiss, a long and slow one. The choices he was making—mostly, his daydreaming of a perfect outcome—would have consequences, eventually.

But fuck, he didn't want to think about them. Not when Aiden's hands were stroking up his sides and down the length of his back so tenderly, like he could memorize every inconsequential nonerogenous zone.

He wanted more Sundays like this, so Aiden could press him into the couch and touch him all over to make up for the days between visits. More nights when he slept over and didn't watch the clock. Whether he would allow himself to have these things in the long-term was a question he didn't want to think about, let alone answer.

It was the beginning of the month. He had about thirty days before Aiden would pay him again. He'd decide before then whether he wanted to stick to the status quo or . . . do what exactly? Be with Aiden for real, no paycheck involved, but not have enough money for next year to help his dad keep the house he'd grown up in?

A little under a month, he thought as Aiden's mouth whisked away his brain power. A month to decide in which way he was going to ruin this fragile, ephemeral feeling he didn't want to call love.

Chapter  11

"**Y**ou're quiet."

Elliott looked over at Aiden behind the steering wheel. "Am I?"

Elliott loved driving. He missed it now that he was close to everywhere he wanted to be in LA. Whenever he was home, he badgered his dad into letting him drive his police cruiser.

He wasn't as good at being a passenger. He got bored too easily, and when he was bored, his default was restless and loud, as Aiden knew.

Aiden's eyes never wavered from the road ahead. "Are you nervous?"

"Now, what makes you say that?"

Elliott had been sitting on his hands for the last half hour to keep them from tapping out maddening rhythms on the dashboard of Aiden's fancy car. He couldn't feel them anymore, but he still didn't take them out. The discomfort distracted him from counting the minutes until they arrived at Aiden's parents' house.

They used to live right in the city. Aiden had been born and raised there, with plenty of trips to the trails on the weekends. He'd told Elliott all about the cabin they had, and how they'd wake up before the sun to make the trip. The new house wasn't as far as that, but it was still far enough that the buildings got less close together, and the terrain started to look a lot more like a desert instead of a tropical oasis hundreds of miles wide.

"You shouldn't be nervous," Aiden told him, as if it were that simple. "They'll like you. If they even notice you, that is. There's probably going to be so many people there that you'll get lost in the shuffle."

"We can only hope."

Aiden flashed him a bright, quick smile. "We'll be there in about five minutes."

The urge to wiggle his fingers disappeared and paralysis set in, stiffening Elliott's neck as he watched scenery go by.

The houses were so nice in this area. Huge, like Aiden's parents' home must be if it was going to accommodate as many people as Aiden had told him to expect. Elliott wasn't sure if he was dreading being mistaken for the help or hoping for it.

Next to him, Aiden took a deep breath. "Are you—"

"Please don't ask again if I'm sure," Elliott said, before Aiden could get it out. "I am. I want to go. It's just difficult for me to feel like I belong here, especially when we're still figuring out what we are."

Aiden took his eyes off the highway long enough to send Elliott one of his tiny smiles. Elliott returned it right away, and the fluttering in his stomach switched gears.

After Elliott had gone home on Sunday, he'd immediately wanted to go back, but they both had their own lives, and Elliott had needed some time away. He hadn't had any contact with Aiden for a few days, even by text. But when he'd shown up for their regular Wednesday appointment, and Aiden had hugged him hello, he'd been hit by conflicting emotions.

Happiness. Disappointment.

Both had been present and accounted for when he'd realized that it wasn't just the long weekend and his illness that had awoken something in them both. This epiphany made things significantly more difficult for him.

Their standard night in had felt more like a date than ever, but the best kind of date. The kind where they'd already broken down the barriers and seen some of each other's vulnerabilities. They had been relaxed around each other even while they were still high on the undefined newness of the relationship Elliott wasn't ready to name.

Aiden threw on his turn signal, taking them down yet another road lined with large houses. "At least Innes isn't coming."

Elliott shrugged, the motion pulling at his trapped hands. "I wouldn't have minded if he was. Have to face him sometime."

Even after he'd started getting paid by Aiden, it had seemed pretty likely that he could go his entire life without having to see Innes again, but getting involved in Aiden's personal life would inevitably lead to a run-in with his past. That was just another bullet point on the Shouldn't He side of his Should He or Shouldn't He list.

Ticktock, ticktock, the calendar in his head chanted. He now had one week less to go until payday. One week less to decide what he would do.

"So, how isolated do these houses get?" Elliott asked, shutting up his own brain.

"Not very. Why?"

"Oh, no reason."

Aiden shifted his fists on the steering wheel and shot him a glance, his eyebrows pulled together. "A likely story. Why do you— Elliott."

"Yes?" Elliott asked innocently.

"There is no way that I am letting you give me road head."

Elliott gasped and finally freed one of his hands to clasp it to his chest like a dowager countess. "I would never! You have no idea how many hours I spent listening to my dad—a cop, you remember—lecturing about distracted driving. I wouldn't even give you a road hickey."

"Good." Aiden nodded, and they drove for a couple of minutes in silence, while Elliott massaged the feeling back into his fingers. "Wait. If you didn't want to do that, why did you ask about—"

"I never said anything about *side*-of-the-road head."

Aiden's laughter flew out the open window as they sped closer toward the Kent homestead.

"Innes has a *daughter*?" Elliott shout-whispered, his hand around Aiden's arm in a death grip.

They were blessedly alone after half an hour of introductions. There were so many people that Elliott was seeing stars—he certainly wasn't seeing any names attached to faces. He'd stopped trying to remember any of them after the fifteenth person had stopped them on their way to the kitchen to find Aiden's parents.

He remembered one name only: Mimi.

Mimi, the one person Aiden hadn't explained his relationship with. At least, not until they were walking away and Elliott had asked. Aiden had glanced at him quizzically, identified her, then let himself be dragged to an unoccupied room.

"I thought you knew," Aiden said, his eyes pinging from Elliott's white-knuckled hand to his face.

"No, I did not fucking know!" Elliott hissed. "It isn't like Innes and I did a lot of talking about our personal lives. And she's . . . she's my age?"

"A bit younger. She just turned eighteen."

Elliott let out a pained wheeze that might have resembled a laugh. "So he had a teenaged daughter the entire time he was fucking me. Including when I was nineteen, *still a teenager*."

Aiden grimaced. "Yeah. I think that's probably why he didn't tell you about her. He must have figured you'd feel awkward about it."

Elliott planted his hands on his hips and widened his eyes theatrically. "Really? Now why would that be? What possible reason would I have to feel awkward about being born within a couple years of the girl whose dad I was fucking? Oh, god." He let his head fall into his hands and moaned. "This is a nightmare. Please tell me she never knew about me. Tell me she never heard my name or saw me in some picture Innes got tagged in on Facebook."

"I don't think so," Aiden murmured, at a volume much more appropriate for such a sordid conversation. "I can't be sure, but Mimi never brought up his arm candy, and she's not the type to stay quiet about that kind of dirt. In any case, she's only just started coming to things like this. Birthdays and Thanksgiving and what not."

"Should I even ask?"

Aiden glanced back at the closed door to the living room behind them, as if staring through it to the girl who stuck out, a skyscraper in a landscape of homey bungalows.

"She and Innes don't talk much, but she wanted to know this side of the family. Mostly to spite her mother, probably. I've only met the woman a couple of times, but she's a piece of work, and she hates all the Kents on principle."

"Jesus. This seems like soap-opera levels of family drama."

"We've got a couple of skeletons, sure. Innes was only just eighteen when Mimi was born, and he refused to marry her mother because they would have killed each other in a year. He pays child support, but other than that, he stays out of Mimi's life, partly because her mother thinks we're all scheming, snobby pieces of trash, and partly because—" His lip quirked humorlessly. "—can you imagine Innes as a father?"

Elliott whistled. "Yikes. Not really."

"Well, there you go."

Like a party balloon deflating, Elliott released a stream of anxious breath. It'd been less than an hour, and he was already exhausted by the meet-the-family outing. He'd expected to learn more about Aiden through his family, but he hadn't expected, or wanted, to learn more about Innes.

A daughter.

The revelation didn't change anything. Innes was as much of a closed book as ever, and Elliott still had no desire to open it for a better look. It did, however, make him uncomfortably aware that there might be more chapters than he'd anticipated.

He hated this metaphor. He wanted out.

"Answer me one thing," he said. "Did Innes actually name his daughter Mimi?"

Aiden laughed. "No. I think she named herself that. But he didn't have a hand in her given name, either. Her mother called her Miriam, and Mimi hated it as much as Innes did."

That sounded more like the Innes Elliott knew, but it didn't settle his nerves in the least.

"All right," he said. "For the sake of my sanity, I'm going to pretend that the last ten minutes didn't happen, so that I can function normally until later, when I'll actually vomit from how creeped out I feel."

"Noted."

"For now, what do we do? I'm sorry, I have no idea where we are or where we're going. I still feel like I'm about the size of a bug in this house, and that's probably translated to the size of my brain."

The house wasn't just big. It was casually, effortlessly luxurious in a way that made Elliott want to crawl up the chimney where he belonged, with his broom and his grimy cap.

Ticktock. Ticktock.

Aiden didn't seem to notice or mind his existential crisis. "You'll get used to it," he told Elliott as he pulled them away from their quiet corner toward the chattering of more people in a room nearby. "I suppose we could go help out in the kitchen, if they need it."

"Don't bother, you'll only get in the way," a commanding voice said.

"Hi, Mom."

Aiden went over and hugged the woman who'd come through the door behind them, which presumably led to the kitchen. Elliott was relieved to have identified where the food was. If he stayed where he was, he wouldn't starve to death if the rapture happened and he was left in this maze of a house.

"And you must be Elliott," Aiden's mom said, extending her hand.

Elliott shook it firmly. "It's nice to meet you, Mrs. Kent."

The Kent genes seemed to have overpowered hers for the most part, because she and Aiden didn't look much alike, physically. Her coloring was lighter, her eyebrows nowhere near as majestic as Jill's. Despite that, there was something about her kind but inescapably scrutinizing stare that reminded Elliott of Aiden's intense gaze.

"It's Kent-Graham, actually."

"Oh, sorry—"

She waved her hand. "It's fine. I took my husband's last name at my parents' request, but I only committed halfway. My name is very unlike my marriage in that way."

Elliott laughed a little hesitantly. She had the same deadpan delivery as her son, and while he'd gotten used to Aiden's jokes, he couldn't be sure he'd understand hers.

"But please, you must call me Catherine."

Elliott deliberately relaxed his posture, reaching deep to find the calmest, most confident version of himself. "Catherine, then. Are you sure we couldn't help in the kitchen?"

Crossing his fingers behind his back, Elliott chanted, *Please say no, please say no.* He wasn't a bad cook, but he hadn't had a lot of practice, living in a dorm. If the kitchen was as well-appointed as the rest of the house, he'd be worried over breaking a butter knife worth hundreds.

Catherine held up her hands. "Oh, no. They're at the stage when too many people in there would only make things more difficult. Come outside with me, instead. It's a lovely day."

She led them through the busy kitchen to the backyard, where people were milling about, eyeing the door they'd come out of, as if staring would make the food arrive faster.

Catherine smoothly introduced them to more people than Elliott could possibly have remembered, and he could suddenly see in her the brilliant lawyer Aiden had told him about, the other Kent in Kent, Kent & Morris.

Even when she got distracted by the younger members of the clan, wiping messy chins and exclaiming over newly loose teeth, it was surprisingly easy to imagine her as a prosecution-crushing genius. It was in the way she moved people to her will without them even knowing they were in motion, not in a mean-spirited manner, just an inexorable one. She was quickly embroiled in an impenetrable crowd, so Aiden steered them away, and Elliott followed him gratefully.

In the back of his mind, he was constantly aware of Mimi. Aloof and reserved, she stuck out of the group. A part of the festivities, but also not. She didn't appear to know everyone as well as they all knew each other, and she didn't attempt to keep up with the lightning pace of the conversations around her, staying conspicuously silent instead.

Despite her separation, she looked a lot like the rest of the Kents, with her lips pressed in a hard line. She looked like Innes, especially around the eyes, which freaked him out a little bit, but he got used to it pretty quickly, especially since he was so busy meeting all the other people in Aiden's family who *also* looked like Innes, and Aiden's dad.

Jill must have done a good job downplaying the significance of Elliott's presence, because he never got the grilling he'd prepared for. Everyone was too busy talking about the minutiae they'd missed in each other's lives to pay much attention to the stranger in their midst. It was a cheerful sort of disregard. It didn't feel the same as being ignored by Very Important Pricks at parties, because it wasn't a deliberate snub.

Elliott was leaning on the picnic table waiting for Aiden to come back from the bathroom when Catherine cornered him.

"You haven't been together long, have you?" Her powerful, glinting stare pinned him in place.

"No," he said. With any other person, he might have delayed and asked how long constituted as *long*, but Catherine would have seen through him.

She smiled like a proud mother cat. "I knew it. You have that look about you both, like you're afraid that the next thing you say will be the deal breaker. I wouldn't worry, though."

"No?" Elliott asked.

Behind her left shoulder, Aiden was making his way toward them, panic on his face.

"He's in deep with you. I can see it. I know my boy. He might be almost thirty now, and as much of a closed book as ever, but I can still tell. You aren't leaving him behind in that, are you?"

Across the patio, Aiden was waylaid by an elderly relative. He threw Elliott an apologetic look, then went right back to listening to his great-aunt or grandmother. He listened intently, with his customary tense almost-frown, but Elliott could tell that he was happy here, surrounded by people who knew him and his stern face and knew how to see beyond it, to the true empathy inside.

"No," he answered Catherine. If he wasn't falling already, then he was clinging on to the edge with a pinky finger.

They ended up planting themselves in a corner of the backyard and not moving except for more food—burgers and salads and sickly sweet birthday cake, like a proper spring barbecue—while a revolving stream of cousins and aunts and uncles occupied the seats beside them.

"I like your family," Elliott said, during one of the rare times that they were alone.

"They like you too," Aiden said, smiling back.

One of the best parts of the day was seeing various children toddle up to Aiden and press their sticky hands into his elbow, chatting up a storm while Aiden listened and made appropriate noises, even though their babble was unintelligible.

"They're like cats," Elliott told him, laughing at Aiden's perplexed expression when a two-year-old stumbled drunkenly away after presenting Aiden with a treasured stuffed bear. "They've fixated on the person who cares the least about them."

"I don't mind kids," Aiden said, shrugging. "But I don't know what to do with them."

Elliott fixed him with a level stare. "Really? You don't mind them?"

"Most of them." Aiden rolled his eyes to the clear sky above them. "Honestly, I feel bad. I like Jim a lot. He's one of my favorite cousins because we have a lot in common. I just hate his kid so much. He's such a horrible child. But they seem to like him, so that's all that matters, I guess."

"I've heard it's easier to like your own kids than other people's," Elliott pointed out. "God knows, my parents were the only ones who liked me when I was a kid."

"Yeah?"

"I was awful. Too much energy, not enough impulse control. I never *tried* to annoy anyone, but there are only so many knock-knock jokes you can memorize and spout rapid-fire in a permanent outdoor voice before people—mostly teachers—start to lose their minds."

"I bet your dad's proud of you. And your mom would be too, if she were here."

Elliott's smile faded.

"I'm sorry," Aiden said. "Was it insensitive of me to talk about her?"

"No, of course not. It's no big deal, really. I'm used to reminders that she's gone."

"Is that something you get used to?"

Elliott blinked. "I— Why wouldn't it be?"

Aiden grasped Elliott's hand, which was dangling between the arms of their patio chairs. "She was your mom. I wouldn't expect that you'd get over her not being there."

Aiden's palm was warm against Elliott's. Elliott looked down at it, trying to come up with one of the normal placating brush-offs he gave to other people who expressed more concern than a simple *I'm sorry for your loss*. It'd been ten years since she died, so he had a lot of them, but none seemed appropriate for what Aiden had said.

"No," he said, finally. "You don't. Every once in a while, I think I've reached the point where I'll stop missing her. And it's true that I don't miss her in the same way I did when she'd only been gone a month or a year. I just wish she was here, for all this important stuff in my life. She'll never know I got into UCLA. She won't see me graduate. She'll never be able to brag about her son, the professor of ancient history. It burns that she's missing all of it."

"She'd be proud."

Elliott's hand tightened around Aiden's before he could get it under control. He let Aiden's fingers slip from his grasp. "Sure. Well, enough about my tragic backstory. What's the synopsis of your teen drama? Were you the athletic type? The likeable nerd? Did you sneak off to Mexico for your eighteenth birthday? I want to know all the season finale scandals."

"None of the above." Aiden rubbed a stubbled cheek and his unfocused eyes turned in the direction of the picnic table surrounded by his family. "I was a boring child."

"Nooo, don't tell me that," Elliott whined. "I already know you're a huge dork in your old age. Don't ruin young Aiden for me as well!"

Aiden shrugged. "Hey, you asked."

"Yeah, I did." Elliott sighed. "I brought this disappointment on myself. No locker room fist fights over someone's honor? No academic decathlons skipped so that you could audition for the school musical?"

"Nope. Sorry. If anyone had academic decathlons to skip, it was Jill." Aiden shifted a bit, seeming suddenly ill at ease in the chair he'd occupied for almost an hour. "She was the really smart one, in that overachieving, rule-following way her teachers loved. I was only on the basketball team and student government because they were great on college applications."

Elliott hummed. "Interesting. I would have thought you'd be one of those kids who were effortlessly amazing at everything." The kind of kid he used to hate for no reason other than petty jealousy.

"Nope. I'm the middle child, and middle of the road in every way. Smart, but not as smart as Jill. Hardworking, but not as driven as Shannon. A good lawyer, but not as good as—"

Aiden's head dropped. They both watched as he laid his hand down on the arm of the chair and relaxed his fingers individually, until none of his knuckles were white with tension.

"Innes," Elliott finished.

Aiden nodded, a sharp dip of his clenched jaw. "Always compared with him, but somehow always found wanting."

Elliott winced. That had to be tough, when Aiden was clearly so well aware of the unfortunate similarities between them. Elliott never brought them up anymore, not even as a joke, because Aiden always went tense and still, like he was now.

"Are you so sure about that?" Elliott hazarded.

Aiden laughed at the same time as someone else on the porch across the lawn, though they couldn't have sounded more different. "Oh, yeah. 'You'll be just like your uncle,' I've been told, like it's supposed to be a compliment. It happens all the time. So similar to him, but never as *good*."

"Yeah, maybe not." Aiden's eyebrows flew up at Elliott's easy capitulation, and Elliott took his hand. "Maybe you aren't as great at winning cases. Not yet, anyway. But I can tell you what you're better at right now. You're better at caring about the people you're representing. Getting people to trust you unconditionally. Letting your family know they're loved. You're better at lots of stuff."

Aiden smiled and his grip pulsed around Elliott's hand. "Thanks." The tension in his shoulders loosened, but the worry and frustration in his eyes didn't completely disappear.

"Well," Elliott said, his big mouth flapping without his express consent. "If you get too tired of being compared to him, you could always get out of the lawyering game."

Aiden's eyebrows popped up and he smirked. "This again?"

"Sorry." Elliott probably didn't look it, though. "I was just thinking, you do have stuff that makes you happy."

"Like what?"

"Your donations. Your football games. Charity work, you know? You could spend time on that."

"Maybe."

"Hell, you could do anything you wanted." The paper plate balanced on the arm of his chair nearly took a dive as he gestured expansively. "You could take up interpretive dance."

"Yeah, that's never going to happen," Aiden growled.

"You more of a ballet guy?"

"You've seen me dance. You know I don't have that kind of coordination."

"Yeah, me neither." Elliott winced. "There's a reason I didn't turn to stripping as a career option."

Aiden laughed, loud enough that a couple of people looked over.

"But I'm serious, Aiden," Elliott said. "You should think about it, at least."

"I've already told you, my mother—"

"I've met your mother. That woman adores you, and I can tell you now, having known her for a couple hours, she'd still love you to bits if you did something that made you happy."

"I know." Aiden's voice was soft and fond, and his shy smile made him look young, like Catherine Kent-Graham's son rather than just one of the many Mr. Kent, esquires.

"Then why are you still working a job you hate?"

He waited, but Aiden didn't deny it. When they'd talked about it before, the word *hate* had never passed Aiden's lips. It still hadn't, but the longer Aiden stayed silent, the harder it would be for him to turn around and say it wasn't true.

The conversation floated away, and they moved on. They watched the kids run around for a while, and then Elliott remembered that they were still holding hands, and he stroked his thumb along the tops of Aiden's fingers until Aiden broke the silence.

"I gave myself a mushroom cut once because all the cool kids on TV were doing it."

Elliott sat straight up in his chair. "No way."

Aiden rubbed the back of his head. "Yes way. Only my mother knows about it, though. I needed her to buzz all my hair off when it failed completely."

"No way! Pics?"

"Absolutely not."

"Crap."

"Hey, lovebirds!"

They both looked. Jill was making her way across the lawn, a plate full of food in her hands.

"Are you just getting here?" Aiden accused. "After all the grief you gave me about showing up?"

"I'm a busy woman, Aiden," she said, waving her hand in his face so forcefully that a deviled egg almost toppled off of her plate. "I'm putting in an appearance. Jim and Sheila should be grateful for that. Don't waste time being pissy with me, though. I've come to do my sisterly duty and cut you loose before they start unwrapping the presents. If you leave now while everyone's still sleepy and dumb from too much cake, no one will even bat an eye."

Aiden sighed, looked at Elliott as if for his opinion—Elliott shrugged—then stood up, stretching his arms high over his head.

"So, you want to make a run for it?" Elliott asked, standing up himself, shaking out joints gone stiff from sitting in the hard chairs for so long. He scanned the backyard, which was steadily growing more gilded with the setting sun. He'd almost forgotten how many people were surrounding them.

"Yeah, let's do it." Aiden kissed Jill on the cheek, ignoring her indignant squawk as something finally did tumble off her plate into the grass. "Thanks, Jill."

They said goodbye to everyone they passed, receiving hugs from some and distracted waves from others—and were on the road and heading back to the city in no time.

Elliott didn't fill the car with chatter on the way back, but it wasn't because of nerves this time. The party had gone as well as it could have, considering that he'd been intensely aware of how different he was from everyone he'd met. Experiencing what a large family felt like had been strange for him—the only child of two only children—but also exhilarating.

It was almost dark when the houses going by started to look like the ones Elliott had grown up with.

"Thank you," Aiden said quietly as the streetlamps illuminated them both in stark bars.

"No problem. I was glad to come."

He shook his head. "Not just that. Thanks for not freaking out and running away from this craziness. And for talking to me. I'm happy to listen."

Elliott leaned over and pressed his lips to the underside of Aiden's jaw, keeping them there for four streetlamps' passing. When Aiden's arm wrapped around his shoulders, he moved in as close as his seat belt would allow, resting his head on Aiden's arm as they drove away from one home and toward another.

Chapter  12

"**I**'m here. Can you buzz me in or something?"

Elliott stared, wide-eyed, at the door to his room, the poster of Alexander the Great staring back. Of course, Aiden wasn't at that door. He was downstairs, on his phone, waiting for Elliott.

Outside of Elliott's dorm.

"Uh. Give me a minute."

"Okay. See you soon."

They both hung up, and Elliott wasted precious seconds looking around the room, cataloguing all the little messes he hadn't bothered to clean up because he hadn't planned on Aiden being so early.

He was still in his pajamas, for god's sake.

But Aiden couldn't be left to cool his heels in the lobby, especially if he'd worn his theater-going duds. He'd stick out way too much. Raking a hand through hair he'd actually spent time and effort on, Elliott quit stalling and headed out of his room, patting Alexander on his armored chest for good luck.

"Hey," Aiden said as Elliott met him on the sidewalk. "Traffic was better than I'd expected, for once."

Elliott was about to assure him it was fine and make a joke about coming too early, but Aiden kissed him before he could. Elliott melted into it, letting his hands tangle into Aiden's soft hair. They were so good at this now, knowing every little thing that would make each other clutch and reach for more.

The air was warm around them, but their mouths were warmer, taking and giving and devouring sweetly.

"Get a room!"

The voice came from a window above them, and the shouter was already gone when they turned to look, reminding Elliott how visible they were.

"Well, I do have one," Elliott said, roughly.

Aiden reached for his hand and squeezed it. "Lead the way."

"You positive?" Elliott asked, taking them both through the door. "It won't take me long to get dressed. You could stay down here, avoid the prison cell."

"I'm sure it's not that bad."

"Uh-huh." Elliott punched the elevator button. "Wait until you see it."

At the end of a ride in a box that still smelled of last night's revelry, there was the long walk down the hall to Elliott's room. Most people were at the dining hall at this time of night, so they saw no one, but Elliott jumped at every sound.

"Wow," Aiden said when they made it inside the room, his back to Elliott. "It's . . ."

"Awful, I know, but it gets the job done." The words were falling out of Elliott's mouth without his input, though he didn't truly believe them.

It wasn't the Ritz, but he liked his room. He'd made it as cozy as he could, with a carpet the colors of Greece's flag and posters plastered everywhere that the stuffed bookshelves didn't cover the gray concrete. It was four walls of sanctuary, a private little oasis for him to be exactly who he was at the moment. The door had a solid lock, and there was no one on the other side who wouldn't go away if he just pretended to be asleep.

"I was going to say that it's really you."

Elliott blinked. "Oh, yeah?"

"I like the pictures," Aiden said, gesturing to the wall next to Elliott's bed that was covered in photos of his parents and Kevin, with any available space cluttered by memes and memos. "And this guy . . . whoever he is."

"Oh, that's Alex. But he's Mr. Great to you."

Aiden laughed, and Elliott started to relax.

While they admired Alex's chiseled features, a knock sounded on the outside of the door.

"Shit." Elliott still was wearing his flannel pants and thin T-shirt. If he opened the door and someone on the other side saw Aiden, they'd probably think—

Think what? That they were together? It was true, in a way, and there was nothing unsavory about it. He had a friend, who might become officially more than a friend. People could infer what they wanted.

"Give me a minute," he told Aiden, and opened the door before he could change his mind. "Hello?"

"Um, hi?"

It was Amanda, a girl who always spoke up at floor meetings. She was normally right in the middle of planning for social events, so they hadn't talked much, outside of him casting his vote against a group bowling adventure.

"I'm so sorry to bother you," she said in a rush, already backing away, her eyes flicking to somewhere behind Elliott. "I didn't know you had company, I'll just go—"

"No, it's fine. Did you need something?"

"It's nothing, I just wondered . . ." She paused, then took a deep breath, her chest inflating as she started to resemble the girl who'd gone to bat for earlier quiet times on their floor. "Would you look at my essay?"

Elliott eyes widened. Until then, he hadn't noticed the thick wad of paper in her hand. "Oh. Why?"

"I'm an undeclared major, and I took an early American history class. It's kicking my ass, honestly. I didn't do that well in our first quiz, so I really have to nail this paper."

"Oh." He glanced down at what must be the essay itself, clutched tightly in Amanda's hand. "You know I'm a classics major, right?"

"Oh, yeah, I know. I was just talking to someone who's in one of your classes. He said you get A's on all your essays."

"I— Who?"

"It's Matt? Matt Solak. He's in your—"

"Early Christian History, I remember." The guy who'd sleepily asked him to join a study group a lifetime ago, when Elliott's biggest worry had been whether or not to take Aiden as a client.

Despite the warm, fizzing realization that Matt actually was impressed by him, and not in a last-ditch, exploitative way, Elliott's gut reaction was to say no.

Amanda seemed nice, but there was still a chasm between them. He didn't know her well enough to be certain she would actually take his advice. She might take up his time, instead, then ignore his critiques and blame him for her bad grade and tell everyone—

When had he become so cynical?

Since forever, said a voice that sounded suspiciously like Aiden's.

Aiden, who was sitting behind him, waiting for their date. Aiden, who dealt with the actual scum of the earth on a daily basis, and still believed the best of Elliott.

Elliott could do the same for one person. Especially a girl who wasn't that much younger than him, with no reason whatsoever to do him dirty.

"Yeah, I can read your paper," Elliott said.

"Amazing! I'm not looking for fact-checking, I just want to see if it makes sense." She dug a blue-polished finger under her eye. "I wrote it so fast, I have no idea if it's all a fever dream."

"No problem. I can check structure and citations and stuff."

"Oh my god, that would be so amazing." She held out the paper. It was a little wrinkled, but the title was neatly printed. "It doesn't have to be right away. I don't have to start worrying about it until after midterms. I only knocked it out so early because last semester, I ran out of time and wrote five essays in two weeks."

Elliott winced, thrown back to his own first term, running on caffeine to study for three different exams at the same time, checking his phone to see if the furnace in their house was fixable or dying an expensive death. "Ouch. Only need to learn that lesson once."

"Yup. Thank you so much for this, Elliott. What kind of cookie do you like?"

"Uh. Chocolate ones?" He flicked the corner of the papers a couple times. In his head, he started calculating how he'd fit it in between his own study and class schedule, and dates with Aiden. If he pushed reading his Poetry and Prose chapter to Sunday night, he could—

"I make amazing chocolate chip cookies. I'll bring some to you."

"That's . . . amazing." He was already looking forward to delicious smells coming from the cramped kitchenette.

Her smile was brilliantly wide for a few seconds, but with a hiccupping gasp, she seemed to remember what she'd gotten in the middle of. "Oh my gosh, I'm going to go. Have a good night! Just knock on my door. Or text me!"

She was already disappearing around the corner when Elliott realized he didn't have her number, but it was okay. Like she'd said, he knew where she lived.

He let the door swing shut and turned back to see Aiden perched on the bed, his face pulled into creases that normally disappeared when Elliott was in his presence.

"Everything okay?" Aiden asked, his grip on Elliott's thin covers tightening.

"Yeah, completely. That was a . . . sort-of friend." Elliott hadn't had time to panic, he realized, setting the essay on his desk, apart from his other piles of papers.

Tomorrow, he'd get to work on Amanda's paper, and maybe they could sit down somewhere and talk about it without him freaking out about things that weren't worth worrying about.

It might be fun to actually talk to another student. He couldn't get back the times he'd run away from conversations like that one, but it would make a nice change.

"She seems friendly."

Aiden's voice was calm and even, but now Elliott looked closer, he resembled a poorly scanned copy of himself. A little pale, a little fuzzy around the edges.

"You okay?" Elliott asked, sitting down next to him and taking his hands, a good foot of bed between them.

"I'm fine," Aiden said, too quickly, then he grimaced. "It's just . . . strange. To be here."

Elliott's abdomen tensed with instant regret. He should've made Aiden wait downstairs. "Sorry."

"No, don't be. It's not you." Aiden's scrunched eyebrows loosened long enough for him to smile ruefully. "It's all me."

"Oh, boy."

"I'm twenty-eight, Elliott," he blurted.

Elliott blinked. "Congratulations. I'm twenty-one. Both of our ages start with a two. How about that."

"I'm very well aware of how old you are. But you make it easy to forget." Aiden's face fell and he tried to take his hands away, but Elliott held firm. "That sounds like I'm blaming you, but I'm not. It's just, when we're alone, I forget because I feel like I can talk to you about anything and you truly understand. When we're out, and other people are around to see, I can see what they see. A college student and the desperate perv he has to put up with."

"It's not like that." Elliott took a breath to gather his thoughts. "Look. The reason why you can talk to me is because we get each other. If we were really so far apart in life experience, we'd run out of things to talk about, wouldn't we? I never talked with Innes as much as I do with you. That's gotta mean something, right?"

"Maybe," Aiden said, though it was easy to see that he wasn't convinced.

Elliott struggled for long seconds, then ended up saying, "We could stay home?"

He didn't actually want to, but wasn't that what he was supposed to do? Didn't people in relationships make sacrifices? If he was going to find a way to fully commit to Aiden, he'd have to get used to compromise.

His worry faded when Aiden shook his head. "No. I don't want that. I can't wait for our date tonight."

"Good."

Silence descended on their small predate get-together, and the longer it stretched, the more aware Elliott became of how ratty his pajamas looked next to Aiden's crisp pants and button-up shirt. They were also surrounded by Elliott's room, which couldn't have been more different from Aiden's sleek, stylish, adult apartment.

Aiden sighed, finally taking back his hands. "I'm sorry to ruin everything. Seeing her next to you was jarring. She seemed like a child."

"She probably is. Or was, recently. She's a freshman. Might have just turned eighteen."

"You never seemed that young, but you must have been."

"Well, I was nineteen when I started college." He shrugged as Aiden clearly did the math in his head. "Early birthday, gap year, you know. It worked out that way."

"A year or two shouldn't make that much difference."

"Aiden." Placing his hands on Aiden's cheeks, which were prickly with long stubble at this time of day, he forced him to meet his eyes. "You didn't steal my youth away from me. Neither did Innes. I'm an adult, but only because I grew up."

"It's not just age. There are reasons why your profession is illegal."

"Bad ones." Not now, he decided, and buttoned his lip against a rant of epic proportions. Aiden had heard it all before, and agreed with him. His issue was with safety, and so was Elliott's.

"Undoubtedly," Aiden said. "But some good ones too. It's about taking advantage of people."

Elliott lurched forward and wrapped his arms around Aiden's drawn-in chest. "It's all okay. Give yourself a break," he murmured in Aiden's ear, absorbing the disbelieving huff with his body. "If it hadn't been you, it would've been someone else, and I hate the thought of that. I—"

It would've been so easy to say everything he wanted to say. Elliott could make it real by telling Aiden how he truly felt. They had time. They could hash out what they were, what they both wanted them to be.

But he wouldn't. Not for two weeks, anyway.

Elliott took his arms back, letting the opportunity dissipate, though he didn't let Aiden get far. They kissed, long and slow, on Elliott's bed until he finally had to pull away.

"You're not getting out of our date that easy," he said, walking backward to his closet. "Prepare yourself for tragedy, baby, because the Greeks are in town tonight."

"Somehow, that's actually kind of uplifting."

"You just wait."

Elliott threw his hands up as he exited the theater. "Incredible! The actors—"

"I agree."

"That set design. The music!"

"I think it really fit, but what do I know?"

"Euripides would be proud."

"Would he?" Aiden raised his voice over the chatter of theater patrons. "I don't know anything about him."

"He's essentially Top 40, but for Greek literature. *Bacchae*, *Electra*. The groovy greats, you know? And tonight's show, of course. My favorite."

Aiden stopped to look back at him, but soon kept moving with the surging crowd headed to the lobby. "*Medea* is your favorite? Not that I'm disagreeing with you, but why?"

Elliott hadn't meant to go off on a tangent. When they'd first entered the theater, he'd been a bundle of nerves, hoping he hadn't made a mistake by sharing a part of what he loved and hoping Aiden understood.

But all his coaching to remind himself that it wasn't a big deal and Aiden didn't have to like the play to like Elliott went out the window.

"Sorry," he said, as he wound down from explaining exactly why *Medea* was a superior play to *Bacchae*, still in the lobby half an hour after the show had ended. "I get a little crazy about this stuff."

"I don't mind. Honestly."

Aiden was smiling down at him, his body at ease. He hadn't reached for his keys in his pocket or started inching toward the door.

Elliott had every reason to believe him, but that he did was still a surprise.

"Thanks," he said, lacing his fingers with Aiden's. "And thank you for coming. Want to get out of here?"

"Sure."

The lobby had mostly emptied out, except for a few stragglers like Elliott and Aiden, too caught up in themselves to notice the ushers checking their watches around them.

As they stepped out the front doors, Elliott stopped in his tracks.

"Professor Salter?"

Stupid, Elliott scolded himself as his teacher turned around. If he'd stayed silent, they probably would have escaped without being seen. As it was, Elliott dropped Aiden's hand and pasted on a wide smile.

"Elliott!" Professor Salter said. "Nice to see you. Couldn't resist the siren call of Greek drama, could you?"

Elliott laughed weakly, panic ratcheting up with every second spent with his two worlds colliding. "Nope. I'm weak for a good tragedy."

"So I gathered, from your passionate defense of *Antigone* in Poetry and Prose the other day."

Elliott felt himself color, but he was still compelled to continue the debate. "It's the best of the trilogy. It's criminal that *Oedipus* gets all the publicity."

"To be honest, I agree with you," Salter allowed, his eyes sparkling. "But a bit of spirited debate is good for the attendance record." With a polite purse of his lips and an extended hand, he turned to Aiden. "And this is?"

"Aiden, a friend," Elliott blurted, to keep Professor Salter from filling in the blank himself.

He needed to calm the fuck down. This wasn't his worst nightmare: an instructor making correct assumptions about how Elliott managed to keep himself from being crushed by debt.

This was a date, and he could date whoever the hell he wanted.

"Wonderful. Perhaps a new devotee." Professor Salter smiled absently after the handshake, then seemed to dismiss Aiden's presence entirely. "It's fortunate that I caught you. It's early, but I think you'll be interested to know that the faculty is considering hiring a few upperclassmen to help with grading next semester. Assisting the assistants with first- and second-year essays, you know. There's a small honorarium involved, but it would mostly be a boost for anyone with an eye toward grad school and teaching."

The nervous flutter in Elliott's stomach picked up its pace, but he managed to eke out a surprisingly casual, "Oh?"

Professor Salter's eyes were sharper than they were when he painted his students pictures of civilizations past. "The postings will be up sometime this week. Look out for them. Do you have experience with giving critique? Other than your own work, of course."

"Uh, not yet. But I've just agreed to take on a project like that." It felt like bragging, but he forced himself to lift his chin and treat this afterhours conversation like a job interview. He had an ace, and he would use it. "Another student in a history course asked for my help with a paper. I'm looking forward to it."

It was—amazingly—the truth. This time, the opportunity to influence someone with his knowledge felt right. He deserved it, and would be good at it. Why shouldn't he be excited to help Amanda?

Professor Salter didn't call him out on his showboating. He just narrowed his laughing eyes a bit and rubbed his chin like Elliott was a newly discovered bronze-cast statue. "Glad to hear it. That's something else to tell the scholarship committee, when they call. I got an email from them this week, actually, although you didn't hear it from me. Your list of qualities to recommend you is growing by the day."

If the theater lobby wasn't so vivid around him, Elliott would have thought he was dreaming. "Wow. Thank you."

"No need for thanks. Just don't slip up now." A playful, wrinkled finger shook in Elliott's face.

"I won't."

Professor Salter's eyes sparkled like a kindly wizard instead of a well-respected history teacher on his day off.

"Anyway, I must go. It's not quite a golden chariot to take me to Athens, but my ride awaits."

"Good night," Elliott called, and Professor Salter ambled down the street.

If Elliott had thought he was embarrassing himself with enthusiasm in the lobby, it was nothing to his thrilled monologue on the way to the car.

"Oh my god, a junior teaching assistant! That would be so awesome. I might have to take on a couple more people for tutoring. It'd be worth the time. And if they give me a good scholarship for next semester, maybe I can replace my laptop," he gushed as they buckled their seat belts. He'd been saving in dribs and drabs, any penny he could spare between his tuition nest egg and monthly help for Dad, but wasn't anywhere near the cost of something good.

"Is it broken?"

"Not yet, but it won't last long. I've been backing up every project like a mad man for the last few months, and it's driving me crazy."

"If you need it now, I can pay for one."

The revving of the engine as Aiden turned on the car was loud to Elliott's ears.

"Thanks, but no," he said, after a pause that seemed to last forever.

Aiden didn't look at him, checking his mirrors instead as he prepared to pull out. "You sure? I wouldn't want you to lose your work because of a technical—"

"I said no," Elliott said, and winced at the way it snapped in the small space.

Aiden's hand froze on his turn signal, then fell to his leg. "I only want to help."

"I know, but you're not actually helping, and I don't think you're listening. We've had this conversation before."

"Have we?"

Even in the low light of the car, Elliott could tell Aiden's confusion was genuine, and that made his flare of irritation all the more difficult to tamp down.

"Yes," he said, and it didn't come out as neutral as he'd wanted. "And you didn't get it then, either."

"I'm trying to understand."

"Are you? Because that's not what I'm hearing."

Aiden's sigh was tight and expressive. "I won't miss the money, if that's what you're worried about. It means nothing—"

"That's the problem!" Elliott exploded. After that, it was a lot easier to speak quietly again. "It's nothing to you, but it's a lot to me."

The car didn't move, and neither of them spoke for a while. Elliott started to wonder if this was what all fights were like, or if it was especially difficult for him, who couldn't keep his convictions inside, even though they were still in the odd limbo of employer/boyfriend.

For two more weeks, anyway.

"Okay, look," he said, when he couldn't bear one more second of not knowing where they went from there. "Have you ever heard those pop songs about independent women paying their own bills? Girl power and whatever?"

He heard Aiden suck in a small breath, then it came out as a laugh, and suddenly the tension was half as heavy.

"Sure," Aiden said. "Why?"

"I'm not a woman, and I'm not that independent, but I do need to pay my own way, with money I earned. Otherwise, you'd be doing exactly what Innes tried to do: throwing money at me like I should be grateful."

Another laugh, accompanied by a shake of his head in the dark. "So, I can't buy you the things you need, but I can pay you, then you can buy them. Is that it?"

"Yes. If you put it that way, it sounds stupid, but the transaction is important to me."

"Okay."

More silence, but it was lighter, like a recovery period, not another wound.

"Are you angry?" Elliott couldn't help asking, even though he knew the answer.

"Not at all. I was thinking. This is our first argument as a couple."

"If we were a couple." He let a smile creep onto his face as Aiden pulled out of their space.

"That's right," Aiden said, heading onto the road. His mouth quirked in a sideways smile. "I forgot. I'm your *friend*."

And just like that, the evening wasn't ruined. They'd weathered a storm, and were strong enough to come out the other side.

"Oh, yeah. My pal."

"Stop. You're bringing up terrible memories of my high-school crush."

"My good buddy."

"I will turn this car around."

"And take me back to your place? Deal."

Chapter 13

Elliott let his door slam shut and collapsed into his desk chair. It'd been a long day, but he was buzzing, first from test adrenaline, second from the meeting he'd just had with Amanda, nailing out kinks in her thesis that were almost as satisfying to resolve as an orgasm.

Midterms were as tough as he'd expected, which meant he thought he'd done pretty well on all of them. It was hard to know, but he felt good about his prospects of a small scholarship for next year.

What he wasn't feeling good about was the phone in his hand. He'd sent a text to Kevin, asking him if he had time to video chat, not giving the reason for the call: some bad news.

His phone *ping*ed. He grimaced and read the screen.

Sure, dude! Kevin had sent, to Elliott's disappointment. *Gimme a minute to get upstairs?*

Awesome, Elliott typed back, then dropped his phone on the desk like a hot coal and drummed his fingers next to his keyboard until the laptop chirped.

"Hey, man!" Kevin said, his pixelated face smiling at Elliott. He was still in his uniform, probably sweaty and tired from vet-technicianing nervous animals all day, and yet, he hadn't told Elliott to buzz off. What a good friend. "What's up? Ready for spring break?"

"More ready than you, you poor nine-to-five schmuck."

Kevin sighed—as if he didn't love his job to pieces—then he smiled widely. "Yeah, it's tough being an actual functional adult, instead of a wittle student, avoiding the real world."

Elliott scoffed. "As if, small-town girl, you just keep living in your lonely world."

Kevin rolled his eyes, still smiling. "But for real, are you ready? All your exams are over, right?"

"Done and dusted."

"I bet you aced them."

Elliott pushed away from the desk, leaning back in his chair to crack his stiff neck. "You have more faith in me than I do, pal."

"I know. I always have." Kevin's grin gained a fondness that Elliott could see, even across hundreds of miles, through an itty-bitty screen. "So, what's happening? I don't think you called me because you wanted to gaze at my beautiful face." He placed his hands under his chin and batted his eyelashes coquettishly.

Elliott pretended to gag, then he paused, nervous, unsure of how he'd say what he needed to say. He decided, after tense split seconds of deliberation, to lay it all out plainly. "I wanted to tell you I'm not coming home for break."

Elliott had expected to see Kevin's face fall—Kevin showed everything, always—but it was still tough to see. It was important to tell him over video, though. It was harder to keep from feeling guilty, but he'd wanted Kevin to be able to see his face, and his regret.

"Dad's going to feel obligated to pay my bus fare, and it's way too much. And don't even try to tell me you won't take a couple extra days off work."

He had other reasons that he couldn't share. This way, he wouldn't have to skip out on a week of work, or debate with Aiden over whether he deserved vacation pay.

After a pregnant pause, Kevin nodded. "Yeah, you're probably right. So, it's cool."

"It isn't really." As confident as Elliott was in his decision to stay, he was mourning the loss of time with his dad and Kevin.

"Yeah," Kevin agreed.

"Being an adult sucks," Elliott grumbled.

"Yeah."

"I am sorry, Kev," Elliott said, leaning in to his webcam until his face was huge in the display. "I know we'd planned to do so much, but coming home . . . it just wouldn't work."

There was a bit of buried relief, though, deep in the darkest parts of himself. No, he wouldn't see the people he loved, but he also wouldn't see the tangled weeds of his mom's old herb garden encroaching closer to the house.

Kevin tilted his head, smiling his familiar, easygoing smile. "Hey, it's okay. I get it, man. You gotta do what you gotta do." His gaze sharpened and he crossed his arms, leaning them against his desk, like Elliott. "So, is it cartoon-watching lawyer guy who's keeping you from coming home?"

Elliott startled, losing his balance and almost braining himself on his lamp. "What? Why would you think that?"

Kevin blew a loud raspberry, then wiped it away from the screen on his end. "Please. As if anything else could keep you away. Yeah, you have your other reasons, but you didn't let those stop you before. Logical assumption: you're sticking around because of some special person." He grinned while Elliott gaped in silent shock. "Plus, you look happy. Happier than I've seen you in a while. You've always loved doing what you're doing. Your history thing, I mean. So it must be something—or someone—new in your life that's putting that smile on your face."

"Oh." Elliott huffed. He shouldn't be surprised that Kevin saw through him. He'd been able to keep a lot of his life choices secret through distance alone, but there wasn't any hiding this. He might as well admit it. "Yeah."

Kevin grinned triumphantly. "That's what I thought. Can't hide from me, dude."

"Guess not."

"So it *is* the same guy you were seeing before?" Kevin asked, his eyes wide with his interest.

"Yeah, it is." Elliott clamped his lips shut. They were tight with his smile and bursting to spill every detail about Aiden and the limbo they were in, but saying it out loud felt like a bad idea. If he said anything, it'd jinx the whole thing, and he needed all the help he could get.

He still hadn't made a decision about Aiden. He had spring break to decide, essentially, which was why he wanted to spend it alone, or as close to alone as he could in a building with a few hundred other people. Even if he told Kevin a highly edited version, Kevin would have opinions about the whole situation, and Elliott didn't want to be influenced by anyone. He was already being guided by enough factors as it was. He didn't need any more food for thought.

"What happened to being casual?" Kevin questioned.

Elliott lifted a shoulder. "We casually slid into being more than that. It was a bit of an accident."

"The best love stories often are."

"You think so? Well, then, ours must be the greatest love story ever told, because we were caught completely by surprise. I'm still not even sure it's real."

"Why do you say that?" Kevin's eyebrows had gathered together and he was doing his best *I'm your therapist, tell me everything* face, all concerned eyes and thoughtfully pursed mouth.

"Well, we haven't talked about it," Elliott said, tacking on, "much," when Kevin's face got a little thunderous. "We're sort of seeing how it goes, but without . . . talking. Or labels."

"Elliott."

"Yes, Kevin?"

"Are you going down a path that'll get you hurt?"

Elliott winced. "Maybe?"

"Why? You're twenty-one, not twelve. You know relationships don't just happen. There's effort required, and communication."

"Hey, I am putting in effort!" Elliott protested. "I totally took him on a date."

Kevin did not look impressed. "*A* date? Singular? You've only been on one date, outside of your . . ." He made a vague gesture that seemed to mean *Inadvisable Non-Romantic Conjugal Relations*.

Elliott sat up straighter in his chair. "Not exactly. We've had dates. Lots of them. But the context was different, so they didn't really mean what they mean now, even though we're doing the same things."

"Uh-huh," Kevin said, his eyebrow raised sky high.

Elliott sighed. "It's complicated, okay? It always is when you don't meet someone in a coffee shop and fall in love at first sight and date for show because you're obviously soul mates."

"So uncomplicate it," Kevin said, with no mercy. "Talk to him, be honest about what you want, and do it sooner rather than later. Because I will be there to pick up the pieces, but I won't enjoy it, and neither will you. I love you, man."

Kevin meant well. Elliott was getting a little choked up, in fact, at Kevin's heartfelt attempt at giving him advice. Elliott wished it were that easy. What he wanted was a very difficult question, one he'd tried to answer many times during the last weeks.

He wanted to graduate at the top of his class. He wanted his dad to stay exactly where he was but without the crushing worry that one missed payment would mean the end of their hard work.

He wanted to have a normal relationship, in which he cared for Aiden—loved Aiden, a voice in the back of Elliott's mind whispered—without compromising his other goals.

If he figured out the perfect solution to all of his problems, UCLA would have to give him an honorary doctorate. It would only be fair.

"I'll try," he said, smiling valiantly. "We can't always get what we want."

"You can," Kevin insisted. "You can do anything you put your mind to, including your mystery man. Many times, and in many positions that I don't need to hear about."

"Yeah, that's never been a problem for me and him."

"Don't want to know! Seriously!" Kevin put his fingers in his ears.

Elliott grinned and leaned on the table, his chin in his hand as he watched Kevin sing tunelessly to block out TMI details that weren't coming. He didn't need to go home for break. Kevin brought the feeling of home to him over a fuzzy screen, every time.

Elliott's hands weren't shaking, but only because he was clenching them in the pockets of his sweater.

"Hey," he said when Aiden appeared in the hall in soft, clean clothes, perfect for Elliott to collapse into.

He wanted to. He felt like he was only just letting the exhaustion of three years of school catch up to him. The past two days of spring break, he'd been alone in his dorm, sleeping or reading for hours, only surfacing when he couldn't ignore his hunger pangs any longer or when Amanda came and hauled him into the common room for some fresh air.

He couldn't say he minded, however much he grumbled about villains disturbing his slumber. It was strange how quickly someone he'd ignored for so many months had become accustomed to mom-ing him into taking care of himself once he'd opened his metaphorical—and literal—door to social interaction. Kevin would have approved.

"Hey." Aiden stepped over Elliott's discarded shoes and pressed him to the door, kissing him hard against the unyielding plane. Elliott let his hands roam, giving them something to do that wasn't plucking anxiously at his sweater's pocket lint. Aiden's mouth distracted him well enough that by the time his hands came up to card through Aiden's hair, messing up the work-appropriate style, they weren't trembling at all.

When it was over, Elliott smiled. Did he look as happy as he felt?

"Hi," he said, some of his tension releasing its grip on his body.

"Hello," Aiden said, smirking. "How's the vacation going?"

He pulled Aiden by the arm to the couch. "Oh god, it's amazing. I never knew there were so many hours in a day."

"There aren't twenty-four, like usual?"

"Maybe that's usual for you, but when I've got an essay due and three chapters to go over with Amanda, there's definitely less than twenty."

"Oh, are you still meeting with her?"

Aiden's arm had come around Elliott's shoulder, but it didn't stay there long, dislodged by Elliott's eagerness.

"Yeah, actually. She asked if I'd keep working with her, which is awesome, because it's great practice, and I actually enjoyed it. We're going to meet once a week." Out of the corner of his eye, he caught Aiden's face, devoid of any expression other than attentiveness. Elliott rushed to add, "Don't worry, it won't interfere with . . . you know."

With a quizzical squint, Aiden smiled a little. "I wasn't worried."

"Okay. Good."

Aiden didn't appear to notice the tension. Elliott sure had, though. It felt like his every attempt at conversation was going south.

"Do you miss home?" Aiden asked, softly.

Elliott blinked and squirmed a bit on the couch, the nerves coming back full force. This was what he needed to get used to: personal questions that went beyond idle chatting during a slow part in a movie. If he was going to start something with Aiden, he needed to stop being surprised that Aiden cared.

"Yes, but no more than usual. It isn't long until summer break, though, and I'll go back for a couple of weeks then, and really get some quality bonding time in."

"That's great. You know I wouldn't mind if you went back, right? You could go tomorrow, skip our dates on Friday and Sunday."

Elliott scratched his thumb lightly on the seam of the leather cushion between them. "I know. I just wanted to talk to you instead of going back. I wasn't sure if it would take me the entire break to work up the nerve."

Aiden sat up straighter. "Talk? About . . ."

"About us." Elliott laughed, half-heartedly. "That makes it sound so serious. Like we're in a soap opera. Riccardo, we must talk. I've fallen in love with your evil twin brother."

Aiden widened his eyes comically and played along with a completely straight face. "You mean, my evil conjoined twin brother, who was separated from me at birth? That evil twin brother?"

"That's the one. Not to be confused with your other, non-twin brother, the one who dated my sister and left her at the altar, then dated me and left *me* at the altar."

"Oh, no, I could never confuse the two. Curse him for stealing you away."

Elliott snorted and couldn't resist giving Aiden a quick, closed-mouth kiss. "It's not that dramatic. But we do have to talk."

"So talk," Aiden said, his expression honest and open. "I'm a lawyer, I talk about serious things way too much. It's your turn."

"What, and I don't talk too much?"

"You talk about everything and nothing. You talk about what's in your head, and there's a lot going on in your head. But, at the risk of sounding completely cheesy, you very, very rarely talk about what's in your heart."

The heart in question pounded. "You're right. That's so cheesy, I wanna grate it on my pasta."

"Yeah, yeah."

"I wanna pair it with some expensive wine. Melt it—"

"Okay, I get it. It was corny." Aiden shot him a quelling look. "But my point still stands. You only let me see parts of you. Which is fine. I like what I see." He placed a hand over Elliott's fidgeting fingers.

"Good," Elliott croaked. He cleared his throat. "I mean, I'm glad. I like you too."

"Well, thank god."

Aiden's smile was a tender slant, so familiar and valued by Elliott that he was worrying about losing it before he'd even started talking. The anxiety that had been simmering in him for nearly a month started to boil over until words were pouring out unchecked.

"I do this for a reason. My job, I mean. I don't have a rich family who can pay my tuition. I didn't play a sport or overachieve in high school enough to get the good scholarships." He looked down at his hands, away from Aiden's patient gaze. "I could do what everyone else does and take out loans that would bury me as soon as I graduated. Let my dad flounder and lose the house after barely holding on to it for years. Or I could work every spare minute and see my grades suffer for it. I could do a bunch of things to make it unnecessary for me to make my living from having sex and maybe it'd be easier than I think it is. But I do this job because I want to and I have the balls to. I do it so that I can have the kind of life I want."

"I get that," Aiden said softly, and Elliott forced himself to meet his eyes.

"Do you? If you do, then you understand that I can't stop out of the blue to fall in love with you. I want to." He reached out and straightened a piece of Aiden's dark hair that had been messed up by Elliott's fingers. "I'm already most of the way in love with you. It'd take one more tiny push and I'd be done for."

"Me too," Aiden said, even as he leaned in. They kissed again, high on their revelations. Elliott could have kept on kissing him for hours, but he pulled away instead.

"If I loved you like that," he said. "It would be easy for me to rationalize a decision to quit, but it wouldn't fix all of my problems."

If the roof on the house fell in, and the bank wouldn't lend Dad money to fix it, how could Elliott look him in the eye if he hadn't done all he could? And if he stopped working now, and allowed himself to rack up debt for the rest of his undergrad and then his master's degree, the work he'd done for the past two years would be undercut. He'd end up with loans hanging over his head and no home to go back to. Why had he bothered if he was going to give up when he was two-thirds of the way there?

"But there's a better way." The quaking in his ribs increased. There was no going back once he told Aiden what he wanted. They were already far past the point where they could forget this month ever happened and go back to being strangers.

"A better way," Aiden said, tonelessly.

"Yes. We could be together like we have been this past month, but with no more boundaries. When we're with each other, I could be completely in it, nothing holding me back." He swallowed, his throat clicking. "And when I'm not with you, I could still do my work."

Aiden didn't have a ticking clock anywhere in his apartment, and the fridge was too far away for its hum to help break up the painful seconds of silence that followed. Elliott tried not to fidget and tried not to panic.

"Your work?" Aiden repeated slowly. "Sex work, you mean."

Elliott's optimism took a hard blow.

"Yeah," he said, still forcing a smile. "I'd have a client, or clients, maybe, but I'd be *with* you. You see? It could work perfectly. We could make our agreement null and void starting this month, and then it wouldn't be weird. We wouldn't have to worry about the money coming between us. We'd know our relationship was real, not like this halfway state we've been in this month, with you as a client but also my boyfriend."

"But I . . ." Aiden leaned back, staring at Elliott hard, like he was waiting for him to say *Gotcha!* "Elliott, I know you didn't want to define what we were to each other, but I sort of assumed that the agreement we had was already void."

Elliott's fists clenched in time with his stomach. He asked, numbly, "Why would you think that?"

"Because we were dating." Aiden huffed and his hands twitched in front of him. "We were falling in love, doing the exact opposite of what we'd agreed on."

The agreement. Sex and physical intimacy, no-strings companionship. There were a hell of a lot of strings now.

Aiden still looked baffled. "You met my parents."

Elliott pushed himself backward, putting his knees between them. His breath rose and fell harshly in his chest as he said, more angrily than he meant to, "And that meant that what we both agreed to didn't count anymore? What did you think I was going to do? Live off of your charity?"

Aiden stiffened and his jaw tensed, hardening in a way that reminded Elliott of the way he'd been before Elliott had truly known him. "Well. In a way, yes. I don't think of it as charity, but I assumed—"

"That I'd let you pay my way? You'd just . . ." His arms flew up in front of him, and his thighs quaked with the urge to get up and pace. "Take over paying for everything I needed with nothing in return?"

Aiden looked him right in the eye, lifted his chin. "Yes."

Elliott lost the battle with his legs, stood up from the couch, and put distance between them. He crossed his arms over his middle and placed himself behind the overstuffed leather chair, his mind fuzzy like white noise.

Aiden had been *dating* him the whole time. Having sex with him, paying for his bus fare, fighting to pay for more, all while being his boyfriend, not his employer. Elliott hadn't even known.

"You thought I'd be okay with that," he said. "Just letting you provide for me."

Aiden shrugged, but his body was tense, so it came off as an aggressive roll of his shoulders. "Husbands and wives don't always make the same salary. Stay-at-home parents—"

"This is not the same, and you know it," Elliott snapped. "That's a partnership. It's a decision people mutually make after years of dating, and there's usually children involved. As much as I love my degree, I don't think it's on the same level as a *helpless infant*. What if you started to resent having spent the money on me?"

Not *if. When.*

Aiden's chin lifted mutinously. "I wouldn't. It'd be my choice, and I'd live with it, regardless of whether our relationship panned out."

Elliott scoffed, and it made his throat burn. "Sure, you think that now. Down the road, though, what if I decide I want to break up with you, but I can't because where am I going to get tuition for my next semester? I could tough it out, put up with a relationship I don't want to be in until the day I graduate, and then bam, you're dumped. You think you'll still be okay with having shelled out all that money?"

The press of Aiden's lips was stubborn and bleak. He shook his head. "You'd never do that."

"How do you know?" Elliott demanded. "We can't tell the future. And what about you? You might start to think of me the same way I'd think about myself. As a leech and a user. I couldn't stand to see myself turn into the kind of person who'd stay with someone they didn't love just because they need to know where their next meal ticket will come from."

Elliott's mouth tasted bitter around the words. This wasn't how it was supposed to go. He'd had a hundred rebuttals planned out in his head, but they hadn't been anything like that. He wanted to cover his ears and walk away, but he felt sick at the thought that Aiden might take that as his final answer on whether their fragile connection should be allowed to fully form. One big miscommunication was enough for him for one day.

His chest ached at the tiny, treacherous thought that maybe he *should* walk out and never come back.

Aiden stood up, taking a tentative step toward the chair Elliott shielded himself with, but ultimately holding his ground. "It wouldn't be like that. I don't do nice things for people just because of what it'll get me. I'm not like—"

"Like Innes?" Elliott's wretched satisfaction cheered quietly at Aiden's nearly unnoticeable flinch. "How do you figure? You think just as little of me as he does if you think I'd be okay with you being my sugar daddy."

Aiden was as angry as Elliott had ever seen him, his fists clenched at his sides. Elliott wanted to snatch back the words.

"No, I don't," Aiden gritted. "I'm not like him at all, and I think it's a bit hypocritical of you to be angry with me for thinking 'so little' of *you* when you try to compare us. We might be related, but we are nothing alike, not least because we wanted totally different things from you from the beginning. He would have been okay with you having other people on the side, but I'm not."

And there it was. The final blow to Elliott's overly optimistic fix-it to their first—and seemingly last—big problem.

"That's it, then?" Elliott said, his words as brittle and blank as he felt. "No discussion about that? You won't even think about it?"

"What's there to think about?" Aiden said, his slumped posture far from his usual straight-backed confidence. "I wish I could say I was cool with it. Some people could, and I envy them. But the thought of you having sex with someone else while you're supposed to be my boyfriend doesn't—" He made a twisting, clawlike gesture next to his head. "Doesn't click."

"It wouldn't be the same with someone else as it would be with you." Elliott grimaced at the whine in his own voice. "How can you know that it wouldn't work if you don't give it a shot?"

Aiden shook his head slowly. "I just do. I'm almost thirty, Elliott. I know myself well enough by now to know that. I get that monogamy is a— What do you call it? A social construct. But that's what I want and I can't help the way I feel. I just wouldn't be able to let it go. Not with you."

Elliott's body temperature shot up, and his cheeks began to prickle. Shock and the wave of anger that came with it chased away his achy sadness and the urge to plead and cajole.

"What do you mean, 'not with me'?" Elliott asked.

Aiden didn't answer right away. He looked at the floor instead, his jaw moving back and forth.

"You think you could keep it impersonal," Aiden said, after a while. "Separate your sex life from your love life."

Elliott managed to keep from stamping his foot like a child having a tantrum. "Of course. Why wouldn't I?"

Aiden let out a breath that was almost a laugh, but too fragile and viciously sharp to be real. "How do you know that you won't fall in love with the next guy too?"

Elliott stumbled away from the chair he'd taken refuge behind, his fingernails scraping across the top of it. All the air in his chest had been stolen, as if he'd been blown back by a blast instead of softly spoken words. His chest burned as he filled it with enough oxygen that he could scream for a long time if he wanted. He didn't. He turned away from Aiden and walked toward the door without another word.

"Elliott, wait," Aiden said. Elliott could hear his footsteps behind him. "I'm so sorry. I didn't mean it like that. I just think that if you don't make a clean break, you might always wonder if you made the wrong choice."

Elliott didn't turn around. He kept on his straight path to his shoes and his escape. "Well, I think the answer to that question is already pretty clear," he couldn't keep from saying. "I chose to give us a chance, but apparently that was the wrong one, because you think I'm a slut who'd get heart-eyes for anyone who told me I was pretty."

"I don't think that," Aiden said, from a few feet away, a distance Elliott appreciated more than he could say. He was so angry, he felt like he would shake apart if Aiden touched him. "It's my fear talking, my fear of losing you before I even had you. I never thought that, and I never will."

He glared down at his shoes as he shoved them on, regretting taking them off in the first place, and spat, "Are you sure? You might change your mind in a fucking second, with no reason or logic behind it. Because that's so easy, right?"

There was a muffled thump, as if Aiden had punched the wall, but Elliott still didn't turn around, not even when Aiden said, "I'm sorry. Please believe me," in a voice so urgent and wrecked that it made Elliott's throat tighten, despite his righteous fury.

He shook his head, his shoelaces blurring in his hand. "No. I'm leaving. I'm not coming back, either. This isn't going to work, so there's no point. Consider this my resignation."

"Elliott, please, don't. Just listen—"

"I'm done listening," he said, his voice reverberating against the walls in the cramped hallway. "Now please excuse me, I have a résumé to update so that I can go out and find a new job—or, wait, no. A new person to fall madly in love with. Because that worked out so well for me last time, didn't it?"

"You haven't done any listening at all, only talking," Aiden said, suddenly loud and urgent. Elliott finally looked at him, in spite of himself. Aiden's face was pale, his eyes wide and wild. His calm and cool demeanor had shattered at last. "Maybe if you'd let me talk for one minute, I could convince you that you don't have to do this anymore."

"'This'?"

"Working. Being a prostitute," Aiden said, enunciating every letter clearly. "However well-paid and comfortable you might be, I can take care of what you need. I know this is frightening for you, but I would never trap you. You can trust me."

Elliott flinched away, even though Aiden hadn't moved. He put his hand on the doorknob but didn't push it down. "God, please stop. How many times do I have to tell you, this isn't *Pretty Woman*. I don't need saving. Nobody is forcing me to sell myself."

"Except yourself. You've convinced yourself that you want to, that you have to, but the truth is, you're scared to stop and think about how much you hate it."

Elliott bristled, his spine snapping straight. "I don't hate—"

"Yes, you do," Aiden said, loud, slow, and clear, like what he said was law. "There's nothing wrong with what you do. Did. Absolutely nothing. But you stopped being okay with it, if you ever were, or else you would never have allowed yourself to fall in love with me. You're looking for a way out. We met at the perfect time. You can stop now."

By the end of his little speech, Aiden's voice was soft and soothing again, though not anywhere near the smooth, even sound of his normal voice. This was so far from normal now. Elliott tightened his fingers on the handle and cursed himself for thinking for a second that he could have something approaching normal. He'd given that up two years ago, when he'd given his number to a stranger who'd wanted to buy his body along with his time.

"No." Elliott sounded steadier than he felt, even to his own ears. "There is nothing perfect about this. Whatever we might have been, it was never going to be anything but fucked-up."

Elliott opened the door and Aiden let him. Elliott kept waiting for another plea, another attempt to convince him to come inside, but there was only the sound of his own feet walking to the elevator. It opened mercifully quickly, and he was alone, so no one could see him lean against the mirror-paneled wall except the eye of the security camera.

There were no tears. Sadness, sure, but anger and a hollow hopelessness covered it up. Resting his forehead on his fisted hand against the cool glass, he kept himself from punching a jagged crack into it by grinding his knuckles against it, leaving smears with his clammy skin.

It wasn't only Aiden he was angry at. He was angry at himself. He'd hurt himself as much as he'd been hurt, and all because he'd been too stupid and besotted to remember that nothing just worked out. Not for him.

His father had taught him to work hard for the things that he wanted, and he'd done that. The moment he'd stopped and simply lived, letting himself fall deeper in love while hoping for a miracle, of course he'd gotten dirt kicked in his face.

He *was* angry at Aiden, though. Every one of his careless words had drawn a little bit of blood until Elliott imagined himself to be covered in it. Aiden didn't trust him. Aiden didn't understand, after all this time, that Elliott needed to look after himself. He hadn't given Elliott's solution a chance. He hadn't thought about it at all, even though it was the only way they could have been together without Elliott feeling like a grasping parasite. They would've finally been on equal footing, and Aiden hadn't considered it for a second.

Biting his lip to keep a rough sob inside, he shook his head at his own unfairness. He couldn't be mad at Aiden for not agreeing to a new situation like that. Aiden had a right to ask his boyfriend not to sleep with other people. But he hadn't wanted to *try*, and in the process of refusing, he'd made Elliott feel like absolute shit.

The urge to scream out his grief and raw pain built up, pushing at his throat until it was tight and hurt more than his stinging eyes. He didn't let it out, but he did wrap his arms around his torso, sink down into a ball, and clench his whole body until every muscle shook and he couldn't hold it anymore.

The elevator *ding*ed and the door opened. Elliott straightened up, walked through the familiar lobby, past the front desk, and the security guard who might or might not have witnessed his near-breakdown. The sun was still shining outside, warm and obnoxiously bright. He couldn't stand the thought of getting on a crowded bus with a bunch of strangers, so he started walking, until he saw a cab and hailed it.

After swinging into the back seat, he slammed the door on the facade of Aiden's apartment. Vaguely, he felt his phone vibrate against his thigh, but he ignored it.

The driver asked, "Where to?"

Elliott opened his mouth to give the address of his dorm, but the words dried up. He was using his anger to chase the sadness away, and once he stopped, he didn't think he could start that engine again. He wanted to cling to it until there wasn't a drop of it left. He wasn't ready to go home and cry into his pillow and eat chocolate until he felt like throwing up. Right now, he wanted to hurt as he'd been hurt.

An address came out of Elliott's mouth. The driver nodded and Elliott switched off his brain as best he could so he wouldn't think about what he was doing.

Because what did he know? He bared his teeth at his reflection in the car window. How did he know he wouldn't fall in love with the next guy?

Simple. He'd never let anyone get close enough again.

The trip wasn't a long one. Elliott tipped the taxi driver generously with money he'd earned from Aiden. He entered the building at a brisk pace, nodding to the security guard, who sat at a desk that was a carbon copy of the one at Aiden's building: sleek and expensive looking. The guard nodded back, then blinked and squinted. Elliott didn't slow down to watch the man attempt to place him. Instead, he entered the elevator, just like he had at Aiden's. Like he had for two years.

This one had walls of opaque bronze instead of mirrors, which he was thankful for. Vindictive wasn't a good look on him.

The door was the same as he remembered. He didn't waste time second-guessing whether he should be standing outside it again. He knocked loudly three times and waited, heart pounding. His stomach plunged. He wanted the door to stay closed as much as he wanted it to open. He wanted the decision to turn back and forget he'd ever come here to be taken out of his hands.

The door opened soundlessly. Elliott didn't say anything.

"Well," Innes said. "Isn't this a surprise?"

Elliott lurched forward and planted his mouth on Innes's in a punishing kiss.

Chapter  14

Elliott pushed Innes back into the room without breaking the kiss, his eyes wide open. Innes allowed him to, but it only took a couple of seconds for Elliott to realize that he was the only one participating. The door slammed behind him, and Elliott finally let Innes breathe, if only for a moment.

"Come on," he gritted, then dove in again, ignoring the sting of collision. He didn't consider stopping because they'd always kissed with an edge of pain. Not like with Aiden, who—

With his vision blurred, the snatches of dark eyes and darker hair were too much like another Kent. Elliott grunted and squeezed his eyes closed. He fumbled blindly for Innes's belt, then with a wet smack of their lips, Innes jerked his head back, and Elliott was left blinking and stumbling forward, but still as far from Innes as his outstretched arms could hold him.

"Wow," Innes said. "You haven't gotten any less good at that without my influence, I see. Elliott, as much as I appreciate spontaneity, this is—"

"Could you shut up?" Elliott said, his voice low and rough to his own ears. "For once, could you not talk and just have sex with me?"

Innes released Elliott's shoulders and backed up, his chin lifting. "I could," he said, his customary smirk in place. "But something tells me that would be a very stupid decision."

"Shut up, shut *up*," Elliott said, taking a step, but Innes moved out of his reach.

"No. I hardly think it's too much to ask to be allowed to speak in my own home. Sound fair to you?"

Elliott clenched his fists at his sides and remained in mutinous silence.

"All right, then." Innes crossed his arms over his chest, looking down at Elliott, even though they were close to the same height. "Why are you bothering me, Elliott? Not that I'm not overjoyed to see you, but I can't help but be suspicious that you'd come here after all this time and suddenly want to pick up where we left off."

Elliott had to physically unclench his jaw to answer. "I want to. Why does it matter to you why?"

"That's the trouble," Innes said quietly, some—but not all—of his habitual condescension gone. "I'm no shrink, but something tells me that you don't really want anything to happen."

"I do," Elliott argued.

"Quit lying to yourself. You've obviously been through the ringer," Innes said, bluntly. "'Scared rabbit' was always a good look on you, but only when it was an act. This? You pretending you want me after all this time? Not an act I'm interested in. So, if you wouldn't mind, I was having a lovely evening with a bottle of Chablis—"

"Would you stop acting like you're so goddamned noble?" Elliott hissed, getting up into Innes's space and grabbing him before he could move away. "Just—just kiss me, touch me, whatever."

He lunged, his only goal to shut Innes up by occupying his mouth. This time, when Innes pushed him away, it was more than firm. Elliott stumbled and had to grab a coatrack to keep his balance. His face flamed, his anger far beyond reason or logic, but Innes's cold eyes and sharply pointed finger stopped him from saying anything in his own defense.

"That's enough," Innes said. "You need to cool it."

Elliott wiped a rough hand over his mouth. "Why? You never wondered what was going on with me before. As long as you got your dick wet, I could've had the worst day of my life, and you wouldn't have cared. Why start being concerned now?"

Innes blinked. "That's . . . Well, it's not completely untrue, but it isn't the whole truth, either." He crossed his arms again. "I didn't particularly care if you were getting any emotional fulfillment when we were together. I certainly wasn't, and I assumed you liked it that way. But I never said I didn't care about your well-being as an abstract concept."

Elliott scoffed. "Oh, screw you."

"If this is your version of being seductive, I think you need to brush up on your technique. I taught you way better than that."

Elliott shifted restlessly on his feet. "You never gave a shit about what I got out of it when we fucked. You never cared if I wanted to or not, why do you care now?"

"That is not true." Innes's voice was sharp and sudden as a whip crack, and Elliott, with his jangling nerves, jumped a fraction. He stared, wide-eyed at Innes. Gone were the smirk and the low-lidded eyes that looked down on everyone in their path. Innes was still, unmasked in a way Elliott had never seen him, and angry too. He seemed almost as angry as Elliott himself.

"You can insult me all you want," Innes said. "A lot of it might be true. I don't give a damn about whether you think I'm a good person, but don't you ever accuse me of ignoring whether you wanted it or not."

"I—" Elliott stuttered.

"I might be an asshole, but I have never and will never have sex with someone who doesn't want it."

It was such a shock to hear Innes speaking so frankly that Elliott couldn't summon a word. His mouth worked like a fish while his brain blue-screened and reset itself. Innes did nothing but glare until he came back online.

"I'm—I'm sorry," Elliott said. The words tasted bitter, but a knot in his chest went slack as his anger drained away.

"Good." Innes rolled his shoulders, and then the lazy lean was back. Well, *lazy* was the wrong word for his standard posture: one knee slightly bent, his weight braced on his back foot, his chin up to show the best possible angle of his impressive jawline, which was as clean-cut as Aiden's, but unsoftened by stubble.

Elliott's stomach clenched at the reminder of Aiden. The effort of trying not to think about him made his throat ache.

Coming here had been stupid, he knew that. He would have hated himself if Innes had let him go through with sex. He already hated himself a little bit for coming in the first place, and for pushing himself on Innes. He'd wanted to hurt Aiden by proving him right, somehow. *See, I'm as untrustworthy as you said,* he would've been able to say. *What a bullet you dodged, eh, asshole?* But he would've only made himself more unhappy.

Fingers snapped in front of his face. "Earth to Elliott. You with me, space cadet?"

Elliott blinked rapidly. "Yeah. Sorry."

Innes raised an eyebrow, a gesture so reminiscent of Aiden's that it caused another flare of anger and grief in Elliott. "You really do look awful," Innes said. "You need to take your teenage angst out of here. Go home, call your father, and get him to put the fear of the law into whoever it is that's made you want to make terrible decisions."

"I'm not a teenager. And you don't want me to do that."

"Why not?"

Elliott let out a harsh bark of laughter. "Didn't your family tell you? I'm your nephew's new plus-one. Or I was."

Innes blinked and his hand came up to idly stroke his chin where a villainy goatee might have been. "Oh. Yes, I heard a rumor that Aiden was dating someone. I didn't know it was you."

Elliott grimaced. "'Dating' is too strong a word."

He struggled to keep his eyes on Innes's as Innes teased out what he meant by that. Innes was a smart guy, so it didn't take long for his eyes to widen.

"Ah," he said, neutrally. "It's like that, is it? That's . . . interesting." A long pause followed, in which Elliott fought not to squirm and Innes failed to keep the surprise off his face. "I have to say, I didn't think Aiden had it in him. From his bitch-face whenever I showed up with you, I thought he'd rather be crucified than pay for sex."

Elliott thought back to the gala he'd attended with Aiden. The night he'd started to lose his grip on his professional distance. He'd forgotten how curious he'd been about why Innes had canceled. He'd assumed that it'd been about him and Aiden, but perhaps that had been a bit conceited of him.

"You really didn't know about it?"

"No," Innes answered. "Why would I? Aiden hardly texts me details on his sex life." He shuddered theatrically. "There's a mental image I didn't need. Thanks so much for that."

"No problem." Back when he'd been Innes's pay-per-view boyfriend, he might have rolled his eyes, but he couldn't manage it now.

"Why did you come?" Innes asked, point-blank. "Trouble in paradise?"

Lots of reasons. All of them shitty. To prove Aiden right, yes. But also to make what had happened with him mean less.

When he came down to it, he'd wanted to show himself that what he'd done with the nephew was just the same as what he'd done with the uncle. Now, a little more rational, a little more calm, with the anger leeching away, he saw how messed up that was, and how untrue.

Nothing about it was the same. Innes, he'd walked away from with ease. He was going to be attached to Aiden for a long time.

"No paradise," Elliott said flatly, the strain from all the bullshit emotions he'd felt today catching up to him and dragging his energy down. "That's not my style. Just trouble. The unfixable kind."

Innes's mouth twisted in a not-quite-smile. "Are you sure? I mean, for a lawyer, Aiden puts his foot in his mouth a lot. But did he say something that was really that unforgivable?"

It wasn't so much about what he said as what he'd implied, Elliott wanted to explain. He'd offered to make all of Elliott's dreams come true for the low, low price of his self-respect.

"Ye—" Elliott started, then he frowned. "Why are you asking? What happened to your bottle of wine?"

Innes waved his hand in the direction of his kitchen. "It can wait a few minutes. We might not be close, but we're still family, Aiden and I. I don't want him to be miserable. He'll be hell to deal with in the elevator at work. So, if I can act as a couple's therapist for you two now, I'll save myself some trouble later on."

"How generous of you."

"You know me. Selfless to the core." Shameless satisfaction with his own despicable self glinted in Innes's eye, bringing back all the times Elliott had wished they were more alike. It would have been much easier than butting heads, like they always had.

Even at their most intimate, they hadn't been anything close to friends. Both of them had been aware that they were a business transaction to each other, which would put anyone on edge.

Beyond their inability to trust each other, they just hadn't liked each other that much. It wasn't as if they'd had a lot to talk about when they weren't having sex. Innes had flaunted his privileged upbringing in a large and wealthy family in a way Aiden never had, and Elliott hadn't been able to relate.

At nineteen, Elliott hadn't been at the same point in his life as Innes, either. There was only so much that they could have had in common. Certainly, they were both intelligent, and could've talked about current events, but that would have been boring. They could've discussed their tastes in music or books or art, but there hadn't been much overlap there, either. Elliott read textbooks on topics the everyman would probably find boring. Innes only read books he found in airports that he could finish before his flight landed, regardless of whether or not he hated them.

Now, here Innes was, waiting for Elliott to pour his heart out about his problems with a blood relation.

Elliott was grateful that Innes had put a stop to a bad decision, but that didn't mean he was going to tell him anything. He had people who actually cared about him for that. People who would take his side, no matter what. That was what he really needed.

Elliott took in, then blew out a large breath. "Thanks for your generosity," he said, wryly. "But I'll pass on your offer."

"Suit yourself."

He turned to leave, but the part of him that his parents raised right stopped him. "I really am sorry."

Innes tugged the cuff of his sweater delicately into place over his wrist. "You said."

"For coming here, I mean. And for getting…" A sweeping gesture that encompassed all of Innes was the closest Elliott could get to saying *getting handsy when it wasn't wanted.*

With a quirk of his lip, Innes nodded. "It's fine. We all make mistakes." His voice was surprisingly benign, but any kindness was immediately negated. "Like that tragic shirt. You pick that out of the lost and found?"

All was right, at least in this part of the world. Elliott shook his head. "See you later, Innes. Maybe. Hopefully not soon."

"Why hopefully?" Innes asked. "You don't want to run into me at the family Christmas party? Aiden would be disappointed, I'm sure."

Elliott's jaw clenched. "He'll get over it. He'll have to, because *we're* over. You and I aren't going to end up as in-laws."

"Maybe that's for the best." Innes grimaced. "There's no way it wouldn't have been weird."

Elliott let himself out with a last wave of his hand. The elevator ride down to the lobby was a lot more composed than the ride up. The desk attendant still didn't seem to have placed him, but nodded at him as he went by. Elliott was willing to bet the guy would remember who he was later that night, and he was glad he wouldn't be there to see the guy recognize him as apartment 15A's booty call.

Once he was in the fresh air, his impetus ran out. He stood on the sidewalk, looked up at the cheerfully blue sky, and wondered what he was supposed to do. Coming all the way here had only moved him along geographically. It hadn't moved him from one stage of grief to another. The anger was still there, simmering instead of boiling.

The screen of his phone glowed when he checked the time. He checked his texts too, finally remembering that the phone had gone off in the cab.

Dad: *When do you get your midterm marks back again? You probably rocked it. Those Greeks won't know what hit em. Off to work, but call me tomorrow. Love ya, kiddo.*

Elliott turned off the screen and tucked his phone under his sweater and into the flimsy pocket of his shirt, right against his chest.

Go home, Innes had suggested just now.

Not all of his ideas were bad ones.

When the cab slowed to a stop outside a small house with a slightly overgrown lawn on a quiet street, Elliott was slouched in the back seat, feeling all the aches and pains of a long drive.

His eyes were stinging and sandy as he used the debit machine to pay, already regretting the expense. As he fumbled with the buttons, he told himself it was only from the unhealthy amount of caffeine in the energy drinks he'd downed on the earlier bus ride, and not from the thought of worrying about money even more than he already did.

"Have a good night," the cab driver said as Elliott opened the squeaky car door and pushed out of the low seat.

Fat chance. "Thanks, you too," he gritted out, grabbing his hastily packed gym bag, which felt heavier than it actually was.

The steps needed to be swept, he noticed as he trudged up them. They were sprinkled with old grass clippings and a few seasons' worth of dirt and leaves. From behind him, the lights of the departing car swung across the house, lighting up the door for a split second before Elliott knocked on it. Then knocked again a few times before it was unlocked from the inside.

"Hello?" Kevin said, his sleep-scrunched, confused face peeking out. "What time is . . . Elliott?"

"Hey, man," Elliott said. "Sorry I woke you. I just needed—" His voice broke. "I needed to come home."

Right there on Kevin's doorstep, the tears he'd held back for hours decided they couldn't wait anymore. Before he could wipe them away, Kevin was grabbing him and pulling him in, holding him tight as he crumbled, soaking the shoulder of his cotton shirt.

Neither of them said anything else, half in and out of the doorway, with the light of dawn barely fizzling on the horizon. Kevin was steady, warm, and uncomplicated. After months—years—of complicated, he was exactly what Elliott needed while his hopes came crashing down around him.

Chapter 15

The kitchen was in a state. It always was, no matter how many times Elliott's dad tried to put snack foods back in the cupboard, or quit leaving bills and receipts in the middle of the table.

It was the hub of the house, the first place Dad stopped when he got home after a long night shift, and the first place he unloaded his pockets. It was also where they gravitated to on days like this.

"I was thinking pancakes."

Elliott moved a pile of broken-down cardboard boxes destined for the recycling bin to the floor and sat in the chair. "You sure you have enough room? Or clean surfaces?"

"Get outta here. It's as clean as any kitchen, it's just cluttered."

"Pancakes it is, then."

They hadn't even been made yet, and Elliott knew they'd taste bittersweet. Watching his dad putter around making them was fun, but after four days, this would probably be the last meal they had together before Elliott got on a bus to UCLA in a couple of hours.

Observing in silence, he could pretend that was the only reason, and that he wasn't remembering sitting at a different table while someone else made food for him on a quiet Sunday.

"Here we go." A steaming plate crowded with pancakes landed in front of him. "Not too bad, if I do say so myself."

"Smells great."

They ate as soundlessly as they'd cooked—or Dad had cooked—because after being home for three days, Elliott still didn't have the energy to talk about anything more serious than the neighbors down the street getting a divorce.

He'd cherish every moment of the visit though. It had been exactly what he needed, even if it hadn't fixed everything.

After the food was gone, Elliott washed the sticky syrup from his hands, then checked his phone. A text notification made his heart leap, then plunge.

Amanda: *How was the Roman Empire cut in half? With a pair of CAESARS!! LOLOLOL see you Tuesday!*

He smiled, even as he sent back a rolling eyes emoji and chastised himself for hoping, for a second, it was Aiden.

Shoving the phone away, he tried to take over cleaning duty from his dad, without much success.

"It's only fair," Elliott argued, wrapping the butter back up in tattered foil. "You cooked, I should clean."

Dad shook his head while he picked up clutter from the table, wiping the surface down before replacing each item exactly where it was. "Most of this isn't your mess, and I don't mind."

"I know you don't, but I don't either."

While they worked, Elliott rushed to fit in the last bits of his life he hadn't told his dad yet.

"I tutored—" He stopped and redirected to keep his lies in place. "I had a new client for a while."

"Not anymore?"

"I think we're friends now? We're going to continue with her tutoring sessions, but she keeps dragging me out for coffee." *Dragged* was a strong word. On both occasions, Elliott had gone willingly. Just thinking about it made his chest warm.

"That's good. You need dragging sometimes." Dad was smiling, but it was the tight one he used when he was blustering past his worry.

"I'm not a hermit, I promise." Or at least, he hadn't been when he'd been seeing Aiden regularly. Amanda's request for more tutoring sessions couldn't have come at a better time, since he had more of it on his hands than ever. No more late-night cuddling sessions for him, until someone else . . . Aaand those thoughts would lead nowhere good, so Elliott shook his head to clear it. "Where do you want this pile?"

"Oh, just leave it on the table."

"You can't do that with everything, Dad, or you won't be able to see the wood." He managed to find a place for the stack, but not before a couple of brightly colored flyers fell to the floor. He crouched to pick them up and actually looked at them, with their pictures of crisp lawns and impressive houses.

"You can just leave them on the top, there," Dad said, already straightening the rest of the papers in an attempt to neaten a mess that wouldn't be neatened by anything less than a bonfire.

"What are these?" The question was redundant. He could see exactly what they were, but that didn't answer his questions.

His dad wasn't a hoarder. He was crap at tidying and organization, but he only kept things that were important. And he wanted the pair of pamphlets from local realtors right on the top of the pile.

His dad had gone still. That was more damning than anything he could have said.

"I've been waiting for the right moment to tell you." Dad's strong fingers thumped against the scratched table in a broken rhythm. "It hasn't come yet, so I guess this will have to do. Elliott, I'm going to sell the house."

The confirmation was just as gut-wrenching as it would have been without the warning. "Why?"

"Why not?"

"Because you've worked so hard to keep it. So have I." Elliott's bones were tired from working, and from the worry that he wasn't doing enough. "Over ten years, scrimping to pay the mortgage every month, and you're just giving up?"

Dad's shoulders were rounded, but his face showed only patient confidence. "It's the logical way to go. I'll be retiring sooner than both of us think, and right now, the only thing this place has going for it is the location. Someone will pay a good amount for the property alone, someone with money who can knock it down and build their dream house."

"Knock it down?" The edge of the kitchen counter bit into his fingers. He hadn't even noticed he'd backed up into it. "Dad, you can't." Anger had eclipsed his shock. Everything he'd done to save this place, and this was how it ended?

"I know it's hard, but give it some time to sink in and you'll see."

"You can't. Not after so long."

"Keeping this place won't keep her with us." For the first time, his dad's calm cracked, his mouth tugging down with heartache. "Brick and mortar are just that. We'll either remember her or we won't. Having this place won't make a difference."

Her ghost was there now. Next to the fridge door, stealing a drink from the milk carton. By the sink, singing while she did the dishes. At the table, her bright smile was the first thing Elliott would see in the morning when he came downstairs.

She stole his breath, and she wasn't even real.

The chair creaked as his dad got up, walking through her apparition to put his hands on Elliott's shoulders.

"Listen," he said, like it was easy to do over the roaring in Elliott's ears. "It's hard for you right now. It's taken me a couple years to wrap my head around it, but this is the right thing. If I can get as much for the house as the appraiser says I will, there'll be enough left over after paying the rest of the mortgage to take care of all my debts."

Instinct made him try to argue. "Our—"

"No. My debts. We'll see, but there might even be enough for me to cover your next semester."

The bottom dropped out of Elliott's stomach. "Dad, you don't—"

"It's only fair. We're in this together, right? We can have all of that, and we only need to let go of this place."

More silence filled the kitchen. His dad's hands fell from Elliott's shoulders, hanging limply at his sides in a mirror of Elliott's position, but with all the weight of life slumping his shoulders.

"It's falling apart, son, you know that." The softness of his voice didn't lighten the blow. "The roof won't last, the basement—"

"I know. That doesn't make it easier."

Elliott couldn't stay there. Pleading eyes and old ghosts crowded him, and escaping was the best option, so escape he did. Again.

The start of a new habit, perhaps, but this time, he didn't run away into the arms of a big mistake. He got as far as the garage before his steam ran out and he was alone.

Dad's tool bench was tucked into the corner, covered by rusty wrenches and bent screwdrivers, with a sun-bleached camping chair next to it. The fabric rasped when Elliott sat down, but it held, more sturdy than Elliott felt.

The house. Gone. Probably soon if it'd already been appraised.

He didn't want to cry again. He'd already done enough of that on Kevin's shoulders on his first day home, switching between righteous anger and grief at the drop of a hat, or one reminder of—

His phone materialized in his hands before he'd really thought about it, chasing away thoughts of Aiden by opening his email, checking his calendar, his texts, anything to keep his mind off everything.

He ended up flitting between two pointless games, unable to concentrate on either of them, so when a call came through, he picked it up in seconds and asked, "Did you know?"

Kevin answered right away, to his credit. "Not fully. But he had some questions about my neighborhood, what the rent was like. I wondered, especially when he didn't seem that worried about the basement. I didn't know, though, so I didn't want to tell you until it was for sure."

"It's okay." His shitty week wasn't Kevin's fault. Nor was it Dad's. "Did he call you?"

"Yeah. He sounded really cut up." A nonjudgmental silence followed, for Elliott to process his guilt before Kevin asked, "Are you okay?"

"I'll be fine. It's just . . ."

"Tough."

The air in the garage was stale and smelled of metal and gasoline. Elliott sucked it down, Kevin's anchoring presence—even over the phone—helping to clear his head.

Kevin cleared his throat. "You remember when we met?"

"Of course. At the hospital."

"The north parking lot. We had fun, right?"

They had, pretending to be superheroes and ninjas, even though they'd both been on the cusp of being too old for games like that. While Elliott's mother lay dying, they'd become inseparable.

"That lot's gone now," Kevin said, interrupting vivid sepia-toned memories.

"Really?"

"Yeah. Couple years ago. They put the parking underground and built a new wing."

"Oh." He hadn't driven out that way since he'd started at UCLA. "Cool."

"So, you know. The memories are still there."

Elliott smiled into the phone, holding it with both hands. "Wow, when did you get so cheesy?"

"Hey, I'm just trying to help!"

"I know. Thanks." The sound of his feet shifting echoed around the garage. "It's not that I think she'll really be gone if we lose this place. We have enough photos, and I'll never forget her. It just feels like giving up, that's all."

"Well, maybe it's okay to give up. You could use a break, man. You deserve it."

Did he?

Last week hadn't been the first time he'd run away from something. He'd wanted so badly to get out of his small town, leaving this house and his dad behind to drown in academia, with no guarantee he'd be able to make the most of his degree.

Wasn't he as much to blame for giving up something he'd forgotten to cherish? He'd been so caught up in keeping the house that he'd lost sight of why he wanted it in the first place: For Dad. So he'd have something when Elliott was gone, chasing dreams and running from bad memories.

"You still there, Elliott?"

"Yeah," he rasped. "I'm gonna go, though."

"Okay. But talk to your dad. Don't leave town mad."

"Good advice." Whether he'd take it wasn't so certain.

"You know it. I'm always right."

After they hung up, the garage was silent again. The light coming under the door had changed from the white of morning to golden midday, but he didn't move.

Behind him, the door squeaked open. He didn't look, because those heavy footsteps down the stairs could only have been one person.

"We should get going soon," his dad said. "Are you packed?"

"Yes. Just need to grab my bag."

There was only one chair in the garage, but Elliott's dad found a flat, mostly clean part of the tool bench to lean on, his arms and legs crossed as he contemplated the concrete floor. "I'm sorry to have sprung this on you so quickly."

Elliott shrugged. "It's okay. I don't think you could have done better."

"Give the idea some time to grow on you. Trust me. It's the right thing."

The canvas arms of the camping chair crunched under his hands. "I do trust you. Logically, I know it's the right move. The medical bills are one thing, but the house needs more funds than we'll ever have to put into it. But when will it stop feeling like we're quitting the marathon five hundred yards from the finish line?"

"I hate to be the bearer of bad news, son, but we're a lot farther than five hundred yards from victory. And even if we did get there, what would be the cost?" Dad slid across the bench closer to Elliott, probably picking up a few splinters on the way. "It's like the poor guy in that book your mother used to read you. The one who ran a marathon to some city to tell them the Greeks won."

Elliott couldn't help a small smile at his father's enthusiasm. "Pheidippides."

"Gesundheit. He finished the whole thing, then dropped down dead. Maybe if he'd passed on the torch to someone else, he wouldn't have—"

"Dad, I can see you trying to relate to me, but you don't have to." It came out sharper than he'd meant it to, but he softened it with another smile. "I'll take that time you said I should. Let me come around to the idea."

"Okay."

"Where are you going to live?"

"I figured I'll get an apartment. Something small, close to the station. Easier to keep clean, right?"

Elliott nudged his dad's knee with a toe. "Nah, you'll just shove the same stuff into a smaller space."

"Maybe. There'll always be space for you, though, kiddo. My couch is always open."

Out of nowhere, the guilt he'd been fighting off ratcheted up, and all he could do was stare at his phone in his hands, wondering over and over if there was more he could have done, places he could have trimmed his budget. Useless, now, but what if—

"You'd better cut that out right now."

He looked up to see a chastising finger and a pointed glare in his direction. "What? I'm not doing anything."

"Uh-huh. Sure. I saw that look on your face the day you got accepted into UCLA. I won then, and I'll win now." Dad's knees cracked as he crouched down so that the two of them were on the same level. "Kiddo, you might not be ready to hear this, but I'm happy, and not despite the fact that I'm selling this place. It's partly because of that. It's gonna be like starting over. Making new memories."

It was the perfect thing to say—something Elliott could remember later on tonight when he was lying awake—but it didn't take away his guilt. It just changed it, because he knew exactly what his dad was talking about.

The presence of his mom in every room was as claustrophobic as it was precious, and by the end of each summer, he was always dying to get back to school to have a break from it. With the option of trips home taken away, the relief was dizzying.

"We should head out," Dad said, straightening up and shaking out his legs.

"I'll get my stuff." Elliott stood, but before he could shuffle to the door, his dad's hand settled on his elbow.

"By the way." Dad's salt and pepper eyebrows—when had that happened?—were low over his twinkling eyes. "If you try to send me another penny, I'll disown you."

Elliott grimaced. "Come on, Dad—"

"No, I'm serious." He tipped his head. "Okay, not that serious, but serious enough that I'll just send it back. That's a promise, so don't even try."

It was a conversation they'd had before, when his dad's pride was at its most bruised, but this time, there was a steely core to the oath. Elliott could tell he meant it, so he cleared his tight throat.

"Okay, Dad."

"You're gonna be fine, right? I know you've been really down this break, and I respect you enough that I won't pry. But you won't keep whatever's bothering you inside to eat away at you, right?"

Elliott wanted to say that everything was fine, that he was having a normal college experience and that his heartbreak—which he'd spoken of only briefly on his first day back—was the run-of-the-mill kind.

Someday, he'd be able to tell the truth.

"I'll be all right," he said, for now. "Promise."

With one tug on his arm, Elliott was wrapped in a warm, solid hug.

"I should have told you all this days ago." Dad's voice rumbled through Elliott's bones. "So you could process a bit before you left, but I was selfish. I wanted to enjoy the days I had with you."

"It's okay," he murmured in his father's ear. "I miss you."

"You're still here. How can you miss me?"

"I just do. I'll see you again soon, I promise."

"I'll hold you to it."

They broke apart, both of them blinking fast.

"All right, kiddo, let's shake a leg."

While his dad started the car, Elliott procrastinated the end of his trip, trailing his fingers along the walls, cataloguing each detail.

If this was the last time he saw the place when it was whole and untainted by realtors putting a brave face on it, he wanted his memories to be crystal clear.

His thin mattress squeaked as he collapsed back onto it.

He didn't feel recharged, exactly. He was still as tired from the tangled mess of his emotions as he was at the beginning of the break, but at least he'd been topped up on parental guidance and affection.

Brotherly love, too. Kevin probably knew he hadn't gotten the full story, but he was a good enough friend not to press for details. All he'd done was agree and curse Aiden's name, which had been exactly what Elliott had needed.

There wasn't enough room to stretch out all the kinks from the bus, but he put his hands on the concrete wall behind his head and pointed his toes to the footboard. The trip had been long, with little to do but think about Aiden, the fight, all the words he wished he could take back, and what he was going to do.

He reached for his phone and read some emails he'd been ignoring. There wasn't much. The campus bookstore was having a sale, a professor had sent an email about office hours, his floor president had called a meeting, the scholarship committee—

Heart sluggishly pounding, Elliott clicked the email.

Dear Mr. Meyer, we are pleased to inform you that you've been awarded a scholarship. Please RSVP to the presentation ceremony . . .

Wasn't life funny? At the end of one of the worst weeks of his life, a bit of good news. Maybe he'd be able to buy that laptop after all with the extra tidbit in his savings account.

Sending off his response to the ceremony invite—yes, duh—was the work of a moment, then he was all caught up. Then, following a long-rehearsed pattern, he opened his banking app.

He had his last month's pay in his bank account. He nearly sent it back until he remembered that they weren't simply ending a relationship, they were terminating a business arrangement. If he refused to take the payment they'd agreed on, then he was going back on everything he'd told himself about keeping it professional.

So he was back to where he'd started at the beginning of the year. A little better off, now that his dad had put his foot down about helping out, sure. But he still had to pay for his living expenses, pay for a useless degree he loved.

Even if he made his mythical tutoring side hustle a reality and earned one of the teaching-assistant spots, they wouldn't cover everything. A regular job with more hours might, but then he couldn't study as much as he did now, or beg for extra projects like he'd planned to do in his final year—

No. He wasn't done. He'd find someone else. Although, it'd probably be someone worse than the two who'd come before.

No one was lucky three times in a row.

He drifted in his bed, too tired to get up, too hungry to fall asleep fully.

Then his phone rang.

Before he looked, he knew it wasn't Kevin or Dad. And who else—besides the new addition of Amanda, who usually only texted in emoji hieroglyphics—would call him?

Aiden's picture lit up the screen, and Elliott had to fight to stop himself from stroking the crinkle of his forehead. (Elliott remembered taking it, batting away Aiden's hands, laughing at Aiden's exaggerated annoyance.) Instead, he declined the call.

His hands shook as he did it, but the pain was far away and it still felt right. This was something he was supposed to do in order to move on, wasn't it? He'd never been in a real relationship, but didn't people say a clean break was better?

Maybe he'd be ready to talk to Aiden someday. For now, there was no point in causing himself more pain when there was no way their relationship could go back to what it was.

When his phone rang again, he declined once more, then blocked Aiden's number.

Chapter  16

Adulting is hard, Elliott typed out, carefully crafting a string of emojis, and sent it to Kevin.

Cry me a river, Kevin sent back immediately, but he followed it with, *What's up?*

I'm at a rEcEpTiOn, Elliott painstakingly emoted. *There's so many fancy people here.*

Is that for your scholarship? Did you find out how much $$$?

KEVIN CHAN. You're such a gold digger. I'll have you know I'm hobnobbing with important people. I'm NETWORKING.

He hadn't actually done any networking yet. He'd meant to, and dressed up a little for the occasion. He'd seen a few former professors, and a teacher's assistant he'd really love to pump for useful information about the application process, but putting himself out there like that, right now . . .

Perhaps by the end of the night he'd stop feeling so fragile, like he'd crack if someone looked at him wrong.

His phone buzzed again.

Kevin: *Yeah, but would you go if you weren't getting a scholarship?*

Elliott: *Nah, u kno me.*

In truth, the awards reception was a small price to pay for—probably—a few hundred dollars in scholarship money every semester. He'd never missed one, even though it wasn't strictly mandatory, only strongly encouraged in the letter he got with the good news twice a year.

The money was only part of the reason why it was worth it to stand around a lobby in the Humanities building, hiding next to the cheese tray until the actual ceremony happened in the auditorium.

However much the award ended up being, he'd put it away in his laptop fund, and maybe he'd be closer than he thought. (Or maybe that was wishful thinking.)

But no matter the drama of his love life—completely normal, he supposed, however alien it felt—his grades hadn't noticeably dipped. *And they won't*, he reminded himself. At least, not because of any love life. He didn't have one anymore.

That part of his college experience was over. But if he didn't get a move on and get over it, he'd be paying for it out of pockets that weren't that deep.

The heart-pounding panic was shoved aside by the buzzing of his phone.

Are you lurking again? Kevin was seriously telepathic. That was what Elliott got for a decade of friendship.

Elliott: *Whatever do you mean?*

Kevin: *You're doing your wallflower thing, aren't you?*

Elliott let his eyes wander to the wall he'd been hugging and the table he'd hidden behind. *Maybe.*

Kevin: *SOCIALIZE.*

Elliott: *WHY.*

Kevin: *Why not?*

Elliott: *Good question.*

Elliott's fingers froze on his phone. He had seen Amanda standing with someone when he'd made his beeline to the refreshment table, but it had taken him a second to realize he knew who she was sitting with. Friendly, overtired Matt, who must have found himself a tutor if he was here. Seeing them talking to each other had been, at first, a shock, but of course they were friendly, even if they occupied two different spaces in his mind.

They'd waved, he'd waved back, then . . . not gone over. He and Amanda were just at the point where he'd consider her a friend, but Matt was another case entirely. So instead, he'd resumed ignoring them, along with anyone he might connect with on a human level.

But were they so different from him? A few years separated them, but years meant nothing when it came to connection. Aiden had taught him that, at least.

Sinking his phone into his pocket, he took his uncharacteristic extroversion by the reins and rode it all the way to the small huddle Amanda and Matt had made for themselves by the wall.

"Hey," he said elegantly.

"Hi, Elliott," Amanda said, brightly, setting his worry to rest. "How's it going?"

"I'm not complaining. Not yet, at least. If they let the dean get on the microphone again, I might revisit that policy, but only if I don't die of boredom."

Matt snorted into his paper cup of coffee.

"I'm good, though, really," Elliott said. "You?"

She shrugged. "I'm not complaining either. Except about how little this scholarship helps. A couple hundred bucks isn't going to make much difference either way, but thanks, I guess? I'll be a slave to my student loan for a month less." She brightened, her eyes going mischievous. "And thanks, also, to Elliott, whose help probably saved my grade point average at least a few points."

She gave an over-the-top bow, complete with a flourishing hand, and nearly missed Elliott's embarrassed grimace as a result.

"No way, you would have earned it by yourself."

"Maybe, but you helped, and I have a little less to worry about, money-wise. So thank you, again." This time, she rested her palm on his shoulder for a second, her skin as warm as her smile.

"No problem." He'd always known he wasn't the only one worrying about the cost of his education, but it was nice to hear it out loud. The other part of her short rant interested him more, though. "So, they told you how much you're being awarded?"

"Yep. They didn't tell you?"

"No. I thought it was a new rule or something, maybe to get people to actually show up to these things." Pressing his hands to his cheeks, he gasped. "What? You mean the hour-long congratulatory speeches and warm sparkling cider aren't enough of a draw?"

Matt laughed again, then grunted in surprise when Amanda knocked him gently in the shoulder. "God, you were so right," she said.

Matt blushed and stared into his drink, and Elliott waited for Amanda to elaborate.

"He was telling me how funny you are for weeks before I even talked to you," she said, clearly unfazed by Matt's embarrassment.

Elliott forced a laugh. "I hope that's ha-ha funny, and not weird funny."

Matt spoke up for the first time. "Early Christian History is the only class I never skip because you and the professor getting into it is so hilarious."

"I— Thanks."

The coffee cup squeaked as Matt passed it from one hand to the other. "I don't make a habit of talking about you behind your back. It's just between us two."

"I got used to hearing about your showdowns with Salter," Amanda piped up. "And now I make him give me a recap every week."

"You don't make me do anything," Matt said, rolling his eyes with a fond smile.

"Except laundry, slob."

Elliott watched them bicker, content to sit back and let them navigate the waters of new relationship territory. It wasn't pre-hookup flirting; they were obviously past that. This was the exciting middle ground between chemistry and intimacy.

Missing the time when he'd had that for himself hurt, but the consolation was being a part of a small cluster, instead of firmly on the outside of it. It was easy to picture himself craving more of this easy affection, and maybe he'd let himself give in to that craving.

He couldn't have what Matt and Amanda had with each other, but maybe he could have their friendship.

"Did you keep going with that study group?" Elliott asked, and he knew how abrupt he sounded only from the way Matt's and Amanda's eyes widened in unison.

"Uh, yeah." Ruefully smiling, Matt gave a thumbs-up. "I even learned some things instead of just drinking coffee."

"Awesome."

"You should come!" Amanda piped up, never one to be forgotten. "I can't always go, but I'm there some of the time, and Matt's there all of the time, now, on pain of death and flunking. It's a good group, you'd like it."

"I think I will," Elliott said. What was stopping him, really? He was already friendly with a couple of regulars. Even if he ended up as an unofficial tutor for the group—was that conceited? He thought he deserved a little bit of conceit, at least in this area of expertise—it would probably be a good thing. He'd read in an article that the best way to learn something and never forget it was to explain it to someone else, and he was inclined to believe—

"Elliott!"

Professor Salter took Elliott's hand before he'd remembered to offer it, shaking it enthusiastically.

"Hi, Professor."

"Please, call me Dave. This isn't high school." He dropped Elliott's hand after he seemed to realize he was still pumping it up and down. "Congratulations, by the way. Can't think of someone more deserving. And excellent move with the tutoring before the break, there. That really clinched it for the committee."

"Uh, thanks?" He flicked his gaze to Amanda and Matt, then back again. "We're all grateful for the help."

"Oh, I'm sure." Professor Salter's hand flapped between them, the rough fabric of his brown suit waggling around his wrist. "But you must be especially so, yes?"

Elliott blinked, even farther out to sea than he usually was with Professor Salter. "Pardon?"

"Ah." Wild eyes squinted as he scratched at his whiskered cheek. "Now that you mention it, that was something I was meant to keep to myself. No matter! It's done now. I'll see you after the ceremony."

"Okay?"

"Ta!"

The doors to the auditorium opened for the people waiting in the lobby clustered in impatience, and Professor Salter was lost in the crowd.

"Ooh, I want a good seat in the front," Amanda said. "You can sit with us if you like."

Amanda's face was so open and accepting that he didn't even feel bad that he'd reached his limit of social interaction for the day. "Thanks, but I'll grab a place at the back."

"Okay." She dragged an unresisting Matt away. "See you later!"

There was no fighting the herd of students and professors making their way to their seats, so Elliott didn't even try. He was swept along, not looking where he was going, too busy wondering what Professor Salter—he didn't think he'd ever be able to call him Dave—had meant. What was he supposed to keep to himself?

"Oh. Hello, Elliott."

His knees locked. The voice was so familiar, yet jarringly out of place.

He turned to face her, pasting on a bland smile. "Hi, Jill. How are you?"

"Fine," she said, coolly. Her brown eyes, so similar to Aiden's, were more glasslike and cold than he'd ever seen them.

How much did she know? Aiden wouldn't have spilled everything, but they were close, and he deserved a good wine-and-bitching session with his sister.

"Are you getting an award tonight?" Jill said.

"Yes." Someone jostled past him, and he shifted his feet.

"Wonderful." She smiled, small but not ungenuine. "We're sponsoring one. Well, the family foundation is."

"That's great. For which department? If you don't mind me asking," he tacked on, even though he was deadly curious.

She shrugged and her lips tilted with her chagrin. "I don't know that much about it, if I'm honest. I agreed to it at the family meeting about where we wanted to donate this year, but Mom and Dad took care of it, like usual. They couldn't be here, so we're representing the Kent family."

Elliott's chest tightened. "'We'?"

"Jill? They want us to sit down now. The announcements will start soon."

How many times in a few hours could his heart sink, leap, or pound before he started to worry about its health?

Elliott turned around quickly to the familiar, deep voice. Aiden stood beside them, tall and straight-backed as ever, in a pristine suit and tie. He didn't look surprised to see Elliott; he met Elliott's panicked gaze calmly and with the same guarded politeness as his sister, although his eyes looked several degrees warmer.

"Hello, Elliott," he said, and Elliott's throat went as dry as a desert.

"Aiden," Elliott blurted, instead of greeting him like a normal person. "Um, I— I'm going to . . ."

Elliott ran away. He might've walked briskly instead of actually sprinting, but that didn't change the fact that he was running from a conversation he wasn't ready to have. He made it to a seat in the corner of the auditorium, and ducked down as far as he could without actually putting his head between his knees.

It was fine. He was a grown-ass man, and so was Aiden. They could occupy the same space for one evening without anything happening. Aiden wasn't vindictive or a drama queen. They could handle this.

After a couple of deep breaths, Elliott uncurled from his protective crouch. The room was filling quickly, but he could still pick Jill and Aiden out right away, in the front row, sitting shoulder to shoulder, their dark hair gleaming under the fluorescent lighting.

Elliott couldn't stop staring at the backs of their heads with the intensity of a cat watching a fish swim around its tank, hoping that Aiden would turn to his sister so that Elliott could see his profile. He didn't know if he was hoping for the expression on Aiden's face to be carefree and happy or solemn and strained. The first one was preferable, but he probably wasn't a good enough person.

The award ceremony passed without him paying much attention. There wasn't a lot to pay attention to, and Jill's shiny hair dripping down her shoulders as she tilted her head to hear Aiden whisper to her was much more engaging.

He felt like a total creep, but not enough to stop. Most people stalked their exes on the internet, looking through pictures and wondering what might have been if they'd done this or that differently. Elliott just had the fortunate/unfortunate opportunity to do it in person.

". . . recipient of this new award is Elliott Meyer."

The sound of his name startled him out of his wistful daze. It was showtime, so he covered his shock with an Oscar-worthy smile. He stumbled to his feet, tripping over some lady's purse in his rush to get to the stage and shake hands with the ancient board member who'd been handing out envelopes and reptilian smiles all night at the pace of a sloth with an attitude problem. There was no envelope, though. At least, not in the hands of the octogenarian presenter.

"We are lucky enough to be joined by two members of the Kent family, who have generously sponsored this scholarship," the master of ceremonies simpered, and Elliott tripped again as he approached the little stage they'd erected. Jesus. How many surprises could he get in one night before it was hazardous to his health? "Please join me in giving them a hand."

The applause wasn't as loud as the roaring in his ears. Jill was the one who handed the envelope over and shook his numb hand, smiling brightly as she posed for a picture with Aiden standing bodyguard-style at her shoulder. Elliott probably looked like a deer in the headlights.

He barely remembered getting back to his seat. All he could do was stare at the envelope in his hands that bore his name and the Kent Family Foundation banner and wonder if Aiden had done this because he hated him. Had he put this money in Elliott's hands because he'd actually listened to Elliott's explanation of his discomfort with taking money for nothing? Was he fully aware that taking this money would make him feel more dirty than he ever had, because it came with no strings except for the ones Elliott had tied on himself?

He didn't open it. The rational part of his brain was sure that the irrational, emotional side of him which was firmly in control would rip up the check as soon as he saw it, and as much as his fingers itched to do just that, he didn't want to regret it later.

The rest of the awards were given out quickly. Or maybe he spaced out while they went on and on, only waking up when it was over. He joined the line of students, proud parents, and sponsors who were trudging back to the lobby and the exit, far too slowly for Elliott, who imagined two sets of brown eyes pinned to the back of his head.

The door was in sight, and it was all he could think about. When he'd come to the ceremony, he'd expected a boring night of glad-handing with the rich people who funded the next generation, punctuated by a brief moment of pride that he was on that small stage, accepting a gift that acknowledged his hard work. It'd gone so differently, and he just wanted it to be over.

When he finally extricated himself from the crowd, he power walked toward the exit, and was so close to escaping when his shoulder was taken in a firm grip.

"Elliott!" Jill said, brightly. "Congratulations!"

"Thanks." The envelope crinkled audibly in his hand.

"I can't believe it was you who won this," she continued, her smile seeming genuine but tentative. "We all saw the shortlist of people they were considering, but ultimately, it was the college's decision, and I'm so glad it was you."

Elliott blinked, wary of her warmth, but distracted by her words. "What?"

"I know you and Aiden aren't . . ." She squared her shoulders and went on. "But you were clearly the best candidate, and we're still allowed to be happy for you."

"Yeah," he croaked. "It's great. Can you thank Aiden for me?" He couldn't do it himself. It would end up sounding too bitter and too angry.

"I could," Jill said, her eyebrow lifting. "It'd be better if I thanked my parents instead. They were the ones who made this happen."

"I— Really?" Elliott said, twitching backward to see her face clearly. "He got them to consider sponsoring UCLA, though, right?"

"Well, he voted in favor of it back in December when we made our charitable donation decisions, certainly. We didn't know why he had a vested interest back then. Hell, we didn't know about you at all. But no, he didn't push for it more than any other cause."

"Oh." Elliott glanced down at the envelope clenched in his fist. He smoothed it out, running his thumb over the letters of the Kent Family stamp.

They hadn't known. They hadn't picked him out of a list of worthy applicants just because they recognized his name as their cherished son's latest flame. Aiden hadn't given this to him as an insult. He'd *earned* it.

"Elliott?"

"Hmm?" He glanced up from the letter and realized he'd been staring at it in silence for longer than was socially acceptable.

"Are you okay?" Jill's face was pinched and cautious.

"Fine," he said, but his voice was too high to sound truthful.

"You look tired." Her words were as blunt as her gaze. "And sad. Do you know who else looks tired and sad?"

Elliott's eyes skittered away, staring at the reflective glass of the door that was, temptingly, mere feet from them. He could guess who she was talking about, but that didn't mean he wanted to hear it.

"I don't know what happened between you two," she went on. "All I know is that one day, my brother was happier than he'd been in years, and the next, he was quiet and acting like his world was ending. He told us not to think badly of you, that it wasn't your fault. I don't know you very well, but I'm inclined to believe him. But the way he seems now? How heartbroken he is? I don't think he'd purposefully sabotage your relationship. So if it wasn't your fault, and it wasn't his, then why are you making yourselves miserable?"

"It's a lot more complicated than that," he said, with the edge of a whine.

"Do you care about him?" Jill demanded.

He stayed silent.

"Do you love him?"

His whole body cringed away from the word. "I—"

"Jill, enough."

Aiden was there, once again having snuck up on them. Elliott took advantage of Jill's distraction and fled, hoping he'd find another exit somewhere.

"Elliott, wait," Aiden called after him.

Elliott huffed and slowed to a stop in the middle of a long hallway that was, thankfully, deserted. Against his better judgment, he turned around. "Can't go anywhere without a Kent in my way."

Aiden winced. "I'm sorry. I won't stop you if you want to leave."

"What do you want?" Elliott asked, then winced himself. He sounded a lot more angry than he was. Right now, he was tired and confused from his flip-flopping emotions. Scared, relieved, mad, sad, relieved again. He wanted to escape, but this was also the most alive he'd felt in days.

"I'd like to talk," Aiden said, unperturbed, his face as granite-hard as usual. "We left everything in such a bad place."

"What's there to talk about?" Elliott shrugged, his helplessness weighing him down. "Honestly, I'd like to know. I'm not angry with you anymore. You see providing for someone without repayment as a way to show you care. I see it as a tab I have to pay off. You don't want to be with me while I'm working with a client. That's okay. It doesn't make you a bad person. It's how you feel, and I respect that. So where does that leave us? I still need money and you still can't give it to me."

"Have you opened that letter?" Aiden asked.

Elliott blinked from the non sequitur. "No. I haven't exactly had a moment to myself, and even a money-grubbing ho like me knows better than to rip it open in front of everyone—"

"Stop that," Aiden snapped. "Don't put yourself down like it's a meaningless joke. I don't think that about you, and you don't think it either. Or at least you shouldn't."

"Sorry," Elliott said, automatically, though he wasn't sure if he was apologizing to Aiden or to himself. To everyone who'd ever cared about him despite his flaws.

"Would you open it now? And read it?"

Elliott nodded jerkily and started to peel up the seal of the envelope. He mangled it, shredding it beyond what was necessary. He had a sudden flash of crystal-clear memory: his mom opening bills and letters at their kitchen table, him watching, fascinated, as she split the paper from its glue easily and without giving herself a papercut. It'd been one of the things that meant true adulthood in his young eyes, along with shaving and making a box of chocolates last more than a day.

There was only one sheet of paper. He frowned, confused. He'd expected a letter informing him of his duty to send a thank-you note to the donors, as well as a check. Instead, he skimmed the single folded sheet until his eyes landed on the words *in the value of full tuition for the remainder of your schooling.*

"Wh-what," he stuttered. "What does this mean?"

"Exactly what it says," Aiden replied, his expression neutral, but not hiding a spark of excitement in his eyes. "The Kent Foundation doesn't do anything by halves. You won't have to pay for school next year, and after that as well, as long as you plan to stay at UCLA, and keep your marks as high as they are now."

"Yes, of course," Elliott said, still staring, dazed at the paper in his hands. "But I thought this wasn't . . ."

"This is the way my parents wanted it," Aiden insisted. "The college agreed to it. It's yours now, the funds are endowed, and they can't be taken away for some petty reason like, say, the recipient and the donor's son dating, but it not working out."

Elliott looked up at Aiden at that. The small smile that touched his lips was sad, but it was still a smile.

"Thank you," Elliott whispered. Crunching numbers in his head was second nature. This changed everything. His plans, his backup plans, they'd all be unnecessary, now that he had this.

"Why are you thanking me? Thank the college. It was based on GPA and the professors' recommendation."

Elliott took a steadying breath. "This just seems way too good to be true. I'm going to wake up in a couple minutes and still be where I was. This is like a scene from a movie, and life isn't like that."

"No, it isn't," Aiden agreed.

"My whole life, if I wanted something, I had to earn it. Nothing comes for free."

"This isn't a handout," Aiden argued, his hand slashing in a firm, quieting motion. "You applied for scholarships and were awarded one based on your own merit. You did that yourself. You'll end up where you want to be because you got yourself there. You don't need me or anyone else. All you need is a leg up, which you've earned through hard work. You could have done it without this." Aiden jerked his chin in the direction of the crumpled letter in Elliott's hands. "I know it. But you don't have to."

Elliott let the words sink in. His dad—and his mom, when she was alive—had told him to work hard, be his own person, and get what he wanted in life. He'd done that. He'd tried to make them proud.

He nodded and couldn't keep the joy off his face as he read the words *academic merit and dedication* over and over.

"I can stop," he said. "Working, I mean."

"Do you want to?"

Elliott considered that. He wasn't ashamed of what he'd done. He had no reason to be. But he felt a little giddy with relief at the thought that he might be able to stop spending so much emotional labor by fighting with himself on bad days. He wouldn't have to put on the right mask to get what he needed.

"Yes," he said, lifting his head proudly and meeting Aiden's eyes. He didn't need to explain himself or his decision, so he didn't offer anything more than that.

"Congratulations, then. I'm happy for you," Aiden said, so softly it almost didn't carry across the short distance between them in the quiet hallway. "I love seeing you smile like that. It reminds me . . ."

Elliott's heart pounded quicker in his chest. "Is this all you wanted to talk about, Aiden?" He lifted the decimated envelope.

"No." Aiden took a step closer, and Elliott wanted to step back, hide from the dangerous feelings he'd thought he'd left behind, but he held his ground. "I wanted to tell you that I'm sorry."

Elliott kept his silence. His fingers itched to smooth away the sadness etched in Aiden's forehead. They'd both said things they shouldn't have. Elliott had stuck the knife of a comparison to Innes right where it would hurt Aiden most. Aiden had let his own fears and his own comfort with taking money he hadn't earned project onto Elliott.

They'd both messed up, and they both deserved forgiveness. But before Elliott forgave Aiden, he had to know if Aiden knew what it was that he'd been so torn up about.

"I'm rich," Aiden said, after a few moments of visibly composing himself. "And I got that way so quickly because my parents were rich before me. I know how privileged that makes me. I never needed to work a day in my life. It never was about working to live, for me. I've never lacked anything, never had to make difficult decisions about what to save up for, what I can afford to buy this week. It's hard for me to understand."

"I get that," Elliott said, his pulse pounding. "But I need you to. I can't just—"

"I know." Aiden stepped closer, and this time, Elliott allowed him to crowd into his space. "I did a lot of thinking in the last week. I thought about what it might be like to be in your shoes. To fall in love with the person who was supporting you financially, while knowing that the axe hanging over your head could fall any second because they decided it wasn't worth it anymore."

Elliott's whole body flushed with warmth.

Aiden reached out a hand, slowly enough that Elliott could lean away, but Elliott let him brush a thumb over his open, trembling mouth. "And to feel like every kiss," Aiden said, "no matter how freely given, could be measured against the cost of how much money was being spent, and found lacking."

The pent-up air in Elliott's lungs left him, and he slumped forward onto Aiden, his head leaning on Aiden's firm, familiar shoulder. He'd missed Aiden's warmth more than he'd even admitted to himself. Aiden's arms came around him tentatively, then tightened further when Elliott shuddered with relief.

"Trust you to say it better than I ever could," Elliott said. His eyes were stinging, and his throat felt two sizes too small, but he wouldn't cry now.

"Hey, it's what I do." Aiden shrugged with the shoulder Elliott wasn't leaning on.

"You understand." Relief and happiness coursed through him.

"I think I do. So, I'm sorry."

"It's okay." He sniffed loudly, grossly. "I am too, for comparing you to your uncle. You're nothing like him. You both paid me, but that's where the similarities end."

"I am like him, though, in some ways. We're both part of this family, no matter how much I dislike his inability to be nice to average humans. I don't have his ruthlessness, and I definitely worry more about your age than he ever did."

Elliott's heart tugged with pity at Aiden's struggle. "It's not a big—"

"I know. At least I'm getting there." He winced, but he didn't look as pained as he had the other times it'd come up. "I might have had a bit of help with that."

Elliott felt his forehead furrow. "From who?"

"Jill." Aiden shuffled his feet, his eyes drifting away from Elliott's face. "She knew you and I were having problems. I couldn't have kept that from her if I tried. But I sort of . . . led her to believe we'd broken up for different reasons."

"Oh."

That explained the chat they'd had just now. Jill had probably been trying her best to keep her distance, because that was what sisters did with their siblings' exes—or so Elliott guessed—but she hadn't blamed him for Aiden's insecurities. It made sense.

"She read me the riot act," Aiden said, his lip quirking. "Reminded me that she's about your age. If she brought home someone as old as me, I wouldn't freak out, because I trust her to make her own decisions and know what's right for her."

Lifting an eyebrow, Elliott bit back a smile. "Just like that, huh?"

"She might have repeated it a few times, but it's starting to sink in." Aiden's face went serious. "I trust your judgment. You've been nothing but sure of yourself since we met. Innes must have seen your strength too, or he wouldn't have pursued you. We're similar in that way too. Actually, the same thing that attracted him to you was probably what drew me in." Aiden grimaced. "Will that ever not be weird?"

Elliott shook his head and smiled, and for the first time in days, it felt like it wasn't going to break his face. "It's unlikely. It'll be our cross to bear. Our skeleton in the closet that we can horrify the next generation with when we're older."

"You want to get old with me?" Aiden said, softly.

Elliott blinked and his whole body spasmed with shock. How had they gotten to this point? It seemed like a few minutes ago, they'd been nothing to each other, and now he was picturing them in matching rocking chairs yelling at neighborhood kids to stop watering their lawns because of the drought.

It was his knee-jerk reaction to say *No, of course not.* But that wouldn't be entirely truthful.

"I—I mean, it's probably too soon to tell, right?" Elliott stammered. "I'm twenty-one. It's only been a few months, and we weren't even really dating for most of it."

Aiden's chest shuddered with laughter against Elliott's. "Relax. I wasn't proposing marriage."

"Oh. Good." Elliott cringed internally at his overreaction. "Are we dating right now?"

Aiden went perfectly still, and the small, barely there movements of their swaying, clinging embrace stopped completely. "That depends. I want to date you."

"Why?" Elliott asked.

"I already know that I love you." Aiden took Elliott's face in his hands, stroking his bruised under-eyes with his thumbs, looking for all the world like he'd never been happier. "What I want now is to know you, inside and out, with no pretenses. I want to be with you, and listen to you, and make sure you know you're on equal footing with me. No more paying your way unless you ask me to."

Elliott couldn't stop smiling. It was like Aiden had peered into his dreams and pulled a monologue from their depths, crafting it perfectly and clearly for Elliott to hear.

"You wouldn't mind getting a cheap-ass cheeseburger with me, Mr. Big Shot Lawyer?" Elliott teased. "It's all I can afford."

Aiden's lips stretched in one of his rare, bright, teeth-showing smiles. "I'd love that. Especially since I'll be budgeting a bit tighter myself."

"What?"

"I quit. Handed in my notice a couple days ago." Aiden's grin had shifted into a wild thing, a little crazed, but definitely ecstatic.

"Oh my god!"

"I want to do what I love, like you do. Not totally sure what that is, yet, but I'll figure it out. Charity work, probably."

There was a bright passion shining in Aiden's eyes, and it was easy to believe that Aiden would do great things, and most importantly, things that would make him happy.

"You'll be amazing, no matter what you do. So, plebeian food it is. We can go out for it, if you want," Elliott said, pretending to consider it seriously. "Or we could stay in. Skip the dating phase and go straight to cuddling on the couch."

"You sure know the way to a man's heart."

"I don't know about that." Elliott tugged Aiden down by the lapels of his jacket and kissed him, his lips tingling with the spark of their new, amazing dynamic. "But I seem to have found my way into yours."

"You did. Accidentally, fantastically, inescapably."

"You swallow a thesaurus or something? I thought I was supposed to be the academic."

Aiden snorted inelegantly, then kissed Elliott again, in the middle of a public building, steps away from the thinning crowd of people.

"I think I love you too," Elliott whispered to him when it was over.

Aiden lifted an eyebrow and drawled, "You *think*?"

"Give me a break, here. I've been trying to convince myself that I hated you for the past week and a half."

Aiden took one of his hands and squeezed it tightly. "That's fine. We have time, now that there's nothing holding you back."

"You sure dating isn't too much hassle? What if I don't want to leave in the morning?"

"I'm sure. If you can fit me into your schedule, I'll always want you with me."

They kissed one last time. Elliott thought he heard Jill's heels click purposefully toward them, then away, but he was too busy pressing grateful lips to Aiden's to pay attention.

Epilogue

Five *in the afternoon is a terrible time to try to teach a class,* Elliott thought, not for the first time. The freshman students he was instructing on red figure pottery were visibly wilting, despite his impassioned lecturing.

Hopefully, the actual professor of this class wouldn't hold it against him. He was doing his best, and he thought it was pretty good, considering that it was right around dinnertime for most of them. Or nap time, whichever they were in more need of. The students had started off bright-eyed and bushy-tailed, likely curious to see if their TA crashed and burned during his first attempt to lead a seminar, then they'd been interested and engaged in the content Elliott was exploring.

There was only so much he could do to keep them awake, though. And it certainly didn't help that the ground-floor window of the classroom faced the sun, which was setting at an agonizingly slow pace and boring a hole right into Elliott's eyes.

As he switched topics, giving his notes a cursory glance to make sure he was on track, something glittered in the corner of the window. A car, passing through the half-empty lot. He would have ignored it, except he recognized it right away. The color and model were familiar.

For a brief second, he paused, long enough for a couple of people in the back row to perk up. He shook it off quickly, though, and launched back into his train of thought.

He felt good about the rest of the class. With the end of the allotted time in sight, a few of the keeners sat up a little straighter and listened better. Elliott became more and more comfortable, dropping in one of his prepared quips, hoping he came off as a quirky and amusing teaching assistant, not a desperately uncool one.

He'd expected to feel nervous. He *had* been nervous. All day, in fact. The only reason he wasn't fainting from low blood sugar was because Aiden had texted him throughout the day, threatening him with dire consequences if he didn't eat at least half a sandwich and an apple. He'd obeyed, and felt much better for it, even though peanut butter and jelly had been hard to swallow when his stomach was tight and his hands finely trembling.

But then, he'd stepped up to the front of the room instead of off to the side, and once he'd started talking about something he was passionate about, the nerves had melted away.

He was only in his master's, but his PhD would come before he knew it, and he was ready to kick its ass and become a lecturer somewhere as soon as possible. From the approving looks the professor was giving him from the corner of the room, he thought he was doing okay.

He finished right on time. The professor shouted out a reminder to check their syllabus for next week, which Elliott thought was pretty generous of him. They were in the second half of the second semester. If the students in the class didn't know by now to check their syllabus, there was really no hope for them.

With the room emptying out, Elliott was able to turn his attention to other things. From where he was standing, he could see the car he'd noticed before. He could also see that the car's driver had gotten out and settled in to wait.

Elliott grinned, then quickly packed up his stuff.

With a wave to the professor, he hefted his messenger bag and walked briskly through the deserted hallways. It was early evening on a Thursday. Most of the students had better things to do than stick around an empty building until the sun went down.

When he punched through the door, Aiden's car came into view, with Aiden himself leaning against it. Elliott jogged down the front steps toward him, smiling.

"You look like you drove straight out of a rom-com," Elliott called. "Do I?"

Aiden certainly made a picture. With his button-up shirt and khakis, his dark clean-cut good looks, and shiny vehicle that seemed expensive to even the least-knowledgeable, he was like a model in an editorial.

Few would have been able to tell the slope of his shoulders was different without the weight of a family law firm on them.

"Definitely." Elliott slowed to a stop beside the car, slung his bag through the open window onto the back seat, then pressed his body up against Aiden's, pinning him to the door. "How was your meeting?"

"Good." Aiden nodded decisively, but excitement leaked in behind his eyes. "No promises yet, but they're enthusiastic about the cause, and I think we'll get a legacy commitment by the end of the year."

"You will, I'm sure of it." Elliott stretched up on his toes, leaning harder onto Aiden's shoulders. "I thought I was going to get the bus today."

Aiden didn't seem to mind Elliott's dead weight. "We finished writing that grant proposal early, and I thought you might like a ride home after your first time being a real teacher."

Elliott smiled wider and bounced on his toes. "Yeah, I'm exhausted from my terrible, long day doing my dream job. I might need to go straight to bed."

Aiden lifted his hand and rested it on Elliott's lower back, spreading his fingers in a tickling caress. "You might, huh? Well, I worked extra hard today too. I'll have to go to bed with you."

"What a pair of boring old men we are," Elliott said mournfully, but he wasn't able to keep from smirking.

"I think we earned it." Aiden dipped his head and captured Elliott's mouth in a long, lazy kiss.

And as the sun set around them, casting their evening of simple pleasures in a rosy glow, Elliott knew they had.

Dear Reader,

Thank you for reading Chloe B. Young's *Worth It*!

We know your time is precious and you have many, many entertainment options, so it means a lot that you've chosen to spend your time reading. We really hope you enjoyed it.

We'd be honored if you'd consider posting a review—good or bad—on sites like **Amazon, Barnes & Noble, Kobo, Goodreads, Twitter, Facebook, Tumblr,** and your blog or website. We'd also be honored if you told your friends and family about this book. Word of mouth is a book's lifeblood!

For more information on upcoming releases, author interviews, blog tours, contests, giveaways, and more, please sign up for our weekly, spam-free newsletter and visit us around the web:

> **Newsletter**: riptidepublishing.com/newsletter
> **Twitter**: twitter.com/RiptideBooks
> **Facebook**: facebook.com/RiptidePublishing
> **Goodreads**: tinyurl.com/RiptideOnGoodreads
> **Tumblr**: riptidepublishing.tumblr.com

Thank you so much for Reading the Rainbow!

RiptidePublishing.com